The
Russian Soul

D1798628

Sam Caxton

ISBN- 978-1-7919-8435-9

ACKNOWLEDGEMENTS

Many people read versions of *The Russian Soul* manuscript and gave me constructive and encouraging feedback. Among the many are Olga Medvedeva, Misha Petreski, Sasha Vutchkovich, Chris Kirkham, Vera Tsareva-Brauner, Nick Lackenby, Udoka Ogbue, Eric Brewster, Milosh Puzovich, Dule Padezhanin, Dragan Pavlovich, Kornelius Kvas as well as Marko, Alek and Lazar.

A special thank you must go to Vesna Goldsworthy for all her support and wisdom.

I would like to acknowledge the input of a very fine literary agent, Darley Anderson who suggested, among other things, that I shorten the initial title.

And last but, of course, not least, I would like to thank my wife and agent, Tanja whose life, I imagine, would be marginally easier away from the intoxicating daily presence of the likes of Alex Gorsky, Senka Golovkin, El Guapo Medina, Milla Ivanovna, Aleksey Kaganov, Jack Sailgood, Tom Deutsch, Niusha Khanbaghi, Mark Hodayev and Hadji-Vasillis, all wrapped up in the one and only – Sam Caxton.
I apologise to those whom I failed to list here. What can I say? buy a copy of the book, check the list for yourself, write me an angry e-mail and in the next edition I will add your name so we can all continue to live in harmony and peace.

Finally, I hope you will enjoy reading *The Russian Soul* as much as I enjoyed writing it.

What would your good do if evil didn't exist, and what would the earth look like if all the shadows disappeared?

Mikhail Bulgakov

1

Santa Francesca Romana

Senka Golovkin wore a white shirt and a dark blue tie. He sat in his large window seat with a bunch of papers in his hands and looked down at the thick, ominous clouds sitting between the aircraft and the Alps. Suddenly, the Lear jet encountered turbulence, shook, and took a dive. After a couple of uneasy moments, the plane steadied and continued en route to London. Beads of sweat appeared on Golovkin's forehead. With a shaky hand, he took a handkerchief out of his pocket.

'I'll tell you about the Russian Soul, Alex,' he said and wiped his face.

* * *

Earlier that evening Alex Gorsky walked out of the Casa di Santa Francesca Romana onto the narrow, cobbled street. It was dark and the cold rain was turning into snow. Further down the lane there was a lamp and a yellowish shop window next to which a big black car was waiting: engine running, headlights on. Two men stood next to the car. Kolya, the bigger and older man, had a shaved head, a beer belly and his tweed jacket seemed a couple of sizes too small. The shorter man had thin, crooked legs and wore a black woollen hat. He leant against the door on the passenger's side and kept shuffling his feet.

'*Privyet,* Alex,' said Kolya, the bigger man.

Gorsky nodded and said with a heavy accent: 'Buona sera.'

'*Sera,*' mumbled the young man.

'*Davai, davai,*' said Kolya, 'We are already late!'

'That's fine, you can always blame it on me,' said Gorsky. 'Take my bag and you two can go. I need to take care of some business in town and I'll join you later. Vatayev will be dining at Roma Sparita, I imagine. I'll find you there, right?'

'Yes,' said Kolya. 'He's a man of good taste and habits.'

'What's your business in town?' said Kolya with a sly grin and a wink. 'A woman? Yes, of course, I knew it. You go chasing chicks around Piazza di Spagna while I spend my time with this mute Sicilian!'

'*Napolitano,*' mumbled the young man, disproving both the assertions. Then he shrugged his shoulders, opened the door and got into the car.

'Right,' said Kolya and looked at the Italian as if surprised he could talk at all. He winked at Gorsky and shook his head as if to say, 'He's not really all there!'

'The Boss rang and asked me to collect a parcel for him,' said Gorsky. 'Rest assured, no chicks around Piazza di Spagna for me tonight.'

'Your gun's in here?' said the big man, taking the bag from Gorsky and throwing it into the boot.

'No,' said Gorsky, 'I've got it.'

'OK,' said the big man and closed the boot with a thud.

'Catch you later. I'll come straight to the hotel and you can then take me to the airport,' said Gorsky and waved his hand at the Italian: '*Ciao!*'

The Neapolitan tried to produce a smile. It wilted in the corners of his mouth.

'Strange man,' thought Gorsky walking up the poorly lit lane. 'Hope not all Neapolitans are like him!'

It was a late December afternoon and the city was immersed in drizzle and fog. Cold dampness saturated the air.

'Smells like smoke and feels like snow,' mumbled Gorsky turning right into Lungotevere street. It was packed with slow-moving cars and apparently suicidal motorcyclists, pedestrians running for their lives, all engulfed in a cacophony of ear-piercing sounds. Gorsky felt a tinge of nostalgia thinking back to his little secluded room in Casa di Santa Francesca Romana—the hotel-monastery where he had spent the last couple of nights, courtesy of Vatayev's business partner, the San Egidio organisation. The hotel was near the Vatican and it was popular among clerics from around the world who came to visit the Holy See. Santa Francesca had been the wife of a fifteenth century nobleman. She had lived her entire adult life in the villa, he learnt from a brochure.

After a few hundred steps, he made a right turn onto a bridge over the Tiber and entered the ancient city, a spider web of narrow streets and passages. With each step a silent, impenetrable wall of darkness grew behind his back. By now the raindrops had turned into snowflakes and Gorsky interrupted his march to cast a glance at the little map he carried, struggling to make any sense of it. He mumbled a Russian profanity that involved ice, bears and virgins, then continued towards via delle Botteghe Oscure.

Fifteen minutes later he stood in front of a marble plaque with the name of the street. After another hundred steps towards Torre Argentina he stopped in front of a tiny, poorly lit shop. The sign above read: Antiquariato Pincherle. Gorsky looked at the shop window. In it were displayed a small red rug and a dusty writing desk with a menorah on top. He stepped towards the door and pressed the handle. A bell chimed as he opened the door and entered, and an old woman's voice reached out from the darkened depths: *'Chi è?'*

'A visitor,' said Gorsky, closed the door and stepped forward. The space was so cluttered and the room so dark that he couldn't see his way.

'We are closed,' said the old woman, now standing in a well-lit doorway at the back of the shop. 'But the angel sang for you, visitor,' she said.

'The angel?' said Gorsky. 'I have some business here with Mr. Pincherle; he expects me.'

'Of course, of course, come through,' said the old woman. 'You, are a lucky man, Mr....?'

'Gorsky, Alex Gorsky,' he said, finding his way through the shop that was no more than three metres wide. It felt like a crypt leading to the depths of a cave under a sacred mountain. 'There are more hospitable-looking ravines in Chechnya,' thought Gorsky. There were crystal chandeliers and cast-iron lighting units hanging from the ceiling, pieces of furniture sitting on top of each other, woodturning and gardening tools, walking sticks and horse-riding equipment. The walls were covered with pictures, framed photographs of ladies in period evening dresses, wide-brimmed hats adorned by luscious plumes, theatre fans and parasols; of monocle-wearing gentlemen with thin moustaches, in double-breasted suits with gold watch chains. Against the walls were a couple of desks crowded by inkwells and fountain pens, hand-coloured black and white postcards, medals from distant wars, pipes and tobacco cases, mirrors, compasses, silver paper knives, old dolls, daggers, gilded dining sets and clocks that looked like they had stopped ticking a century earlier. A Luger pistol and a tropical Tarbush fez sat next to a white silk kimono with a cherry tree motif.

Gorsky stood on the only clear patch of floor space.

'This angel will protect you, signor Gorsky,' said the woman. 'That much, I know.'

'Buona sera,' said Gorsky as he finally reached the back of the shop and stood in front of the shopkeeper.

'The Russian gentleman, Mr. Kaganov sends me,' he said. 'The man who came last week to buy the sword. Remember *il russo*, Mr. Kaganov?'

'Oh, yes of course. *Il russo,* the collector from London, *sì, sì,* I remember, come this way!' said the woman and made a gesture inviting the visitor to follow her through the lit doorway. A cat ran ahead, followed by the woman and the visitor.

They walked into a small, windowless office that had a subterranean feel. It featured a desk, the lamp on it the only source of feeble, yellowish light. There were two wooden chairs, a couple of random pieces of furniture, and a framed black and white photograph. An old man sat in an armchair and the cat leaped straight onto the blanket covering his lap. One hand on his walking stick, the man began petting the cat with the other. Dark glasses obscured most of his face. In the middle of the office stood a Chinese man in an elegant dark coat. He held a long silver box in his hand.

'Buona sera,' said the old man and Gorsky returned the salutation.

'This is Mr. Zheng,' said the old man to no one in particular, and turned to the new visitor. 'And you are?'

'My name is Gorsky, and I am here on behalf of Mr. Alexey Kaganov, the Russian collector who came to visit you last week.'

'Oh, I see. Yes, I remember,' said the old man. 'Mr. Kaganov, of course. He was amazed to see the little bundle we had here and the sword, of course, Caravaggio's sword!'

'Yes, the sword,' confirmed Gorsky. 'I was instructed to collect the sword.'

'This fine gentleman,' the old man said pointing at Mr. Zheng, 'came all the way from Beijing to purchase a unique sword that belonged to the Japanese master poet Matsuo Bashō. This sword, you see, can cut words in mid-air, as soon as they are spoken but before they are heard.'

The Chinese man nodded slightly and a hint of a smile appeared in the corners of his mouth.

'I must be going,' he said. 'Nice to meet you.'

Gorsky nodded back, but before he could say something appropriate the man was gone. Light on his feet, quick, interesting character, he thought before turning his attention to the host.

'Do you want to take your coat off?' asked the woman.

'No, thank you,' said Gorsky and took a seat. 'I came to see you, signor Pincherle as...'

'I know,' said Pincherle. 'I know.'

'You know?'

'You came all the way from London on behalf of the Russian collector, Mr. Kaganov?'

'I did.'

'Shall I bring the parcel?' asked the old woman.

'Yes, please do,' said the man. 'As per our agreement, Mr. Kaganov has transferred the money and the documents are ready for you. The artefacts are yours to take to London.'

'Artefacts? Is there more than one?' asked Gorsky. 'I thought there was just the sword?'

'The bundle, there are the letters of course,' said Pincherle, 'And yes, there is the sword.'

'I didn't know about the letters.'

'Mr. Kaganov came about the letters first, you see. His interest was primarily in this little bundle. It was very important to him. It was so important that he read them

twice while sitting in that very same chair. Only later u.
decide that he wanted the sword too!'

The old woman left the room and the old man turned
toward the visitor, trying to discern the contours of his face.

'*Slavo?*' said Pincherle.

'Yes, *Russo,*' said the visitor.

'Have you been in a war?' continued Pincherle and
tapped the floor with his walking stick.

'No, I haven't,' Gorsky said with a frown. He didn't like
questions about the war. He had no answers. He too only
had questions.

'No, of course not,' said Pincherle, leaned back in his
chair and stroked the sleeping cat. Then his lower lip
trembled.

'I can tell men of war, you see,' he suddenly said and
tapped the floor again. The cat woke up, raised its head and
looked around before deciding to continue napping.

The old woman came back with a long wooden case that
she carefully placed on the desk. She took out a
handkerchief out of her pocket and wiped its lid.

'He asked you about the war, didn't he?' she said. 'I
apologise. He does that to all our visitors and that's why he
has no friends left!'

'My friends are all dead. They died in the war,' said
Pincherle. 'They are all dead.'

'Please forgive the old fool!' the woman said and
continued to wipe the lid while Pincherle hung his head and
sat, still stroking the cat.

Gorsky approached the desk. The old woman moved
aside and invited him to inspect the case. It was just under a
metre in length and fifteen centimetres wide. It featured two
keyholes, with little keys in place, but the lid was already
unlocked and Gorsky lifted it.

ry rare artefact, Sir,' said signor Pincherle. said to have belonged to the collection of nte who, in the year 1600, lost it in a game ...as to Michelangelo Merisi Caravaggio, the painter. The story has it that this game of cards took place in the Madama palace the very night that the philosopher Giordano Bruno was burnt at the stake at the nearby piazza Campo de' Fiori. A game of cards played by the Cardinal, Caravaggio and Galileo Galilei, the scientist.'

'May I?' asked Gorsky and signor Pincherle nodded in approval.

'Of course.'

Gorsky took the sword out of the box with both hands, carefully, as if it were a delicate and fragile porcelain vase. He lifted it and looked down the blade's fine edge, felt the weight and balance, scrutinized the shape of the hilt, the cross-guard, the grip and the pommel, the ricasso. He then focused on the blade: 'Very fine workmanship, very fine.'

'Minted at the bottega Guerrini in Milan,' said signor Pincherle, 'Leonardo da Vinci is said to have designed weapons for the Guerrini. Who knows, it might be a da Vinci design. That would be something, wouldn't it?'

'Yes, it would,' said Gorsky as he brought the blade closer and began reading the inscription aloud: '*Nec spe nec metu,* right?'

Pincherle nodded. 'That was the motto of Caravaggio's bunch of drunkards and thieves who fancied themselves as artists. Without hope, without fear!'

Gorsky took the sword in his right hand and cut a circle in the air with it. The weapon felt light, manageable. The handle was small for his hand but it felt as though it were endowed with mystical qualities drawn from the warm ashes of Giordano Bruno, the telescopes of Galileo, the sinister quality of Caravaggio's paintings, the secrets of the Vatican cardinals and the baroque grandeur of their palaces.

'Without hope, without fear,' repeated Gorsky.

He liked this disquieting motto. It struck a chord, recalled distant memories, shapes and apprehensions. It held the scent and promise of the unknown, remote, forgotten and finally perhaps, found. Gorsky was no expert in swords, Italian painters or art in general, but he knew how to listen and he recognized that the cold, timeworn steel had stories to tell.

'This is the sword that killed Tomassoni,' said Pincherle, 'A young man of good Roman stock who had the misfortune to pick a fight with Merisi over a game of tennis. After the murder, Merisi fled and turned fugitive. In Malta, he struck a deal with a Templar knight and exchanged the sword for safe passage to Sicily. Mr. Kaganov liked that part of the story very much. Giving one's sword to the pirates in exchange for one's life.'

'I can imagine,' said Gorsky with a wry smile. He was very well versed in the taste and inclinations of said gentleman. 'Artists brandishing swords are a sure sign of dangerous times. Where did you find the sword?'

'I acquired this and some other items via my Lebanese connection. He bought them, he told me, from a wealthy Syrian refugee,' said Pincherle, nodding.

'An intriguing, complex story,' said Gorsky who wasn't inclined to believe the old man's tales. Too much storytelling, he thought, too much Italian elegance and not enough... Substance. Was that the word he was looking for, 'substance?'

'How do I know that this item is what you claim it is?' said Gorsky.

The old man laughed tentatively. 'There are two ways you can go about it. You either study the subject matter, or you study people, so that you then know when they are lying. Only two ways.'

'There is another one—a third way,' said Gorsky. 'There's always another way of doing things.'

'What would that be?'

'You buy the story too, start believing it, merge it with reality.'

The old man laughed more heartily now and even slapped his knee, startling the cat. Gorsky turned towards the woman and asked her to close the case and hand him the documentation necessary for exporting it.

'Everything is ready,' said the woman. She opened a desk drawer, took out a large brown envelope and passed to the old man.

'Mr. Kaganov has paid for everything?'

'He did, indeed. He did,' said the woman.

'Indeed,' said Pincherle, opening the envelope and taking out a bundle of very old handwritten papers.

'These are the letters,' said the old man. 'They are all in Russian, but a friend translated the first couple for me. Mr. Kaganov was most impressed. So impressed, that he bought them all immediately and asked me not to mention the bundle to anyone.'

'Thank you,' said Gorsky, taking the bundle and the envelope, which Pincherle extended towards him. He glanced at the first page on top of the bundle. The handwriting was neat, the letters very small and every page densely filled. He read the name of the sender aloud, 'Agathon Karlovich Fabergé.'

Where had he heard that name before? He knew that name. He read the first line:

'Sankt Petersburg, 1921. Pis'mo ot voennogo ministra.'

Then he muttered something about the good old days when they called the spade a spade. Smiling, he said: 'A letter from the minister of war. They call them ministers of defence these days, don't they?' He then placed the bundle into the envelope, and slid it into the inside pocket of his coat.

'I'll show you out, Mr. Gorsky,' said the woman as she handed over the box with the sword.

'Thank you,' said Gorsky.

'Buona fortuna,' said Pincherle, picking up the cat from the floor and putting her back on his lap.

Gorsky followed the old woman through the shop trying to avoid the maze of antiques and stalactites. After bidding farewell, he stepped out into the dark street. He glanced at his watch. It was still early and Gorsky decided to walk across the Tiber and straight to the Roma Sparita restaurant. The place was on his way and Kolya would be still there.

'Good,' he thought heading again into the dense web of Roman streets. It took him twenty minutes to reach the Tiber and another ten to cross the Garibaldi Bridge and reach Viale di Trastevere. The thoroughfare was still packed with cars, trams and buses working their way in and out of the city centre. It was a damp cold evening with the few pedestrians bundled up in woollen scarves. Romans are terrified by these few flakes of snow, Gorsky thought, and laughed, picturing the hard-frozen winter landscape of his native Voronezh. Car headlights turned people into shadows scampering across the walls of adjacent apartment blocks. Ambulance and police sirens wailed in the distance. Car horns made people curse aloud and the shadows move faster.

After a few hundred meters Gorsky turned into a narrow pedestrian passage, came out on the other side and continued in parallel with Trastevere. This was the neighbourhood of Casa di Santa Francesca, the part of town where he resided and which he knew well. He soon reached Via Della Luce and continued towards the little piazza at the end of the street. Fifty meters before the neon lights of Roma Sparita he stopped. He held the long box in one hand while the other remained in the pocket of his coat. He tried to discern the shadows in front of the restaurant. There was a shadow in the doorway next to the restaurant and Gorsky saw the contours of a man in a ski jacket. That was the unsociable Neapolitan. Kolya was nowhere to be seen and Gorsky thought that he must be dozing in the car. His black Audi was parked down the street.

At that very moment, he saw Vatayev and Irina coming out. They made a couple of steps in the direction of the Neapolitan. Vatayev was struggling to open an umbrella with one hand while his wife held on to his other arm. Gorsky made a couple of steps, raised his hand and was just about to call out when a shadow jumped out of a nearby entrance and after a couple of quick steps stopped in front of the couple. Next, Irina's scream pierced the night. Vatayev stepped forward and Gorsky saw the muzzle flash of a gun and heard a shot, then another one. He dropped the case and ran. A third blast, and Vatayev fell to the ground. Irina continued to scream until she too was cut down by two shots in quick succession. Gorsky took the gun out of his pocket. He was no more than ten meters away and could clearly see the Neapolitan, who turned the gun in his direction. Gorsky threw himself over the hood of a car, fired a shot and hid behind another vehicle. He got up on his feet just in time to see the weapon dropping out of the Neapolitan's hand and his body crashing against a wall, bouncing back and then falling to the pavement. There was a dark smudge on the wall and it was only when Gorsky came close that he realized that half of the man's face was missing. He scanned the surrounding buildings and rooftops. All was quiet. He picked up the man's gun, slid it into his pocket and took cover behind one of the parked vehicles. Someone else had been shooting—using a large-calibre weapon.

After a couple of seconds, Gorsky managed to crawl towards the immobile bodies in front of the restaurant entrance. Vatayev was hit in the forehead and the chest while Irina had blood all over her neck and chest. He stooped down to check if they were breathing. They were not.

A group of people was now coming out of the restaurant and gathering at the entrance, afraid to step outside.

They don't dare come out, waiting for the police, thought Gorsky, and so the police must be on their way. He reflected that he still had a couple of minutes left. He went to pick up the box he had dropped. He then walked towards the parked Audi. On the front seat a bulky body slumped against the window. It was Kolya. Gorsky opened the door, and looked at his friend's glassy eyes. A small calibre bullet had entered the right-hand side of the skull. Behind the ear, Gorsky saw the entry wound and a couple of drops of blood.

'Goodbye,' said Gorsky. With his gloved hand, he dropped the killer's gun into the car. He pressed the button to open the trunk, got out of the vehicle and picked up his bag. He then crossed the street and walked away. When he felt out of sight of the party gathered in front of Roma Sparita he started to walk briskly. He needed to get away as far and as quickly as possible.

Gorsky would claim that he carried a flute, or a clarinet. That he was a musician, a painter, a banker, or an art lover stranded in Rome. His wife left him for Joe, a rich American with whom she ran away to his Texas ranch and cattle business. Gorsky was Nureyev's long-lost brother or Dostoevsky's grandson. He was in a hurry and the only thing that mattered was getting out of Rome, out of Italy and into the safety of Kaganov's empire. Yes, he would be able to spin a story, to pretend to be someone else, anyone else. All the stories would flow into one and he could tell them in any order, in any language if that helped him reach the airport.

After a ten-minute walk, he hailed a taxi and asked to be taken to Fiumicino.

'Certo,' said the driver and turned up the radio. He was following a live report of a football match from Buenos Aires. A small Argentinian flag hung from the rear-view mirror.

'Boca Juniors,' he yelled and banged both his hands against the wheel. When the passenger failed to display any interest in Argentine football, the driver turned up the radio even louder.

'Good,' thought Gorsky,' he is so absorbed in his game that he will not remember me. Gorsky took out his mobile phone and dialled the contact with the face of a man in his late forties. The phone rang twice.

'Alyo?' responded a voice.

'Senka!' whispered Gorsky.

'Da?'

'Listen carefully,' said Gorsky and looked at the driver who was happily commenting on the performance of his team. 'Vatayev, Irina and Kolya are dead!'

'What did you just...?'

'Shut up and listen. They are all dead and we don't have much time.'

The driver was overjoyed that his team was winning. He kept on shouting and thumping the wheel with both his hands as the car left the city and took the motorway toward the sea and Fiumicino.

2

Agathon and the Minister of War

Half an hour later the taxi stopped in front of the airport. Gorsky handed the money to the driver, waved away the change and got out. He hoped that he hadn't attracted the man's attention. The news about the killings would go public in minutes. All media outlets would report the assassination of a Russian businessman, his wife and two more people.

Gorsky understood why the Neapolitan had to be disposed of. It was a mop-up operation. No traces, no loose ends. There was one loose end, though, and his name was Alex Gorsky. Whoever ordered the hit must have access to insiders who would work this out. They would. The only good news was that the Italian police would not be given the opportunity to question him. His boss wouldn't allow that. No, he certainly wouldn't.

Gorsky entered the airport terminal, walked toward the VIP area, approached the counter and showed his passport. The neatly groomed Italian woman smiled. He said, with an air of quiet authority: 'I am with Mr. Kaganov!' She smiled again and waved him through.

The security officer nodded as Gorsky went out through the gate and stepped onto the tarmac. He had a gun in his pocket—a recently fired Sig Sauer. The VIP badge does wonders, he sighed with relief while climbing the steps up to the jet's door. A man in an aviation uniform waved him in and Gorsky entered the cabin. There were eight large leather seats on each side and in the first to the right sat a man in a white shirt. He had dark, deep-set eyes, short brown hair and a very high forehead made even higher by a receding hairline. His cheeks seemed pale, as if drained of all blood. The expression on his face was one of worry.

'Alex,' said the man.

Gorsky sat down on the left-hand side and dropped the case on the floor underneath the seat. He unbuttoned the collar of his shirt and took off the tie.

'*Privyet*, Senka!' he said.

They were relieved to hear the rising whine of the jet engines, both hoping to be airborne as soon as possible.

'What happened?' asked Senka Golovkin.

'I am not sure myself,' Gorsky replied uneasily. 'I know what I saw but I am not sure I understand it.'

The plane began taxiing. Gorsky asked: 'Did you call our associates in Rome?'

'I did as you suggested,' said Senka. 'I told them to send their public relations person to spin a story about another mafia shoot-out and to explain that the killer was gunned down by his own associates.'

'Do you really think this was an Italian mafia affair?'

'No, I don't,' said Golovkin, 'but you are right, we need to divert the media focus from the Russian connection. Now, calm down and tell me what happened. Step by step, in detail.'

The engines throttled up for take-off and the passengers felt their thrust pin them to their seats. In under a minute they were airborne, en route to London.

Gorsky leaned back in his seat and took a deep breath. He then tried to focus on the things that he had observed, leaving out any conclusions that he might have reached or feelings he may have harboured.

Once he finished, he looked at Senka. Now was the time to start piecing it all together. A working hypothesis was needed and Golovkin was the right man to produce it. They had to understand the reasons behind these murders. Who? Where? Why?

'The police will work out for themselves that the shooter was hit by an elephant gun and not a pistol!' said Golovkin.

'They will,' said Gorsky, 'He was probably hit by both a small calibre bullet and a dum-dum shell. A desperate Italian junkie caught in the crossfire during a merry Russian mafia family shootout? No, the man was connected, he was an insider and the police will soon show interest in the man who shot the killer. The Boss wouldn't want that, Senka, would he?'

Senka shook his head and as he opened his mouth to say something, the on-board satellite phone lit up and warbled. The two exchanged glances and Senka picked it up.

'Yes, Boss, sure Boss, he is here, yes. You want to talk to him, sure,' he said and passed the receiver to Gorsky.

'Tell me,' barked the voice from the receiver.

'Vatayev and Irina are dead,' said Gorsky, 'Kolya is dead too, Boss!'

'How?' said Kaganov.

'Everything was fine until last night,' began Gorsky and retold that evening's story from the moment he left the antiquarian. The Boss listened silently.

'Did you collect the items I sent you for?'

'The sword?' said Gorsky, 'I did'.

'Did you pick up anything else?'

'A bundle of old letters.'

'Good. Keep the bundle safe and bring it over,' said the Boss, 'give me Senka now.'

Gorsky passed the receiver back to Golovkin and tapped the front pocket of his coat as if to make sure that the bundle was still there.

Senka exchanged a couple of words with the Boss, nodded several times and put the receiver down.

'This was strange,' said Gorsky, 'did he ask about Vatayev?'

'No,' replied Senka, 'he didn't!'

'Why Vatayev? He must have been the prime target, right?' said Gorsky. 'Where did the Italian turn up from anyway?'

'Santino is the name. San Egidio's security staff, had clearance from Rome as well as from London.'

'From London?'

'Yes, he came through his uncle's connections, our usual partners.'

'Who's the uncle?'

'Colonel Vargas,' he said after a brief pause.

'Vargas?'

'Yes, Vargas!' Senka confirmed with a nervous gesture. 'What did you pick up from the antiquarian?' he said.

'The sword that the Boss bought last week.'

'Why didn't he take it with him?'

'Needed the art treasure paperwork for export... or something; and there was also the bundle. He bought these letters...'

'The sword is in there?' said Senka and pointed a finger at the long case underneath Gorsky's seat.

'Caravaggio's sword!'

'The artist? The one who killed the pimp of his favourite model?'

'I don't know the details and right now, believe me, I don't really care!'

'Did the antiquarian give you anything else?'

'He did,' said Gorsky and took the bundle out of his pocket. 'The letters!'

'Let me see,' said Senka and took the bundle from Gorsky.

'Agathon,' he muttered the name on the first letter and began reading the neat Cyrillic writing.

While Senka Golovkin entertained himself with the letters, Gorsky went back to the beginning of the evening. The Casa di Santa Francesca Romana, the meeting in the street, the walk, the antiquarian, the Chinaman, the sword and the letters, the old man's tall tales, the walk back across the river, the shooting and the four corpses... the taxi driver, the airport, the flight, Senka...

'Listen,' Senka said abruptly as turbulence shook the plane. He pushed the letters into Gorsky's hands.

'Look at this!'

Gorsky took the letters and leaned back into his seat. Senka was reliable. He had won the youth chess championship of the USSR. He knew how to solve problems, how to read between the lines, to tie up loose ends. Senka was no secret agent or intelligence operative, but Senka knew things. He knew many unusual things. The two went back many years and Gorsky trusted Senka's loyalty, his cool head and analytical skills.

All letters seemed to be written by the same person and the signature was that of Agathon Karlovich Fabergé.

'One of the jewellery people, so what?' said Gorsky. He began reading from the middle of one of the yellowish pages.

When the doorbell rang, I dropped my book. Eerie feeling. After my release from prison we haven't had any visitors. The family had fled the country, there were no friends left either. Some were imprisoned, others too scared to be thought of as my associates.

I walked quietly down the corridor and stood behind the door. I stopped breathing and heard voices, the sound of shuffling feet, a cough. Eventually, I summoned all my strength and opened the door. I found myself facing three shadows. There stood a man in a long black leather coat with a visor hat. A sure sign of a higher standing in the new Soviet pecking order: a People's Commissar. I know the purpose of that office and the sort of men who hold it. Behind the officer—two soldiers, brandishing rifles.

The Commissar shouted his name and then asked for me by name, patronymic and surname. He asked for comrade Agathon Karlovich Fabergé. No, no mistake there. Upon receiving confirmation of my identity, he reached for his purse and presented me with an envelope. It contained a letter from comrade Trotsky, the Minister of War, he said, and held the paper in front of my nose. He had orders to wait for a response, the Commissar said, nodded and clicked his heels in a salute. All so terribly theatrical, my dear Victor.

At first, I hesitated to take the envelope and I stood there staring at the troika. Eventually, I took it and checked the name of the recipient. I was still hoping it wouldn't be mine. I was still hoping the CHEKA had made a mistake, that the Kremlin got it all wrong, that... Maybe the Minister of War wanted to summon someone else, someone completely different, not me again! I gathered enough strength to break the seal.

It was not very long. Leon Davidovitch Trotsky was writing to summon me to Moscow to enable me (ha, ha... To enable me!) to give a contribution to the Revolution with special reference to the newly established Commission for Expertise. The said

Commission was led by a luminary of the revolutionary artistic expression (yes, that's what he called him, a luminary!) comrade Maxim Gorky under the personal supervision of the Premier of the Soviet Union, Vladimir Ilyich Lenin. I was to travel to Moscow immediately and report to Vitaly Fressman, a professor of geology at Moscow State University. Fressman was the man in charge of the inventory of gold, precious stones, jewels and other items of degenerate luxury that had been expropriated from the decadent aristocracy and the imperial family in accordance with the first amendment of the 5 October 1918 Revolutionary Decree on Registration and Protection of Monuments of Culture and Ancient Art, Owned by Private Persons, Societies and Institutions... and so on and so forth.

I read the letter three times and said I would report to Moscow. What else? The commissar saluted and the lot marched off into the desolate darkness while I went to my room and sat back in my armchair. I stared at the flowery details of a rug for hours. I had to think.

Lydia didn't utter a word. She didn't ask me anything. She just sat there waiting. Eventually, I told her that I had to leave St. Petersburg and go to Moscow, to work on that diabolical inventory. They wanted to put my expertise to good use, I told her. That's good, I said. When they need you, they keep you alive, said Lydia. But when they don't need you anymore they send you to Siberia—if you are lucky. We sat in silence for the remainder of the evening. Lydia is a wise woman, you see.

'Agathon?' mumbled Gorsky and cast a glance at his partner who busied himself by looking through the window and wiping his face with a handkerchief. He then returned to the letters.

My dear Victor!

I reported to Moscow on 10 August and was assigned to the coordination of the newly established Division for the Inventory of Expropriated Bourgeois Commodities. I saw mountains of diamonds and gemstones of all colours, shapes and sizes, lakes of silk, rivers of gold and silver jewellery in the process of being broken, smashed by a clueless, fanatical mob of foul-smelling serfs equipped with hammers and rusty bayonets, possessed by soul-devouring greed and a burning desire to avenge a historical injustice. Forty train cars filled with treasure were brought from St. Petersburg alone. These people worked in freezing temperatures, day and night, without electricity, proper tools or skills.

In January 1922, I was transferred to a more important and secretive assignment. Nikolai II Romanov had cleared the Kremlin Armory of all weaponry and converted it into the Imperial Family Treasury. After the revolution, upon strict orders from Lenin, all the Tsar's valuables from around the country were shipped to Moscow and amassed in one place, piled up, tossed around without being properly catalogued. When I entered the Armory, I was left breathless. Nothing, nothing I had ever seen or imagined could compare with that spectacle. No story, no tale, no account or yarn could match the splendour of the gold, the excellent cut of the diamonds, rubies and sapphires, the supreme handiwork of the Italian, German, Dutch, Belgian and French goldsmiths in creating sceptres, necklaces, crowns, rings, watches... There were chests filled with gold coins, piles of golden bars stacked to the ceiling, renaissance and baroque paintings were left leaning against the walls, marble sculptures sitting on precious rugs alongside furniture, chandeliers, silk gowns and tailored uniforms and evening dresses. And nothing, nothing could have prepared me for the spectacle of the sheer volume of it, of the entire Kremlin Armoury filled up to the ceiling by riches.

And, my God, I was the one who prepared these goods for transportation. I was the one who had sealed many a room, safe deposit and freight car in St. Petersburg!

Six months later, my dear Victor, I wrote to the director of the Museum Fund, Natalya Sedova, the wife of the Minister of War, and requested an urgent audience. I asserted boldly in my submission that the matter was of the highest revolutionary interest. It had to do with the Western, capitalist markets!

Can you imagine, Victor? Me advising the communist on capitalist market matters! The Socialist Museum Fund operated under the auspices of the Committee for Enlightenment headed by Lunatcharsky. The main task of the said Socialist Museum Fund was to compile an inventory of all the exceptionally precious and artistically outstanding samples that could then be offered for sale in the West. The Bolsheviks needed enormous amounts of money to feed the starving population, to launch the widely announced first five-year plan, and to start the industrial reform necessary to convert feudal Russia *into a modern, industrial nation. They needed to sell the confiscated assets.*

By July 1922, I knew very well that once the inventory had been completed or the Bolsheviks had realized that the global market was unfavourable, they would opt for a wholesale trade, at which point I would only represent a hindrance to many a corrupt commissar and zealot. I only had one chance.

Natalya Sedova welcomed me by announcing that she didn't have any time to waste. She said she was tired of people like me. People coming with all sorts of pleas and stupid excuses. She hated tears for we had a revolution to run, didn't we? She hated seeing grown men cry. It was so unbecoming, undignified, she explained, and then suddenly asked about my letter.

I explained that I had in my possession the most precious jewel the world had ever seen. A jewel most rare, valuable and yet... anonymous. I said that I had in my possession the Russian Soul, the finest jewel in the world. It was my intention to barter it for the freedom of my family and my own.'

Gorsky read the last sentence twice and then turned towards Senka.

'A jewel called The Russian Soul was in his possession?' he said. 'Who is he? Agathon what?'

'Agathon Fabergé, Alex,' said Senka, 'he was a jeweller and The Russian Soul is a jewel. A very special and precious jewel.'

'A jewel like the Easter eggs the Fabergés used to make for the court?'

'That's right. Just like those Easter eggs they used to make for the Romanovs.'

'So, he wanted to exchange the jewel for a pass to leave the country?'

'Not only that he wanted, he did exactly that!'

'How would you know?'

'It's common knowledge that Agathon Fabergé and his family crossed over frozen Lake Ladoga in a sledge and reached Finland. I think that was in 1927. He spent the rest of his days in Helsinki, collecting stamps.'

'I see. And what would Boss's interest in the letters be? He picked them up because they are in Russian, I imagine!'

'I don't think so,' said Senka, 'Aleksey Kaganov is not the kind of person who trots around the world collecting White Russian émigré diaries for the fun of it. Sentimentality is not exactly his forte.'

'So, why then?'

'What if...'

'What if what?'

'What if the jewel still exists? What if it can be traced? Brought back to the country, it would be a powerful symbol of historical continuity with Imperial Russia. It could symbolize the glory, the power, the future...' he took the letter from Gorsky's hand and read aloud: 'The finest jewel in the world and a symbol of Russia.'

'Fine, it was a precious stone!' said Gorsky.

'No, this wasn't just any jewel,' said Senka, 'The most precious jewels the Fabergés made were those Easter eggs for the Imperial family...'

'Ok, it's an Easter egg, so what?'

'There is a problem with that,' said Senka, 'the list of eggs is well known and documented. Their whereabouts and ownership is known, catalogued.'

'So?'

'So... there is no such Fabergé Easter egg,' cried Senka. 'Officially, the Russian Soul doesn't exist. This most precious of all jewels is not listed!'

3

The Report

A young woman came down the well-lit corridor, stopped in front of a door and knocked twice. The plaque on the door read 'Sir Jack Sailgood, Chief Operating Officer.' The woman's name was Elizabeth and this was her first Foreign Office posting - Moscow, involving occasional trips to Minsk, Kiev and Odessa. It was early in the morning and the smell of coffee lingered in the air.

At that time of the day, Jack Sailgood would usually busy himself with writing the executive summary and then reading the online editions of several newspapers while listening to a variety of Ukrainian and Russian news outlets. That very morning his attention was drawn by a bizarre story featured in all the main Russian media outlets. A colourful group of young people stormed the Church of the Holy Assumption in Voronezh, interrupting the Divine Liturgy to perform a rap number featuring lyrics with explicit sexual content and a dance routine that was subsequently described by Archbishop Alexis as primitive and lewd. According to Pravda.ru, a squadron of police in full riot gear escorted the group out politely. While being pushed out and shoved into the police vehicle the group members yelled slogans in support of transsexuals' freedom to marry in a civil ceremony. The other major daily, Izvestia.ru, concluded that such an act of vandalism was insulting and used terms such as pornography, blasphemy and desecration to describe the act.

A hardly noticeable spark lit up Sir Jack's eyes and a smirk ran over his face. He cried out for the visitor to enter.

Elizabeth walked into the office and waited for Sir Jack to find the right button on the remote control to mute the audio. He then made a gesture inviting the young woman to take a seat.

'Yes, Liz,' he said, trying to look like someone ready to listen.

Jack Sailgood was a man of medium stature with fair hair, light, sky-blue eyes and a piercing gaze. He sported a barely visible paunch—a testament to his longstanding beer-loving habits.

'Sir Jack, terribly sorry to intrude this early,' said Liz and made paused as if to call for attention.

Sailgood shifted in his seat and leaned back in his chair.

'Tell me,' he said.

'WikiLeaks published a new batch of intercepted emails, reports and memos, and some of those contain...'   'Our emails, memos and reports?' interrupted Sailgood.

'No, thank God, no. This time they are not ours!' said Liz emphatically only to conclude that, 'well, not all of them are ours. I mean, just a couple.'

'Just a couple...' said Sir Jack as he massaged his temples gently with both forefingers.

'Some of the messages contain very interesting information, though, about one of our favourite candidates to replace Myshkin!'

'Which one?'

'Aleksey Kaganov, the London-based oligarch!'

'I see.'

'His rating among the pro-Western intelligentsia is currently high as you will see from my report. He's also showing willingness to collaborate. He made contact.'

'That's fine. Apart from that, what makes him such an outstanding candidate?'

'He claims he can produce the Russian Soul!'

'The Russian Soul?' said Sailgood, 'not even the evil spirit-slayer Dostoyevsky made such bold claims. Ha, ha, to produce the Russian Soul!'

'It's a jewel,' said Liz. 'The Russian Soul is a jewel. As you will see from my report, it is one of the famous Easter eggs that the last Russian Tsar used to commission annually over a period of thirty years. Now that the Romanovs have been rehabilitated and sanctified, the importance of this jewel seems to have increased exponentially!'

'I've heard about these Fabergé eggs!' said Sailgood and shifted in his seat.

'Certain people, though, well known to us of course,' explained Liz, 'are becoming nervous about this affair!'

'Some people are nervous because of this egg, you say?' said Sailgood and leaned forward, placing his elbows on the desk.

'Yes, because of the jewel!' announced the young analyst, flushed with pride and a sense of achievement.

'The Russian Soul is the name of this egg?' said Sailgood.

'*Russkaya Dusha*, yes!' said Liz. 'The murder of the journalist Politkovskaya in Moscow, the assassination of Alexander Litvinenko with polonium and the attempted murder of the Russian banker Goluzhny in London. The suicide of Berezovsky in Sussex, bombs in Sofia and Mexico City, attacks in Paris, all seem to be linked to this jewel.'

Jack Sailgood lowered his chin on his hands as if praying. He scrutinized the young woman for a good few seconds.

'Sir Jack,' said Liz, putting a blue folder on the desk. 'You should read this. It's my full report on this case. I stayed up all night to have it ready for today.'

'Sure,' said Sailgood, coming out of his prayer posture and reclining back into his chair, 'I have a meeting with the Chinese today but I promise to devote my full attention to your report as soon as possible!'

'Thank you, Sir Jack,' said Liz standing up. 'Should you need additional information, please...'

'Thank you, Liz,' said Sailgood and picked up the phone.

Later that morning Sailgood took the blue folder from the desk and tossed it into the bottom drawer. It was a busy day. He had several meetings scheduled with the staff from his Odessa office as well as one with his Russian counterpart, Nikolai Patrushev. He liked Patrushev, and what he liked best about him were the first five to ten minutes of their meetings, when the Russian would lament the demise of the Cold War and the KGB.

'Those were the days, Jack,' Patrushev would say, 'when you could count on the fact that your enemy cannot be trusted! And today, what do we have today? We are made to sit here pretending to be chums! Total rubbish, rubbish! Backstabbing has become the ultimate art form!'

On this occasion, the main subject of their conversation was the Ukrainian civil war that followed the Kiev 'coup d'état,' as Patrushev would refer to it, or the 'Russian invasion of Crimea,' as Sir Jack preferred to call it. Since they couldn't find a single point of agreement, they decided to meet again after the forthcoming Foreign Ministers' summit.

Later that same evening, Sailgood met two Chinese colleagues who were privy to information concerning the delivery of Russian antiaircraft systems to the Syrian government. The Chinese also mentioned being in possession of documents listing instances of human rights abuses in Saudi Arabia. To repay such a courtesy, Sailgood briefed the Chinese about some activities of their dissidents in Western Europe. He handed over a document with the addresses, bank accounts and other personal details of some of these dissidents. The Chinese mentioned the technical expertise that they acquired from American top-secret research projects that happen to employ patriotic Chinese scientists. They wouldn't release the names of the projects and of the scientists involved, though.

'Patience,' thought Sailgood. 'Patience.'

It was just one of those regular monthly social engagements characterized by a friendly and collaborative atmosphere that no one took too seriously except, of course, the notoriously suspicious and paranoid Russian Secret Service, the FSB.

After meeting the Chinese, Sailgood decided not to go straight home but to make a stopover at the office where he kept all his paperwork locked behind several layers of security. After an American operative had left his laptop in a Pigalle sex parlour a couple of months ago, Sailgood decided to be even more cautious than usual. The computer contained unscrambled files with the names of several dozen mercenaries infiltrated into Libya with the specific task of murdering Colonel Gaddafi. It also contained a Mossad report on contacts established with potential defectors, high-ranking Iranian officers of the Islamic Revolutionary Guard Corps. Clearly, if such information were to fall into the wrong hands, it would be most unfortunate.

It was late, nearly midnight, and except for members of the security staff there was no one to be seen. Sailgood parked his car in the underground garage and took the elevator. He entered the office, switched on the lights and took off his jacket and tie. He opened a cabinet, grabbed a bottle of whisky and a glass, poured himself a drink and sat down at his desk.

After a sip and a deep breath, he decided to have a look at Dudley-Vernon's blue folder. But once he held the folder in his hands, he looked at it as if having second thoughts. After all, Liz was just trying to impress her superiors and advance through the ranks, wasn't she?

She would do anything to attract attention, wouldn't she? Sailgood mused as he took another sip. The heirs of the Romanov Empire. Bollocks! Let's see what the Russkies are up to now!

He opened the file and started to read.

* * *

Jack Sailgood glanced towards the clock on the wall. It was past midnight and his glass was empty.

'Russkaya Dusha,' he mumbled and sprung up from his chair. Everything has a price. Everything must have a price. It's the most fundamental law of Mother Nature. Even the damned Russian Soul must have a price tag! It might be in roubles but a price tag nonetheless!

He put Liz's folder back in the drawer, closed the drawer, grabbed his jacket and left the office. Once in the underground garage, he walked briskly to his Jaguar, opened the door and pressed the engine start button. He was about to pull the gearshift into drive when he changed his mind abruptly. No, this situation required urgent action. He fished the phone out of his pocket, scrolled through the address list and found the thumbnail of a middle-aged, blond man sporting gold-rimmed glasses. He tapped on the face and waited.

It rang eight times before the sleepy voice of Tom Deutsch cried: 'Go to hell! Do you have any idea what time it is?'

'Tom,' said Jack Sailgood, 'we need to talk. It's about Siberia.'

'Come again?' interjected Tom.

'I can't say any more over the phone,' said Sailgood, 'I need to see you!'

'Yeah,' uttered Deutsch. 'I'm in Odessa.'

'You must get back to Moscow, it's important,' said Sailgood. 'I'll be in your office lunch time tomorrow.'

Sailgood didn't feel like answering questions. He put his mobile back into the inside pocket of his jacket, pulled the gearshift into drive and pressed the accelerator. He drove out and onto the Smolenskaya Naberezhnaya Boulevard.

The night was quiet and there was little traffic, just delivery vans and a couple of taxis. He turned the radio on. They were playing a Vladimir Vysotsky classic, *Ya ne lyublyu,* I don't like. It was sung by a young Georgian with a difficult name. Something like Maisuradze, Maitaradze... ending in -adze, anyway.

Sailgood began humming: 'A million is exchanged for a rouble, let the big changes come ahead, but I'll never be able to like them.'

He liked these lyrics. He really did. Especially now as he drove down the Boulevard in a good mood, rumbling and mumbling along with the Georgian -adze fellow.

4

The Transylvanian theme park

It was one a.m. when Gorsky came out of the building and went straight towards a large, bald man wearing a dark blue uniform. Senka Golovkin trotted along. As the pair approached, the man nodded and opened the back door of a large sedan.

'*Dobriy vyecher,*' said the man.

'*Privyet,* Vanya,' said Gorsky and took the front passenger seat. Senka Golovkin sat at the back.

'Where to?' asked Vanya.

'Shepherd's Bush,' said Gorsky and Senka looked at him with an expression of surprise on his face. 'What for?' he said.

'To pay a visit to our friend, Vargas. I want to hear from him personally about the Neapolitan that he sent to Vatayev.'

Gorsky didn't know Vargas very well. He had only met him a couple of times, and always in the company of the Boss or his business associates. He spoke to the man only twice, and briefly. But that was enough for him to make up his mind: he didn't like the man.

'Since you want to talk to Vargas,' said Senka, 'let me fill you in on some background information. You might find it useful. Vargas's brother Gregor owns a couple of night clubs in Paris and has dealings with many international entrepreneurs, including some not very friendly Bulgarian racketeers who try to squeeze him for a rather handsome sum on a regular basis. Gregor sends his negotiators to discuss the rather unfortunate issue, but these people are just out of a war zone and rough around the edges. This has resulted in a major misunderstanding and a couple of Bulgarians hospitalized. To exact revenge and send a message, the Bulgarians organized a hit on Gregor. This resulted in a most unfortunate incident. Gregor's wife Angelique was hit by a bazooka while driving to the beauty parlour. The episode started a gang war and sparked Gregor's interest in real estate. He approached Bata Negulescu, Vargas' business associate in Romania. At the time, this Bata had just wrapped up a trafficking, smuggling, import-export business and decided to invest his money in Transylvanian tourism. He bought the castle of Vlad the Impaler, aka Count Dracula, and transformed it into a theme park. He devoted special attention to the castle dungeon, where he restored the torture equipment to brand-new condition. That was what sparked Gregor's interest. He inquired into the possibility of a joint venture–a hospitality centre for international VIP prisoners. There's a word for it now... extraordinary rendition is what they call it. But Gregor's brother is a real champion who runs an elite tourist business in the Ukraine - a human safari of a sort. The Boss told me about it; he was very impressed by the innovative dimension of this business. I'm not sure how innovative that can be but... There you go. That's the family for you.'

'What's the business?'

'They pick up tourists in Kiev and take them to eastern Ukraine, close to the frontline between Kiev's forces and the separatists. They arm them with assault rifles or other weapons, as they wish - could be rocket-propelled grenade launchers, AK-47s, hand grenades... And they let them shoot.'

'Shoot at what?'

'They have a price list, apparently. Children and women cost less; they don't shoot back and are easy to approach. The separatist armed forces are the most expensive, obviously. They shoot back and require the use of military tactics.'

'And who are the tourists?'

'Anyone with enough money to pay for it. They have waiting lists, loyal customers, the business is booming. From London to the shooting ground in four, five hours and back in the morning for the opening of the stock exchange. Cocaine and girls are complimentary.'

'Entrepreneurs,' said Gorsky.

'Right,' said Senka and continued. 'So, Vargas has some business interest in that specific venture. And not only that, our Colonel has started a new business venture in London, a cab business.'

'He's running a cab business, you say? What's next, an old people's home, a children's day care?' Gorsky didn't like the man and he couldn't help it.

'It's an aerial cab business. He had imported a couple of choppers from Texas and started a deluxe air taxi service that includes such things as a stocked bar, escorts and other small personal favours.'

'Is that all? I am kind of disappointed. It sounds mild and friendly in comparison with the other ventures.'

'No, there's more, much more to it but we are out of time. We are there.'

The car had come to a stop in front of a restaurant. The bright neon sign on top of the shop window was red, white and green. It read 'Trattoria la Bella Patria.'

'I won't be long,' said Gorsky and opened the door. 'You stay here. Don't move.'

While Gorsky went into the restaurant, Senka leaned back onto the large leather seat.

The restaurant was closed for business and only a couple of staff still busied themselves with cleaning and tiding up. The dining hall featured a dozen tables with chequered tablecloths, black and white photographs of Italian monuments, wreaths of garlic on the walls and bottles of wine on the shelves. Behind the counter stood a large pizza oven surrounded by logs—some of them real and some plastic. A stocky man in his early forties came to meet the visitor.

'Hello,' the man said. 'We didn't expect you.'

'Hi, Haas,' said Gorsky as the two shook hands, 'is Vargas in his office?'

'He is, I think. He's been here all evening,' said Haas and pointed at a door in the corner, next to the pizza oven. 'First door to the right,' he said.

'Thanks.'

Once through the doorway, Gorsky found himself in a long corridor. He had been here before. Once, he thought, possibly twice. He walked to the door and knocked.

'Yes,' he heard, and pressed the handle.

'Gorsky?' asked the man seated behind a glass-and-chrome desk and, nodding in recognition, showed the visitor to a chair. 'Let me finish this conversation. I'll be with you in a second.' He was holding a phone.

The visitor sat in the chair, his hands in the pockets of his dark grey overcoat. While his host was giving instructions about an early morning fresh vegetables and fish trip to the market, Gorsky looked around. He knew of Colonel Vargas and he had met some of his boys. He had been in this very office. He noticed that the framed photographs on the walls were new, and one of them caught his attention. It showed Vargas standing in the middle of a group of young men, all

43

with moustaches and big smiles. They all looked alike—maybe because they were all Moldovan—or was it Romanian? No, no Moldovan, remembered Gorsky. There was also a large colour photograph of the real Vargas, Colonel Vargas, as he preferred to be called, standing in front of a warplane wearing a uniform with decorations. The plane was an old Soviet MIG-15 and the landscape behind it looked desolate.

'That's me in Monrovia,' said Colonel Vargas switching his mobile off. 'It was during my days in Liberia and.... well, Africa in general.'

'Libya, you said?'

'Libya also, but that was before,' said Vargas and pointed at one of the photographs on the wall, 'there's this photograph with a group of young officers. That was in Tripoli.'

'What's this?' asked Gorsky nodding towards a richly designed Italian cuisine certificate that hung on the wall behind Vargas. The name on it was in large print and read 'George Luciano Vargas.'

'Well,' said Vargas, 'Luciano is my, how shall I put it, my nom de guerre! With my real name, *Yoet*, you don't get very far in the pizza business!'

'I hear you run a successful tourist business?' asked Gorsky.

'Well...' started Vargas, unsure whether to talk about his operation or not. 'It's a tourist operation that we started in a couple of African countries. Now we are expanding it to parts of Europe. The business model existed before, in Bosnia in the '90s. We just cleaned it up, recruited better staff and raised the professional level. We now have more experience, access to markets and of course, political support - we are networked, you see?' explained Vargas. He held both hands on his beer belly and carefully waited for

Gorsky's reaction. There was none. The visitor sat immobile in his dark coat. He knew there was more to that story.

'We now operate in the Ukraine too, you see. The Boss helped us with his local connections. Without local knowledge, it is impossible to enter the area, let alone to do business.'

'What's the business, Vargas?' said Gorsky and gripped the armrests of his chair as if to get up. Vargas seemed nervous. He was talking too much, and there must have been a reason for that.

'OK, OK...' said Vargas leaning over the table. 'We pay the locals handsomely. They have a war going on and need all the cash they can lay their hands on. So, we...' Vargas started saying, but his visitor interrupted him.

'Your man, the Italian you sent to Vatayev some time ago, was killed last night. But more importantly and to the point,' said Gorsky and made a brief pause, 'he shot Vatayev and his wife in cold blood. He also shot a friend of mine.'

Vargas picked up the mobile phone from the desk and slid it in a pocket of his dark green jacket. He lit a cigarette.

'Santino?' he said. 'In Rome?'

'That's the name and the place.'

'You were there?'

'I was there.'

'Fuck!' Vargas cried and banged his fist against the desk. 'That little Italian cockroach... I don't believe this! Are you sure he shot them? And who shot him? Who shot the boy, you?'

'He did kill these people, yes. And no, I didn't kill him. Santino, if that is his name, lay low in waiting. When the order came he carried out the task and became a liability. He was killed by sniper fire.'

'How do you know it was sniper fire?' asked Vargas.

'Let's just say that I possess that... skill, we can call it, and that I can tell,' said Gorsky.

'Did you see the shooter?' asked Vargas sucking on his cigarette.

'No,' said Gorsky and pushed his hands deeper in the pockets, 'I didn't.'

That is why he came directly to Vargas. He wanted to face him and see his first reaction.

'I will make my inquiries,' said Vargas, 'the boy came recommended; his cousin worked with my brother in Paris. I will inquire and let you know.'

'Vargas,' said Gorsky and leaned towards his interlocutor in his seat, 'let me make this clear. We lost Boss's deputy and two of his friends. The only known trail leads to this office and... straight to you, Vargas.'

'Gorsky, let me...'

'You don't understand. You fucked up and now there is only one way out for you. That's how it works. I need the name of the man who gave the order.'

'The man who gave the order?' said Vargas and nearly jumped out of his seat, 'What do you...'

'You heard me. People died and you are involved. I don't know how much but I'll find out. And once I do...'

'But...'

'I already told you what you need to do.'

'Right,' said Vargas and nodded. 'Did you speak to the Boss?'

'I did but that has nothing to do with you. You fucked up and you better deal with it, or you'll have half of the Russian mafia coming after you. That's not a threat—that's a promise!' said Gorsky and got up from the chair. 'I'll find my way out.'

Back in the car, Gorsky sat down in the front passenger seat and turned back toward Senka.

'I never liked that man,' he said.

Vanya turned the engine on. Senka was still holding the Fabergé letters in his hand.

'Anything new?' said Gorsky, noticing that Senka had turned rather pale.

'Leon Trotsky must have wanted this jewel badly.'

'Trotsky?' said Gorsky, 'Why would that be?'

'To finance his permanent revolution, to start a new international movement, and to liberate the Soviet Union from Stalin.'

'I see,' said Gorsky and exchanged a secretive glance with Vanya - not those stories again!

'But what's going on?' He knew his friend well enough to understand that this wasn't about Stalin or Trotsky. 'What's happened?'

'I just got a strange call.'

'What call?'

'A call from a police officer,' said Golovkin, 'from Scotland.'

'Something happened to the Boss?' said Gorsky and turned completely around to face Senka.

'His car went off a cliff.'

'And...?'

'It exploded!'

'And the passengers?'

'Apparently all dead,' Senka Golovkin whispered. 'Dead.'

5

From Marange to Khatanga

At half past noon, Jack Sailgood stepped out of the metro train. He liked to travel on his own around the vast city. The Moscow metro system offered a valuable opportunity to develop a feel for the life of the ordinary man, the average Ivan. The vast underground cavern of the Byelorusskaya metro station was not overcrowded at that hour, and one could enjoy the elaborate geometry of the marble floor and the sumptuous ornaments adorning the walls and the vaulted ceiling.

Once past the 35-meter-high escalator and on the street, Sailgood walked gingerly over the slippery crust of ice and snow and turned left into Lesnaya Street. A few hundred steps later he found himself in front of building number three. He approached the locked entranceway, scrutinized the cluster of buzzers and pressed the button next to the name 'Winston and Partners. Law firm.' An indifferent female voice crackled through the speaker: 'What do you want?' 'Jack Sailgood of the British Gas and Petroleum Corporation,' he replied as distinctly as he could.

The doorway clicked open.

When the door opened the panel in the elevator flashed the number five. Sailgood had already managed to take off one glove and was working on the other one. He stepped out of the elevator and into a spacious lobby.

In front of him stood a smiling African American girl.

'Good to see you, Deborah,' said Sailgood.

'Always a pleasure, Sir Jack.'

They shook hands and exchanged pleasantries. Sailgood had been on these premises many times before. He knew some of the employees too. Many were Russian, American and British lawyers specializing in business and criminal law in places such as Kazakhstan, Georgia, Turkmenistan, Uzbekistan and Azerbaijan. Each door bore the name of one of the countries. Sailgood knew that all these sections had one thing in common and that this thing was Tom Deutsch. The man had unlimited access to information and reported to no one. No one within the Winston and Partners structure, that is. So, free was his hand that the company's CEO, Ronald Van Zandt was mildly uncomfortable with Tom's, as he once put it, satanic presence.

They stopped in front of the door with the tag Tom Deutsch, Director of International Operations. Deborah knocked twice and a raucous voice followed by a cough answered: 'Come in!'

Deborah opened the door and Sailgood stepped in. 'You don't need me?' she said. Deutsch coughed some more, nodded and waved his hand. Deborah left the room and closed the door.

'Hello, Jack,' said Deutsch, getting up from his chair to welcome the visitor.

'Good to see you, Tom,' said the Englishman and shook the offered hand.

'Take a seat.'

Jack Sailgood took off his coat, threw it, along with his fur hat and gloves, onto one armchair and sat in the other.

'You should stop smoking, Tom,' he said, watching his host try to squeeze a cigarette out of a pack even before he put out the previous one.

'Stop, you say,' said Deutsch, lit the cigarette and inhaled a good lungful of smoke. 'You know,' he exhaled, 'in this city one must be eternally grateful to providence if one doesn't start abusing drugs... and I mean real drugs like coke, heroin or industrial quantities of vodka.'

Deutsch took another drag, took his time and exhaled: 'I'll quit smoking when I get out of here.'

'Listen to me,' said Sailgood, 'this requires your full attention.'

The American dropped the cigarette into the ashtray and put both his hands on the desk.

'I think I found a way we can strengthen our man's claim to the office in Moscow,' said Sailgood.

'I'm all ears.'

'We traced a jewel that belonged to the Romanovs,' said Sailgood. 'The jewel went missing after the Revolution, but it seems to have surfaced and is causing some commotion now. Someone wants a piece of the Russian action.'

'Russian action?' said Deutsch and took another drag. 'I thought we already had plenty of Russian action? What are you saying?'

'The jewel can facilitate the instalment of our man in Moscow.'

'Kaganov is ready,' said Deutsch. 'He needs to take care of a couple of tiny details himself and we can then proceed with the most colourful and joyful of all the merry revolutions, the one at the Red Square!'

'I have always admired your spirit, Tom. I just hope and pray it won't go as pear shaped as it did in the Ukraine.'

'The Ukraine was a cock-up. The locals are too incompetent and greedy even by Eastern European standards. The Russians are serious people, though. Bigger crooks but reliable in their crookedness. Anyway, you know what I mean. Utterly ruthless and professional. One must give credit when credit is due,' announced Deutsch solemnly. 'So, where is this wonderful jewel?'

'Somewhere in Mexico, it seems,' said Sailgood.

'I thought you said you'd traced it?'

'Well, we traced its existence, that is,' said Sailgood and shrugged his shoulders.

'And where does this metaphysical trail take us, you said?'

'To Mexico.'

'Mexico? As in the big chunk of land south of El Paso, Texas that's home to some hundred and twenty million people?'

'Yes.'

'Would you care to give me some... more refined information?'

'It was last seen in the possession of the artist Frida Kahlo. That's all we know, I'm afraid.'

'So, you should be,' said Deutsch. 'Afraid I, mean... that Kahlo woman died a century ago!'

'In 1954, to be precise,' said Sailgood.

'And how do you suggest we trace this jewel?'

'Well, Tom, it sits on your territory, you see...'

'I see,' said Deutsch with a smug smile. 'We have made some progress. Yes, we did.'

Deutsch equally disliked lagging behind opponents and allies. He believed in efficient information gathering, sharp analysis and decisive action. He would never think twice about wrestling the initiative from under someone else's nose. Initiative was everything—like the opening gambit in a game of chess or a pre-emptive nuclear strike.

Tom Deutsch and Jack Sailgood went back a long time. They could argue about their methods perhaps, but never about core interests or the direction of travel. They also had a little business venture to take care of.

'Jack,' said Deutsch, 'the news from Africa is not good. Mugabe is gone and our little operation at Marange is seriously jeopardized. These new military people seem to be backed by China. The Kimberly Commission is intensifying the pressure on the UN to kick Zimbabwe out and the Africa-Canada Group published a report documenting illegal traffic of diamonds. The value of the black-market trade was set at two billion dollars.'

Sailgood knew that the Marange operation was in jeopardy. What he didn't know, though, was where Deutsch was going with this line of thinking. Did he have a new scheme in mind?

'So, Africa is in the focus of the international public opinion and human rights organizations. Not to mention the World Health Organization and even the Band Aid projects,' said Deutsch and started coughing and/or laughing. 'Harare is now bad for business.'

'Is it?' obliged Sailgood.

'Yes, which brings me to my point, Jack,' said Deutsch. 'Have you had the chance to read this morning's papers?'

'The Russian papers?'

'Yes, the Russian papers.'

'Haven't had the time, this jewel affair took away all my time and imagination.'

'Good,' said Deutsch, 'I can then inform you that the Director of the Institute for Geology and Mineralogy in Novosibirsk held a press conference last night at which he announced their newest and most glorious finding: a crater in the middle of Siberia. It's called Khatanga and it holds enough diamonds to meet the needs of the world market for the next three hundred years.'

'Say that again,' said Sailgood.

'Diamonds, asteroid crater, Siberia, three hundred years... lots of diamonds...' said Deutsch. '*Ponimayesh?*'

'*Da,*' said Sailgood, '*ponimayu*. Are you trying to tell me that Garriburton Global is about to leave the warm climate of Africa and plunge head on into the frozen tundra of Siberia?'

'That's right, my friend,' said Deutsch, 'we need to accept the new geopolitical reality and get a seat at the main table. This is going to be big, Jack, very big.'

'But Tom...'

'Listen to me. Africa is compromised and it is only a matter of time before the whole operation comes under the control of the local state administration and the international trade organizations. Too much visibility equals too much regulation equals less profit and more risk. And for that or even lower risk we can go after the main prize!'

'Siberia?'

'Siberia!'

'Excuse me for my ignorance, but it's hard to see how Siberia could involve less risk? We could continue to work directly with the Harare regime, whatever and whoever that is. These new military people could be interested in acting as guarantors of our investments.'

'Don't hold your breath, Jack. Just another coup in Africa, business and chaos as usual. It will take a decade to settle down. I'm telling you, we're out!'

'I see...' said Sailgood. 'Did you mention a Scotch by any chance?'

'I didn't but it's always a good idea,' said Deutsch and got from his chair to pick up a bottle and two glasses from the cabinet. 'Kentucky Bourbon if you don't mind.'

'I don't,' said Sailgood as Deutsch poured the drinks.

'To our future,' said the American raising his glass.

'To Khatanga,' said Sailgood and downed the drink. 'Tom, do you have any idea of how costly such a deep underground mining operation might be? We are not talking superficial mining here with a couple of picks, shovels and a bunch of semi-naked natives under the guard of a gang of uniformed criminals. We are talking about an asteroid-made crater that's likely to be ten miles wide...'

'Make it sixty.'

'Sixty miles and God knows how many miles deep, in the middle of the Siberian frozen tundra, which happens to be in the biggest country on the planet that is protected by the largest stock pile of nuclear weapons and one of the meanest and toughest armies in the world... and under the watchful eyes of the most feared state security agency in the world, the FSB.'

'Well,' began Deutsch, 'No one said it would be easy, but once our man Kaganov is in office, all the interesting chunks of the country will be up for sale, and thanks to our generous and unselfish support we will be at the head of the line. Most international companies will run for the usual oil, gas and gold, and they will enjoy the full protection of the government assets you just mentioned. It will be a perfectly legitimate enterprise.'

'Why, you want us to start paying taxes?'

'No, of course not. When you are paying the bribes, you don't have to pay the taxes as well. And yes, after the first phase we will not pay for anything anymore, for we will own the place.'

'Will we?'

'Yes, the Dalgan and the Nganasan are local Khatanga tribes whose ethnicity, language, culture and human rights have been heavily suppressed by the Russians for centuries now. Let alone the fact that these people are unhappy with Moscow's lack of investment in the area and are looking for some foreign sponsorship.'

'I see,' said Sailgood. 'Just one tiny detail, Tom. Where do we find the sort of money needed to start this operation?'

'It's not where,' said Deutsch. 'It's who.'

'Fine. Who would that be?'

'That will be one José Saldero Medina.' said Deutsch not without pride.

'The drug lord and mass-murdering maniac?'

'You are getting too old for this line of work, Jack. Too old, too sensitive and waaay too judgmental. Señor Medina is a wealthy businessman looking for an opportunity to invest his hard-earned cash and we happen to be in the ideal position to help him achieve his main objective. It's as simple as that: no politics, no ideology, just good business.' Winded by this little speech, Deutsch started wheezing, coughed for a bit, then hastily lit another cigarette. The wheezing subsided. 'Do you have any idea, Jack, how much the North American drug market is worth? Do you have any idea?'

'Several billion, I would guess.'

'Make it more like fifty, sixty perhaps,' said Deutsch and puffed out a cloud of smoke. 'Fifty billion of newly hatched green American dollars that need to find a safe place to copulate and produce many more green American dollars.'

'I can't see anything wrong in that,' said Sailgood.

'Of course not! The US Treasury Department prints the money, we collect it and reinvest. That's what I call a sound business model and, at the same time, a paradigmatic shift in terms of global strategy.'

'Let's get back to the beginning of this story for a moment.'

'Let's do that,' agreed Deutsch.

'To make any of these things possible, we need Kaganov in the Kremlin.'

'Sounds about right, yes.'

'To strengthen Kaganov's position we need the jewel, the Russian Soul.'

'We do need the jewel.'

'Any ideas how we find it?'

'Sure, I have ideas,' said Deutsch and pressed a button on his office phone. 'Deborah, will you please get our man in El Paso on the line... when? Now! I want to talk to him now!' He then turned to Sailgood and raised his glass: 'To the forthcoming new Red Square revolution!'

'What's the timeline?' said Sailgood coughing and tearing up after taking too big a gulp of his drink.

'Our man is ready to return to Mother Russia and lead the democratic forces into the final battle against the last bastion of the post-Soviet, neo-communist, misogynist, homophobic and backward forces,' said Deutsch and downed the content of his glass.

'The Romanovs are now fully rehabilitated and the Russian Orthodox Church canonized them. Unfortunately, they have no living heirs and the whole thing is largely abstract, metaphorical. They are just recycling the myth, the legend...' said Sailgood. 'That's the Russian Soul, Tom.'

'You mean the jewel? The Russian Soul?'

'The Tsar was replaced by Lenin, then came Stalin and then a long line of faceless apparatchiks. This is a vast country, but full of superstitious, God-fearing people. Russians understand one type of government only, the one that tells them what to do. Our friend Myshkin knows that very well and plays the card of the father of the nation. Alexey Kaganov is right. The jewel is sacred. It holds magical powers!'

'Why would a jewel lost somewhere in Mexico be sacred and magical?' said Deutsch with a wry smile.

'It's called alchemy, Tom. All we need to do is to surround the jewel with an aura of mysticism, sophistication and glory. Just picture Kaganov, the great leader of the Russian world, the one who will restore the glory of the

Tsars, bring peace and prosperity to the masses from the Elbe in the west to the Yenisei in the east, from the Arctic to Mongolia. Kaganov will sit at the table with the Europeans and the Americans and lead Russia from the steps of Asia into the heart of the civilized world of Paris, London and New York.'

'OK, I get your point.' said Deutsch. 'You're missing a tiny detail though, aren't you?'

'Like what?' said Sailgood.

'We don't have the jewel, do we?

6

El Guapo

A black Hummer rolled down the Avenida del Trionfo towards the centre of Ciudad Juárez on Mexico's northern border, Behind the driver sat a man with a hefty moustache. He wore a dark blue jacket over a flowery yellow shirt and wide lapels. Under the jacket, tucked into his belt, was a Colt 38, its grip engraved Pancho on one side and Villa on the other. In the passenger seat sat a man tightly gripping an automatic assault rifle. He wore a Texas-style ten-gallon Stetson hat and a pair of sunglasses. A Toyota UV carrying four armed men rolled ahead of them. Three more Toyotas with more firepower drove behind the Hummer. They moved at high speed cutting through traffic and passing through red streetlights. The party belonged to the one of the local drug cartels and its undisputed boss, the man in the back seat of the Hummer.

Ciudad Juárez is a border town in the north Mexican state of Chihuahua, situated on the Rio Grande opposite El Paso, Texas. The town has the highest number of crime-related deaths in the world, surpassing even that of the whole of Afghanistan at the peak of the war against the Taliban. Drugs, arms, slaves, prostitution, pornography, smut films, domestic violence, street violence, gang-related violence, gratuitous violence... you name it, Juárez had it, and plenty of it. Some claim that the only positive thing about the town was that it wasn't lawless, strictly speaking. The law was enshrined in one man and one man only, José Saldero Medina, El Guapo, the man on the back seat of the Hummer. Next to him was his trusted lawyer and adviser Ignacio Ituribe. The man on the passenger seat was Gonzalo Nieto de Pachenga. *'Paco, para los amigos'*, he liked to say, though he never had any friends.

The motorcade rolled down the Avenida del Trionfo and turned right into Camino de la Rosita, a narrow one-way street. El Guapo's vehicle stopped in front of a discrete and unassuming neon sign that read *'Barrigas—Restaurante tradicional, buena comida y buonos compañeros.'* El Guapo jumped down from the vehicle and stood on the pavement with a mobile phone in his hand while Pachenga and three other men stomped through the entrance to the restaurant. When his right-hand man gave the all-clear signal, El Guapo stomped in too, followed by Ituribe. They passed by a petrified maître d' and walked into the main dining hall where they were met by the proprietor, the cringing, bowing Antonio Barrigas. El Guapo looked around at the patrons. Most of them nearly dropped their cutlery and glasses. They stopped drinking and talking. Some stopped breathing too.

'The Blue Room...' mumbled Barrigas. 'The Blue Room is set for you, your favourite!'

Medina didn't pay much attention to the proprietor. He stood in the middle of the restaurant's main hall and wished everyone a good evening. He apologized for such a rude interruption and mentioned that he would, of course, pay all their bills. Ituribe stood behind him and looked bored. El Guapo congratulated everyone on the choice of the restaurant as this was the pearl of Chihuahua and the envy of many a Texan Gringo. He then invited all the *hermosas señoras y estimados caballeros* to order drinks and food as they wished for they were now, of course, special guests of the *pobre cristiano* José El Guapo Medina. He smiled, shook the hands of a couple of patrons and promenaded towards the Blue Room. As soon as El Guapo left the hall, Pachenga explained that for reasons of security he would like everyone to drop their mobile devices into his men's sacks. A couple of ladies in different corners screamed and Ituribe shook his head. Indeed, the one thing that the Harvard educated Ignacio Ituribe could not stomach was Pachenga's lack of grace and panache. It made his stomach churn.

Once in the Blue Room, El Guapo approached the table and took out from his pocket a Cuban cigar. He placed the cigar on the table and next to it a cigar cutter and a lighter. He took off his jacket and put it over the back of his chair, then pulled the gun out and laid it within reach on the right-hand side of the table. Ituribe took a seat opposite his, dropped a folder he had been carrying next to his plate and put a silver cigarette case on top of it.

'What can I bring you, *señor* Medina?' Barrigas said.

'How about something refreshing?' said El Guapo, 'we are thirsty!'

'Do you want me to bring you a jug of water with ice, mint and lemon...' said Barrigas with a bow.

'I didn't say I was dirty, you peon. I said I was thirsty! Bring me a jug of Marguerita Chamoyada and an iced tea for this miserable creature here,' croaked out Medina nodding at Ituribe who was playing with his cigarette case. 'And I want to order the food now, *rápido!*'

'Sí, señor!' said Barrigas and took out his notebook and pencil. He was ready. He wasn't breathing too well, perhaps, but he was ready to take the order.

'Give me a plate of *tomates rellenos*, then a couple of quesadillas with Poblano chillies and mushrooms, tacos with fish and Chipotle chillies... then, but only once I have finished with the appetizers, I want an *Arrachera, a Brocheta de filete* and...' Medina stopped in mid-sentence and directed a penetrating gaze at Barrigas, '...are the meats locally sourced, or imported from Texas?'

'From Chihuahua, Chihuahua...' cried the restaurateur as if his life depended on it. Perhaps it did. 'Local, all local, I personally go to the market every morning and buy local produce!'

'Good man,' said El Guapo, flashing his impeccable, Hollywood-white teeth. Barrigas hazarded a guess that it was a smile. He showed his own teeth in return and bowed. Juán Barrigas had lived long enough in Ciudad Juárez to be able to smell danger, and danger incarnate came in the shape of José Medina, the Emperor of Drugs, whose operations extended to Afghanistan, New York and beyond, spreading its tentacles into the nerve centres of world power, the dark corners of governments and shady global enterprises. Barrigas had come over to Mexico as a young man from the Spanish Extremadura region which produced Hernán Cortés, the conquistador of the Aztecas. All his life he had tried hard to lose his Iberian accent and he was now trying harder than ever.

'Good man, and bring me a bottle of the Sangre de Cortés, ha, ha... The Spanish bastard drank enough Aztec blood so it's time for us to repay the courtesy. Don't you agree, amigo?' said Medina, flashing his white teeth at Barrigas, who bowed lower than before and again managed to produce a semblance of a smile.

'Bring a jug of water too, for this valiant servant of mine,' said El Guapo and nodded towards Ituribe, 'and to eat?'

'Hm...' said the advisor. He had just extracted a pinch of white powder from his cigarette holder... 'for me a... salad, Caesar salad.'

'A salad,' said El Guapo. 'Give him a salad, a salad!'

'*Muchas gracias,*' said Barrigas, and retreated in a hurry with his precious notebook.

'Stop sniffing and start talking to me,' said El Guapo and picked up a knife from the table to play with. He noticed a large tear drop coming out of the corner of his advisor's eye.

'Hm... our source in the Pentagon confirmed...' said Ituribe closing the silver cigarette case, '...that the US administration is serious about downsizing their military presence in Afghanistan.'

'*Hijos de puta,*' said El Guapo and hit the table with his fist, 'gratitude, is this what they call it, gratitude?'

'Hm ... Johnson pledged to secure our interests in the country post American withdrawal.'

'Tell the Yanks to get stuffed. I had enough of their drivel. No, don't tell them anything, just get in touch with those Taliban gentlemen we've been talking to. Let's talk some business.'

As he said 'Taliban,' the door opened and a waitress brought in a tray with the drinks. The business conversation stopped. Barrigas brought the *Sangre de Cortés*, uncorked the bottle and poured a sip of the red wine in a glass. El Guapo waved a hand at him in a circular motion for him to fill it. 'Skip the niceties, old man.'.

'Talk to me some more,' he said once the door closed.

'Well, the Gringo from El Paso is asking for two things.'

'I already don't like it... asking is too presumptuous, don't you think, abogado?'

'Pleading,' Ituribe corrected himself, 'he's pleading, begging for a meeting to discuss a possible joint venture. It would take care of our cash flow problem—on a permanent basis.'

'I'm all ears,' said El Guapo and picked up the wine glass.

'He didn't give me any details but implied a global business venture and gave me two key words...: Russia; and...'

'And...?'

'... diamonds.'

'Interesting,' said El Guapo. 'Diamonds are always interesting. And what's the second plea?'

'To find a jewel.'

'Me, to find a jewel?'

'It's in Mexico, the legend has it.'

'How are these two pleas related?' asked El Guapo and poured himself some more wine. '*Sangre de Cortés*! Let's drink some more Spanish blood!'

'We find the jewel,' said Ituribe, 'and bring it to the table as our ticket to the big party.'

'How big... this party?'

'Three hundred years' worth of diamond supplies for the whole world,' said Ituribe.

'Ok, let's find the stupid jewel, and...' El Guapo started to say when Pachenga stormed into the room holding a mobile phone and mumbling something about traitors and *hijos de putas.* El Guapo picked up the gun and the phone while Ituribe repocketed his silver cigarette case.

'What now?' cried the King of Drugs. He heard what Pachenga had to say and cried, 'An army column is moving in our direction? No time to waste!'

He put on his jacket, snatched the smoking paraphernalia up from the table and stuffed it in his pockets, then collected his gun. He walked out of the room followed by Ituribe. In the main dining hall, two of his men already stood at the exit waiting for him. As he moved through the room someone dropped a piece of cutlery. Faster than his men, El Guapo turned towards the table the sound came from and fired four shots at the two men sitting there. The ladies in their company screamed and raised their hands. One held a knife and a fork, the other a spoon. The two men lay immobile on the floor.

'Sorry, *señoritas,*' said El Guapo. 'I am in a bit of a hurry.'

He walked out of the door and onto the street and jumped into the Hummer.

'*¡Vámonos!*' he yelled as Ituribe threw himself onto the back seat, '*hijos de putas y cabrónes, chingada madre, hijo de perra...*'

'What happened?' said Ituribe while Pachenga was yelling orders to the driver.

'That *cabeza de mierda y pendejo de la...*' said El Guapo. '... I hate traitors! I hate traitors more than rattlesnakes, more than rats and scorpions put together. When I get hold of that *hijo de puta*, I will feed him to the rats and wild dogs... I will...'

'I see,' said Ituribe.

The column of vehicles moved out of the narrow Camino de la Rosita and sped up the Aucatlán boulevard towards the south and El Guapo's headquarters, a large mansion turned into a fortress that even the local police felt ill-equipped to approach.

'I want to talk to that son of a bitch now. Find him or I'll come to find him myself!' said El Guapo on the phone before turning to Ituribe: 'Abogado, remind me to cut the balls off this *hijo de puta* politician. I pay him good money to buy haciendas, private jets, women and votes... useless, he is useless!'

'Sure,' said Ituribe. 'I will remind you to cut off his balls.'

'What were you saying about those Russians and diamonds?' asked El Guapo.

'I said that we should find that jewel and take it to London.'

'London? Why London?'

'That's where the meeting is taking place.'

'OK, Russians and diamonds, sounds exotic...' said the King of Drugs. 'Smells like money, feels like money... what can I say, all good! Find the stupid jewel and we are off to London. I've had enough of this desert!'

7

The return of The Rose

The compartment shook. The engine droned on to the accompaniment of distant thunder. Uniformed men sat tightly packed together on a narrow bench, their backs against the bare metal fuselage. They stamped their heavy boots against the floor, puffed on cigarettes and laughed while the engine noise grew louder. Laughter and smoke, weapons and kit rattling. One of the men showed his teeth. He clapped his hand against his knee, then laughed some more while wiping his mouth with his sleeve. He then elbowed the man next to him and they both laughed and grinned. The engines roared and the boots kept stomping while behind the row of tiny round windows red lights flashed on and off. Suddenly, the laughter faded away and an eerie kind of cold penetrated the bones. Cold, ice cold. Without thinking, you jump out and plummet toward the dark ground...

Gorsky clawed his way out of the dream. He thought he had screamed. He sat up in the bed, wiped the sweat off his forehead and looked around. He recognized the few pieces of simple furniture, the high ceiling and the tall Victorian windows. No more uniformed men that he couldn't recognize, no more engine roar, no more stamping boots. He had returned to his home galaxy, like so many times before. Next to him, under the bedcover, was a slim body, on the pillow a curl of brown hair. The cover rose and fell slightly, rhythmically, the breathing silent.

'Is she asleep?' crossed his mind. 'I never know if she is asleep or not. It's a mystery to me!'

Gorsky glanced at the digital clock on the windowsill. Seven o'clock. He got out of bed. He had had enough sleep; five to six hours was plenty for him. Deep inside he had always been a believer in being awake, alert, in constant movement.

The body of the Buddha appears to be immobile while his spirit is everywhere, Gorsky mused.

Barefoot, he moseyed up to the window and pulled aside the blind: it was misty, soggy, windy. The streetlamp cast light onto the road lined with parked cars, where a sanitation worker pushed back in place a couple of bins and rushed on. He wore a yellow jacket, had short, blond hair and probably spoke Lithuanian at home. Across the street, a man shut the door, checked his wristwatch, switched on the tiny player strapped to his arm and set off jogging. In his childhood, as Gorsky remembered it, he liked to get up early and prepare the books for school, to have breakfast, to start running before touching the ground while the others were still busying themselves with their shoe laces. He left the room, closed the door behind him and opened a second door a couple of steps down the corridor to the left. In the bathroom, he washed his face and brushed his teeth. As he came out he heard a whimper.

He opened the door of the living room and said, 'Shut up, Knyaz!' to a large Samoyed dog who got up on his hind legs and placed his paws on his master's shirt. Gorsky patted the animal on the head and they went together to the tiny kitchen where he filled a tin bowl with the contents of a box of dog food to which he added some milk. While Knyaz was happily munching his meal, Gorsky retreated to the corridor, closed the door and went into a room that was equipped with a treadmill, a rowing machine, a collection of dumbbells and other sporting equipment. He put his running gear on, hopped on the treadmill and touched the screen: six miles an hour, then eight, ten, twelve. After fifteen minutes on the treadmill he jumped off, sat on the rowing machine and pressed the P1 option on the screen: program one. He bent his knees, extended his arms, picked up the handle, straightened his back and pulled. He pulled hard, with his legs first, then with the back and finally with the arms—the way Pat, the rowing coach, had taught him. Thirty minutes at resistance rate eight, eighteen strokes per minute, one minute and forty-five seconds per five hundred meters split: P1. There was also a P2 and a P4 but those were competition modes. P1 was well suited for contemplation and problem solving. It was a meta-physical mode.

Gorsky worked part-time as an instructor of Russian Systema, a martial arts technique. Following the collapse of the Soviet Union the ban on teaching the Systema was lifted and many former KGB and SPETSNAZ agents who had left the country began teaching it. For Gorsky, teaching martial arts was a way to keep his reflexes sharp and to earn a couple of extra pounds on top of what he was making as a security guard working for Aleksey Kaganov. He taught at a local Kung Fu school, but had private clients too. Clients like the American Air Force Base at Lakenheath, in Suffolk. He liked to 'throw the Yanks around.' They called him Boris, or sometimes Ivan, or the Ivan. Some called him Stripes, for he always wore his Russian military shirt—his *telnyashka*, with narrow light blue and white horizontal stripes, in the style used by paratroopers.

He kept this room locked. It was his private corner. His dwellings were temporary, a compromise, just like a soldier's bivouac. Like some animal species, he preferred to eat alone. He liked his training and his routine. There was a room in his flat that no one had ever entered. There was also his springtime trip: every April he would take off from work and vanish for three weeks. He never spoke about his whereabouts during this period. Whether among Siberian rivers, Scottish Highlands or Norwegian fjords, in the wilderness he felt at home.

It's all about speed, he would reflect when trying to formulate his philosophy. Not the speed of a train, a plane or a bullet. It's about the speed of light!

Alex Gorsky needed solitude and quiet to refocus. He would sit still for hours on end, observing mountains and wild animals.

His girlfriend Kathy once asked him if he ever passed classified information to the Americans. 'Nothing that you can't find on the Internet,' he replied. 'It's funny, you see, they ask me all sorts of questions—soldiers and officers alike. They want to know about weapons, tactics, combat readiness and morale, endurance training and martial arts... They ask everything except the most obvious and the most important question.'

'Like what?' asked Kathy.

'Like, how come I speak English so well? Did I learn it at school or in the army? Do I speak other languages too perhaps? Was I trained in skills other than languages? Why was I trained and how many of us were there in that specific program? They never thought of asking the essential question. Shame on them.'

'Would you have told them?'

'That specific bit of information is not to be found on the Internet, is it?' said Gorsky.

As he was reaching the twenty-fifth minute of the rowing P1 drill the door opened and a long, smiling face with a pair of lively dark eyes appeared through the gap.

'Morning, rower,' she said and waved to catch Gorsky's attention.

'Hi,' he said taking his eyes off the machine's display. 'Morning, baby!'

'Breakfast in ten minutes, because I have to go,' said the young woman.

'Sure,' said Gorsky and increased the number of strokes to thirty-six, lowering his split time to under a minute and thirty seconds. Rowing across the Mediterranean, from Sicily to Libya and back in five minutes!

The small table in the lounge, just outside the tiny kitchen, was set for breakfast. Bacon and eggs, bread, butter and yoghurt for Gorsky, wholegrain cereal for Kathy. And coffee, of course: Turkish for him and decaf with soy milk for her.

'Good,' said Gorsky, taking a seat at the table and drawing his chair closer to the plate. He had completed his jog and his P1 session, had a shower, put a clean shirt on. He looked, smelled and felt good.

Kathy squeezed the mug in her hands: 'Let me recap,' she said, 'I need to understand this. You, Kolya and an Italian are in Rome with Zakhar who has business with the Saint Egidio Foundation. The last evening, before departure, Zakhar and his wife dine in his favourite restaurant. Kolya and the Italian go with them.'

'Yes,' said Gorsky while spreading butter on a slice of bread.

'Now, you weren't there with them because the Boss asked you to fetch that parcel from the antiquarian, yes?'

'He asked me to fetch only one item,' said Gorsky, tucking into the bacon.

'The sword. OK, fine. But once in the shop you are told that there is another item for you to pick up.'

'Yes.'

'The letters, right. You pick up these things and walk across the city to the restaurant,' said Kathy. Gorsky nodded, chewing.

'As you approach the place you see a shadow and stop. You see Zakhar and his wife in front of the restaurant. The shadow comes out into the light and you recognize the Italian. He approaches the two and shoots them.'

'Yes,' said Gorsky, took a sip of the coffee and leaned back in the chair.

'You run towards the spot with your gun out and the man turns towards you. You throw yourself on the ground, he shoots at you, misses and you get up and shoot him. At the same time, though, the man is hit by something that takes half his head off.

'A large-calibre sniper round,' said Gorsky.

'Right. You hide behind a parked car. The shooter disappears. You check Kolya, Zakhar, Irina... All dead. You run. Why? Why did you not stay to talk to the police?'

'The Boss wouldn't want me to,' said Gorsky.

'Why not?'

'No exposure to law enforcement agencies or media,' said Gorsky. 'That's the golden rule. It's part of the job, it says so in the contract.'

'They will be after you, you know? Not that hard to identify the third security man and trace him down.'

'I know, but that was supposed to be the Boss's problem. He takes care of the police, the media and the politicians.'

'The Boss...' said Kathy and took a long sip of the decaf. 'Except that the Boss is dead now.'

'Yes.'

'So, where does that leave you?'

'That leaves me with the letters and a sword.'

'What are the letters about?'

'Agathon Fabergé's letters.'

'Fabergé, the jeweller?' said Kathy.

'Yes,' confirmed Gorsky not without surprise. 'How come you women always know about precious stones?'

'You don't want to know, darling,' quipped Kathy. 'Why would the Boss be interested in hundred-year-old letters?'

'Because of a thing called Russkaya Dusha, it seems.'

'As in Russian soul, spirit?'

'No, as in the jewel!'

'There's a Fabergé jewel called the Russian Soul and the Boss wanted it...' said Kathy squeezing one eye as if aiming at a target, '... only to give it away as a present to Milla Ivanovna?'

'Maybe,' said Gorsky and shrugged his shoulders. 'But it gets even better.'

'Does it?' said Kathy and took another sip of decaf.

'The jewel is supposed to be one of the famous Easter eggs that Nikolai II, the last Tsar or Russia, commissioned for his wife and mother over a number of years. Senka tells me that these eggs are all well known, but that this one - the Russian Soul - is not listed. As if it didn't exist!'

'So, the dead Boss who wants to become president is after a non-existent Fabergé Easter egg jewel?' concluded Kathy setting down the now empty mug.

'Something like that,' said Gorsky.

'I see. But it gets even better, doesn't it?' said Kathy. Gorsky placed both hands on the table and got ready to listen.

'Someone just killed Zakhar, Irina and Kolya, right? And that someone knows that you are the only witness to the murders... that someone might be looking for you now, as we speak!

'Might be,' said Gorsky.

'So, what are you going to do?'

'See Milla Ivanovna...'

'The grieving, widowed wife,' interjected Kathy who wasn't a great fan of the said woman.

'...and give her the letters and the sword. I also need to talk to her. She must know something.'

'Even if she did, why would she tell you?'

'I don't know,' said Gorsky. 'My good friend and two other people I knew were killed. The Boss is dead too. These are exceptional circumstances.'

'How big?' said Kathy and moved the mug from one place on the table to another.

'Really big, Kathy,' said Gorsky. 'The Boss was one of the richest men on the planet. What could be big enough to take such a man out of his comfort zone?'

Knyaz got up from his corner with his tongue lolling, wagged his tail and growled as if he had a say in the matter.

'You're right,' said Gorsky to the dog. 'And you have no idea just how right you are.'

'I have to go,' said Kathy looking at her mobile phone. 'Oh, yes. You might want to know that Milla Ivanovna confirmed this morning's massage session. After all she's in mourning and I am sure she wants to look her best at the funeral.' She stood up from the table, dropped her plate and mug in the sink and picked her coat from the hanger.

'Call me tonight,' he said.

'Will do,' she said and kissed him on the cheek. 'Take care. They are bad. These are very bad, evil people.'

'I know,' he said. 'Don't worry. Trust me.'

'I was afraid you would say that,' Kathy said managing to produce a faint smile. She touched his hand gently then turned around and rushed out of the door.

As soon as the sound of Kathy's steps faded away, Gorsky got up to clear the table. Dishes in the sink, butter in the fridge... Something was wrong, thought Gorsky. Knyaz wagged his tail, the hot water flew into the sink, and the radio announced a windy day... And yet, that smell of rot was present, lodged in his nostrils. He knew it well. He had learnt to sniff it out, like Knyaz would do, like any animal would do. The dishwashing liquid was making lots of foam, a cloud of foam, when the mobile rang.

'It's been confirmed, Alex,' cried Senka Golovkin. 'The Boss is dead. The car collided with a truck and fell off a cliff. Milla Ivanovna flew there in the middle of the night to identify the body.'

'And?'

'She made a positive identification.' said Golovkin breathing heavily. 'I am going to see Milla Ivanovna now; she just came back and she's at home now. I'll be in touch,' said Senka and terminated the call.

Gorsky was left standing in front of the sink overflowing with white, warm dishwashing liquid foam.

Under the watchful eye of the dog, he used a kitchen towel to dry his hands and rushed to the laptop on the living room couch. He logged in and started browsing the daily news headlines: Aleksey Kaganov recently asked to be permitted to return to Russia, FSB, the Russian Secret Police has a hand in the Oligarch's Death? Before Death Oligarch Writes to Russian President Asking for Permission to Visit Mother Hospitalised in Moscow, The Kremlin Behind Oligarch Death - Suggests Source Close to Russian Diplomats, Friends of Late Tycoon Tell Reporter of Recent

Nervous Breakdown, After Zakharov's Murder, Kaganov Dies in Car Crash - Coincidence? The Trail Leads to the Kremlin!

He then wanted to check his e-mails. It was the usual rubbish plus a mail from the gym about the next session, a communication from the landlord about a heating issue, and eventually, a mail from someone completely unknown, someone called Rose.

'What kind of rubbish is this, now?' thought Gorsky and was just about to press enter and dispose of the message when he realised that the name was written in Cyrillic: *Роза*. A Russian woman looking for a husband? He clicked on the icon to open the e-mail. It was in Russian and very brief: 'Find the Russian Soul.'

It was signed, *Роза* - The Rose.

8

Niusha

Gorsky cast a glance at the kitchen clock. It was time to take Knyaz out for his morning walk. He put his coat on, the heavy trekking boots and hat, attached the leash to the dog and picked up the case with the sword. On the second floor, he knocked on a door. A plump woman with a watering can in her hand opened the door. She wore a long robe with a flowery pattern.

'Hello, Alex,' she said and leaned to pat the dog. 'I heard the news this morning...'

'Yes, terrible news, Mrs Paraskevi,' said Gorsky. 'You mean the Boss, right? Kaganov's car crash?'

'Yes, of course I mean that,' said the woman, 'What happened to him?'

'I don't know much myself. I've just received the information from a friend, a colleague from work; he told me of the accident and said the police was handling the case. It is not treated as a suspicious death. My friend, I mean, my colleague said.'

'I see,' said Mrs Paraskevi, 'Terrible, terrible... Do you want to come in?'

'No, thanks. I wanted to ask your husband, Mr Stavros, to have a look at an item I brought from Rome the other day.'

'Yes, sure,' said Mrs Paraskevi.

'Here it is,' said Gorsky and passed the case to the woman. 'It's a sword that I brought over from Rome. It's quite old and precious, the antiquarian said. I just wanted your husband's opinion on it. He's the expert.'

'Of course,' said Mrs Paraskevi, 'I'll pass it to Stavros. He'll be more than happy to have a look at it.'

'Thanks,' said Gorsky. He proceeded down the stairs and onto Kingston Street. At the first corner, he turned right towards Mill Road and soon reached Parker's Piece, a large patch of grass in the heart of town. It was the dog's favourite spot and Gorsky was happy to unleash him and throw a tennis ball around.

The Moustakas were Greeks who had lived in Britain since the late eighties. She was from Thessaloniki in mainland Greece and he was a Cypriot from Nicosia. Sometimes they disagreed about accents, expressions and names for things or food items but one thing they had in common, though. One was never to mention the Turks in their presence. Not even ask for a Turkish coffee or baklava. No, in the presence of the Moustakas, one was best advised not to mention the Turks.

Mr Stavros owned a small antiques shop in town. Before he started this business, he was a curator at the British Museum and versed in Medieval and Renaissance warfare. He was a good person to seek an opinion from. Gorsky didn't believe signor Pincherle's stories. On the other hand, he couldn't quite understand why the Boss would want to buy a phony sword. But hey, the Boss was so predictably unpredictable. It was part of his game, of his 'deadly charm'.

'Unpredictable is good,' Kaganov told Gorsky on more than one occasion. 'Once people start thinking you behave erratically and call you 'capricious' you know you're doing fine. Friends and enemies should be kept guessing. Fear also helps. Instil fear in people around you. Being feared helps, it's good for business!'

In ten minutes, Gorsky and Knyaz reached the intersection of Mill and East Road. Kolya, Zakhar, Colonel Vargas, Senka, the old man in Rome... Gorsky's mind was busy trying to restore some order to the events that took place in the past couple of days. These were not ordinary events but game changers of the highest order. Gorsky felt as if he lacked the key to interpreting such a new reality though. He was sitting in pitch dark while someone was setting off fireworks.

Parker's Piece was diagonally across the road, which meant crossing two streets to get to the common. Before the intersection on the right at the very corner of the two streets and next to the abandoned Christian Zionist Church there was a small park and a playground. At its entrance, on a white, plastic chair sat a man selling pins, badges, balloons and daffodils. His hair was long and white. He wore an aged coat that looked colourful thanks to the many items he sported on the lapels and sleeves.

Gorsky stopped in front of the man and bought another Union Jack pin. He had already bought many of his pins and badges. They had spoken a couple of times. George, he said his name was, was an ex-serviceman. He fought in the Falklands where he was wounded in the head during a very long, cold night. 'The Argentines shot at us and we shot at them...' he explained once. George had no immediate family or friends. A small pension and lots of memories, that's all he had.

'Useless,' he said '... the past.'

George lived in a shelter for homeless people.

'It's warm there,' he said. 'It's OK.'

Gorsky listened and bought more pins and badges. They said hello and goodbye to each other, nodded their heads. George never asked and Gorsky never said anything about his own experience in Chechnya. He placed a couple of coins in George's tiny collection box and said goodbye.

'God bless you,' George said.

Gorsky held the leash tight and was about to press the large pedestrian button on the streetlight when screams and shouts attracted his attention. They were coming from the playground next to the church. He turned around and spotted a group of hooded youths gathered around a bench. They held Scrumpy Jack cans in their hands and kept taunting a girl and her dog. The streetlight turned green and started beeping for the pedestrians to cross. Knyaz was pulling the leash when one of the hoodies stopped jumping and booted the dog with a powerful right-leg kick. The dog squealed and the girl crouched on the bench. Gorsky jerked the leash back and approached the group. At first, they didn't see him coming. One of the assailants poked the girl with a long stick and laughed wildly. As Gorsky took Knyaz off the leash, one of the hoodies turned around and pointed in his direction.

'Oi, what about you? Mr ...' he said producing a broad, fake smile of semi-rotten teeth.

'*Nyet,*' said Gorsky and hit him on the cheek with the open palm of his right hand. The hoody dropped the can, stumbled and fell over on his back at which point the other three hoodies noticed Gorsky's presence and turned facing him.

'And you, who the fuck are you now?' said the tall hoody with a dirty baseball cap.

'Some sort of a knight, I guess,' said a short one and picked an empty beer bottle up from the pavement.

'Yep, shining armour and all that shit,' concluded the one with the baseball bat.

The girl sat upright on the bench now and her Cocker Spaniel sneaked underneath.

'I know your smug face,' said the short hoodie and raced towards Gorsky raising the can. The other three stood in a semi-circle.

'No, you don't,' said Gorsky, moving slightly aside to avoid the attack. He then tightened his big fist and hooked the jaw of the assailant taking him a dozen inches off the ground. As the body landed on the concrete path, Gorsky felt the impact of the baseball bat that hit his shoulder and the back of his head. He grabbed the bat and once he had the man within reach pulled his shirt, brought his face closer and then to an abrupt stop with a head butt. The man's knees gave in and he fell leaving the baseball bat to Gorsky who turned towards the last two thugs. The tall one with the baseball cap tried to run but was stopped by a mighty kick in the groin that came from the girl who was now standing in the middle of the path in full combat mode. The last member of the gang looked at the girl, then at Gorsky who stood a whole head taller. He turned only to find himself facing Knyaz' fangs and eager gaze. He yelled a profanity and ran towards the furthest corner of the park.

'Well, and who are you?' said the girl standing right in front of Gorsky with a threatening note in her voice.

'I'll be fine, it's nothing,' said Gorsky and stroked the back of his head, 'Thank you for asking.'

'Oh, not only that we like to beat people up but we have a funny streak too. What planet did you just come from and what do you think you are doing? They are my mates, you know?'

'Nice people, your friends, very nice. Next time when I'm not around you can take them home to your mum and your teddy bear. Nice little friendship you people have there. Sorry for interfering with your games and good bye,' he said and turned to leave.

'Ok, ok,' she said. 'It did look a bit odd, I must admit. Let me have a look,' she said and made a gesture for the tall man to lower his head. He did so and she began to examine the bump. 'It's already swollen and there's a nice cut too. Some blood, not much but still...'

'You don't sound like people from round here?'

'Russian.'

'Russian, right. You need someone to fix your head.'

'My head is fine, thank you.'

'Nah, come with me. You have some blood in your hair. I live around the corner. Come with me and I can fix your wound and make you a cup of coffee.'

'No need really...'

'Shut up and move,' she said with authority and the matter was settled. They called the dogs, put the leashes on and began walking down Mill Road towards the first street to the left, Collier Road. The girl spoke and Gorsky listened. She sounded English but looked Arab he thought, or maybe not quite Arab but not Greek, not Spanish. She had big dark eyes able to produce an intense, penetrating stare.

'By the way, my name is Niusha,' she said and they shook hands. 'Alex,' he mumbled. 'You're not from around here?' he said while they were walking towards Collier Road.

'Birmingham, if you don't mind. That's where I'm from.'

'That's fine with me.'

'Why did you ask?'

'You asked me first.'

'Yeah, but you are obviously a foreigner. You behave like a bear in a Ming Dynasty vase shop so I had to ask. That makes sense, right?'

'Right.'

'You have a wife at home?'

'I don't have a wife at home.'

'A girlfriend?' she insisted.

'A girlfriend what?'

'Do you have a girlfriend?'

'I do have a girlfriend, so what?'

''What's her name? You will need someone to clean your cut tomorrow.'

'Her name is Kathy.'

'What does Kathy do?'

'Unlike you, she minds her own business.'

'What does Kathy do? I said. 'It's a polite question. Round here we call it a conversation, you see?'

'She works as a therapist and in her spare time is building a country house of recyclable materials.'

'Your house?'

'Her house!'

'Cool, that's cool,' said the girl. 'She does all of that?'

'Yes, she does all of that,' said Gorsky. 'Are you always that nosey?'

'Yeah, I am, why? You jumped into my life, remember? So, the girl invests, right?'

'Yes! She invested some of her savings in it and she hopes to resell the house and maybe earn one for us.'

'Right, where did she get the capital to start her business?'

'Working...'

'What kind of job?' she cried and stopped in the middle of the pavement. 'I see, Kathy was a working girl... you know what that means do you?'

Gorsky stopped and stared at her.

'I think I know,' he said, 'no, she wasn't that kind of working girl!'

'I see, you saved her life as you saved mine tonight, right?'

'No, you're not making much sense, you know?'

'You, big hero!' she cried, 'do you realise that these morons were my customers? They are morons, that's clear, but nonetheless, paying customers.'

'You a working girl too?' said Gorsky with a triumphant little smile protruding from the corner of his mouth.

'No, I sell dope,' she said. 'Nothing major, you know. A bit of hash here, a bit of grass there, some colourful pills... Fun stuff, you see. I don't do hardcore. I have principles. I know it might not look that way to you but I have values and principles, big man. You get it?'

'I get it,' said Gorsky and nodded.

'Of course, you do,' said Niusha. She sounded like someone with serious military training: 'you come with me and you let me thank you for spoiling my business.'

'What, where? I can't go anywhere tonight for...'

'Sure, sure, you see this corner?'

'I see that corner.'

'Come with me!' she ordered.

9

Doing business with women

'This WikiLeaks routine is affecting my nerves,' said Jack Sailgood and put two pills on his tongue. He took a sip of water and swallowed them while going through a pile of printed papers on his lap. 'Can you imagine that they managed to intercept an e-mail that contains the words diamonds, Harare and Khatanga in the same paragraph!'

Tom Deutsch sat on the next seat reading from his tablet computer.

'They can write and publish anything they like, this is a free world we live in. Thanks to people like us, of course,' said the American.

The British Airways flight originated from Moscow Sheremetyevo airport and was en route to London Heathrow. Sailgood and Deutsch occupied two seats in the first-class section. They had important work to do, lots of papers to read and lots of problems to solve. They used to fly routinely in their respective agencies' jets until a couple of months ago when a WikiLeaks dispatch drew attention to the travel expenses of the British intelligence community, which prompted a couple of Members of Parliament to raise this question and suggest that these expenses be brought in line with the diplomatic service standards. 'Administration is administration,' as one MP put it. Flying in the CIA jet was out of the question as eyebrows might be raised about such a cosy proximity. So, here they were in the first-class cabin with one agent occupying the seats in front and the other behind them. The one in front read the ESPN Sports review on a tablet and the one behind was browsing through the latest edition of Country Living dedicated to Shropshire cottages on his mobile phone.

'Jack,' continued Deutsch, 'the more dust flies around, the less visible it gets. The WikiLeaks boys and girls are doing a fine job. We should be supporting their work with some funding if we aren't already!'

'Sure, and I guess you suggest we give Edward Snowden a medal for taking all of our NSA dirty laundry to Moscow!' said Sailgood and dropped the papers onto his lap. 'It might finally encourage others to step forward and buy tickets for Russia and perhaps China.'

'Well, well,' said Deutsch, 'look who's talking... you let that Assange terrorist just leisurely move into the London Embassy of his choice and live there peacefully ever after! What do you call that?'

'We can't do anything about it except what we are already doing. Block the building and wait for him to come out. International law, sorry!'

'Holy cow, international law you say. Did you just say international law? Did I hear you say international law?' said Deutsch. 'Let me remind you, my boy. We make laws, we then apply and enforce them. We have the ability and bear the responsibility to tell right from wrong. After all, we are the Free World and the International Community.'

'So, what do you suggest?' said Sailgood, 'that we storm the Knightsbridge Embassy of a foreign country, take the target outside and shoot him in the street?'

'Oh,' said the American, 'you are so melodramatic, so Shakespearian, that you would make it look like a tragedy at the end. No, I am not suggesting anything of the sort. You just have the Embassy stormed and tidied up and you then

85

issue a very polite and civilised statement where you explain that you are terribly sorry for the collateral damage caused but that you had reports that the Queen's security was compromised and that a terrorist cell was preparing an imminent attack under the auspices of the Ecuadorian Embassy. Done, *finito, Ende!*'

'I see,' said the Englishman, 'the Queen would never agree to it though.'

'What do you mean? You are not going to ask her, aren't you?'

'Well you see...'

Deutsch stared at his partner with eyes wide open unsure whether to laugh at the joke or... did he miss the cue? Sailgood's facial expression was collected and serious. The flight over Belarus was calm and most passengers were busy reading from tablets and listening to music.

'You would have to ask the old lady for permission?' said the American.

'It's called sense of humour, Tom,' said Sailgood who never missed the opportunity to make a casual reference to the British Royal family in his conversations with the American.' Dry perhaps but nonetheless, humour.'

'Fuck you,' said Deutsch, exhaled and pressed the service button. The stewardess came over in a matter of seconds,

'A large Bourbon on the rocks,' said Deutsch and signalled with his thumb at his co-passenger.

'Thank you, Tom,' said Sailgood. 'A Scotch for me, please. Neat, thanks.'

While the stewardess was preparing the drinks, Sailgood and Deutsch sat in silence each with his own line of thoughts and strategy to develop.

'We are flying over Minsk, Belarus, at an altitude of thirty thousand feet,' announced the pilot, 'we'll soon enter the airspace of Poland and then fly over Germany, Holland and across the English Channel. We expect to arrive at our destination soon after ten o'clock. The weather in London is calm, six degrees Celsius with no precipitation.'

The stewardess brought the drinks in large glasses and red BA napkins. They thanked her, scanned her delicate features, nodded in approval and raised the glasses.

'To our enterprise!' said Sailgood.

'To Khatanga!' said Deutsch. He then took a sip from his glass and asked: 'Did your crew report today?'

'From Khatanga, you mean?'

'Yes, I meant from Siberia, Khatanga of course,' said Deutsch, 'they flew there on a reconnaissance mission and to meet the local politicians, right?'

'Yes,' said Sailgood, 'but they had an accident.'

'What do you mean?'

'The helicopter crashed...'

'What, they are dead?'

'No, not all of them,' said Sailgood. 'The pilot survived.'

'Only the pilot survives the crash of a chopper?' said Deutsch, 'there's a first time for everything, I guess.'

'Yes, the Russian pilot survived. The helicopter belonged to the Russian Ministry of Forestry.'

'Did the chopper crash or not?' Deutsch showed signs of impatience.

'It did crash but in such a manner that everyone got finely chopped by the propellers while the pilot managed to escape.'

'I see.' said the American. 'I imagine that this official version of the events was provided by the most forthcoming Russian Ministry of Interior Affairs?'

'Vadim Kudrov in person.'

'Right,' said Deutsch, 'how is our friend Aleksey Kaganov doing in London? Is he getting ready to return triumphantly to Russia?'

'No, he seems to be dead,' said Sailgood and helped himself to the Scotch.

'Dead, you say?'

'Car accident in Scotland.'

'Jack, are you now telling me that our man, the governor of the fuckin' biggest and now also richest chunk of Siberia managed to get himself killed in a car crash? Just like that?'

'Confirmed by the police.'

'What police force would that be? Not Russian, I hope!'

'Scotland Yard,' said Sailgood in a reassuring tone.

'Why does this guy get killed in a car crash a couple of days after the Khatanga diamond mine announcement? This sounds wrong, Jack, plain wrong.'

'Do you remember the Williams case?'

'Not sure I do.'

'It was an MI5 and FBI venture to develop a procedure and the necessary technical expertise and equipment for the analyses of the origin of banknotes. Our man, Gareth Williams, underwent training in London before being sent to Boston to pick your brains. Upon his return, he set up and ran a lab designed to process international deposit banknotes. It was all set and ready to go.'

'I'm all ears,' said Deutsch.

'Well,' said Sailgood and lowered his voice, 'the day before the operation was meant to begin, Williams vanished and was found two days later in the bath tub of his bachelor flat in Pimlico stuffed in a sports bag. Dead, of course.'

'I know that the guy vanished but didn't know the details.'

'Top secret. Not even his family was told.'

'Why are you telling me all of this? What's the connection?

'There is a most interesting coincidence. The first batch of banknotes earmarked for analysis belonged to our man, Aleksey Kaganov. We suspected him of many dodgy dealings but wanted to have something concrete to tighten the screws on him before he is catapulted into the Kremlin orbit.'

'He didn't like it. I suppose.'

'The money originated from a Khatanga Investment Fund in Abu Dhabi and was transferred to London via Cyprus,' said Sailgood.

'Did he sell the Khatanga mining rights?' said Deutsch and shuffled in his seat.

'No. It's more likely to be Afghan drug money,' Sailgood reassured him.

'US dollars from the streets of New York, I bet,' said Deutsch and shook the ice cubes in his otherwise empty glass.

'Probably. That's something we expected Williams and his team to ascertain.'

'You think Kaganov commissioned the hit?'

'I'd say yes. However, the problem grows bigger,' said Sailgood, 'how did the information leak out!?'

'I see your point.'

'What's there to stop the next leakage?' said Sailgood.

'In terms of our Khatanga operation, that leaves us to deal with Kaganov's number two, right?' said Deutsch and signalled for two more whiskies.

'Well, Zakhar Vatayev was assassinated the other day in Rome,' said Sailgood and his partner just stared at the melting ice cubes. 'It was a professional job. His. own security man shot him. The killer then got shot himself.'

'Who got him, the police?'

'No, it was someone who managed to vanish. The Italian police couldn't identify him or trace him.'

'You think it's a Russian underworld affair?'

'Probably, although...' said Sailgood taking another drink from the stewardess. Once the girl turned around and

89

marched down the aisle under the watchful eye of the two agents, he continued: 'Rumour had it that Vatayev was getting close to the Kremlin, too close.'

'Behind Kaganov's back?' said Deutsch and gently shook his glass.

'So, we are led to believe.'

'And why are we now flying to London when everybody there seems to be dead?'

'Kaganov's wife, Milla Ivanovna, is au courant with the Khatanga enterprise and willing to continue the negotiations. She is the beneficiary of the will.'

'I am glad that she is au courant,' said Deutsch with an ironic expression in the corner of his lips.

'The Mexican, Saldero, will be there too so we can conclude the deal to everyone's satisfaction.'

'The jewel?'

'Thanks to your man in El Paso, the Mexican took charge of the jewel.'

'The Banker?'

'Lord Mintbatten, the President of the Rothson, Mintbatten & CEN will be there to meet us and attend to our financial needs,' assured the Englishman, 'As in transferring and investing the Mexican's cash through the proper channels...' said Sailgood.

'Good. Mr Hank says the situation is under control,' confirmed Deutsch before proceeding, 'OK, the situation is not great but seems workable. But do you know what is the one thing that I hate more than anything else?'

'What would that be?' said Sailgood and raised an eyebrow.

'Doing business with women,' said Deutsch. He then shook his glass to hear the comforting sound of ice cubes, 'Doing business with women.'

10

El Guapo Vs Julian Assange

It was ten a.m. when a twin-engine Bombardier jet en route from México City dropped through the clouds and touched down at London City airport. The aircraft slowed down, turned left off the runway and came to a stop in front of the VIP entrance of the main building. The ground staff rushed to produce the passenger boarding stairs and the flight attendant opened the door. Through the opening emerged a ten-gallon white Stetson hat and the face of Gonzalo Pachenga. He clinched a hefty cigar between his teeth while scanning the surrounding area through a pair of gold-rimmed Ray Ban aviator glasses. He nodded his head and rushed down the stairs. El Guapo Medina was the next passenger to appear. He wore sunglasses too, a white suit, a claret red shirt with large lapels and on his feet, brown moccasins with an elaborate golden brooch. He looked around too, sniffed the air and his face turned into a grimace of disgust and made him spit from the top of the stairs. He then mumbled a couple of profanities, took his sunglasses off, stuffed them into a pocket and came down on the tarmac. A woman followed him. In her early thirties, her hair was long and black. She had dark red lipstick, wore a fur coat and high heel boots that made it nearly impossible for her to walk. She managed to scream simultaneously at El Guapo in front of her and at Xavier Ituribe behind her. This was María Guadalupe Quetzalcoatl, Medina's third wife, a strong-headed woman whose whims and tantrums instilled more fear and panic among the cartel's members than Nieto Pachenga's machine gun and the machete combined.

'She used to be a nice farm girl,' El Guapo explained once, 'and then started to watch those idiotic soap operas and turned into one of her heroines. People who make those films should be shot. Right, as soon as I have some spare time, I'll have a couple of them shot, to make an example!'

After Guadalupe came Ituribe and a suite of security staff, a chef, a masseur, a coiffeur and an allegedly famous yogi who went by the name of Vayatta.

The party walked through customs and out on the street. El Guapo, Guadalupe, Ituribe and Pachenga entered the first and longest limo that featured a multitude of aerials on the roof.

'*Vamonos,*' yelled Medina at the driver with a broad hand gesture and leaned back in the seat.

Ituribe pressed the interphone button without looking at the boss. 'The Dorchester, on Park Lane, please,' he said and the turbaned Sikh driver nodded and pressed the accelerator.

'Finally get some use of your stupid Harvard and all those degrees,' said El Guapo before breaking into uncontrollable laughter, 'ha, ha...'

As soon as she managed to fix her make up using a small mirror and portable cosmetics set, Guadalupe banged her foot down and declared that she always wanted to see the Queen's house.

'*Mí amor,*' said El Guapo, 'not now, we go to the hotel first and then...'

'I came all the way...' said Guadalupe while her eyes turned dangerously feline, 'To see that house!'

'María...'

'Nooow!' she screamed, promptly settling the matter. El Guapo gave a nod to Ituribe who pressed the button and passed the instructions to the driver.

The motorcade made up of four limos drove slowly through the heavy London traffic. Medina watched the city through the tinted glass while images of other big cities he had visited flashed before his eyes: Los Angeles, Mexico City, Bogotá, Kabul... He had visited New York City too but didn't have very fond memories of the sojourn. It ended with a bloody shootout in the Bronx that involved the NYPD, the Puerto Rican mafia, as well as a bunch of disgruntled retired members of the local Black Spades gang. El Guapo managed to escape but his younger brother José, El Guerrerito, was fatally wounded and died two days later. No, El Guapo Medina was not fond of New York and preferred not to remember the Bronx. He was afraid that his thirst for revenge would take the better of him and compromise his business interests.

'Oh, he's so tall,' said Guadalupe interrupting El Guapo's train of thoughts. She was looking upwards trying to see Lord Nelson on top of the marble column at Trafalgar Square. 'A real man!'

The vehicle then passed through the Admiralty Arch and continued down The Mall towards Buckingham Palace. Guadalupe was so impressed by St James's Park and excited about the prospect of finally seeing La casa de la Reina that she clapped her hands in joy and screamed a few times.

As the vehicle approached the Palace, Guadalupe ducked looking through the windscreen. 'Oh, the Queen is at home!' she said.

'*Qué?*' exclaimed El Guapo.

'You wouldn't know, would you? You, thick-headed peasant!' asserted Guadalupe, 'When the Queen is in residence... That's what you say, the Queen is in residence and the British flag flies at high-mast.'

'Interesting,' commented Ituribe.

'Sure, sure,' agreed El Guapo, 'just stop screaming.'

The car turned left in front of the Palace and the driver announced that they would have to go around it for there were some road works to the right, on Constitution Hill. 'It's not that big,' commented El Guapo seizing Queen's home, 'nothing special.'

Despite the dense layers of make-up, María Guadalupe's face turned visibly white. 'A peon who crept out of a cave in the heart of the Sonora desert with a pack of snakes is going to give me...' she raised a finger in front of El Guapo's eyes, 'lectures about the merits of classical European architecture?!'

'I could have a bigger and nicer one built tomorrow if I only wanted!'

'You?' she said lowering the finger. 'Where would you have that built? In which one of the two stinky, dusty back lanes of your pitiful, godforsaken Sierra Madre village?'

'Stop me or I'll kill her!' said El Guapo to Ituribe and Pachenga who didn't look enthusiastic about getting involved in this specific dispute. Luckily for them, a mobile phone rang and they both started checking their pockets. 'It's me,' said Ituribe, 'my international number.' He looked at the display and then at Medina asking for permission to reply. Once the permission was granted he pressed the button.

'*Dígame,*' said Ituribe, 'Yes, the flight was fine... Yes, all fine... Thank you.' He then switched off the phone microphone and turned towards Medina, 'it's the Russian secretary. They propose to meet tonight.'

'Tonight?'

'Yes, the wife of the late Kaganov is in charge and she wants to meet you before the official meeting tomorrow afternoon.'

'Wife...?'

'Milla Ivanovna is the name.'

'OK,' agreed Medina, 'tell them we'll be there.'

'One more thing, *Jefe*,' said Ituribe, 'they want us to bring the jewel tonight.'

'The Russian Soul, tonight?'

'This Milla Ivanovna wants to see it.'

El Guapo reflected for a moment and a faint smile appeared in the corner of his lips. 'Sure,' he said, 'sure.'

Ituribe switched the microphone back on, confirmed the details of the meeting and thanked the interlocutor. 'That was Senka Golovkin, the secretary to the late Kaganov and now to Milla Ivanovna.'

'Two top people die within a couple of days,' said El Guapo, 'interesting people these Russians. There might be many things we could learn from them... about all these wars, revolutions and weapons, you know?'

'I am not going anywhere tonight!' Screeched Guadalupe with disdain, 'I need to buy some jewellery first. I need to make myself presentable!'

'Of course,' agreed Medina, 'Ituribe has already booked you at Diment and Van Goor's, the finest jeweller in London. Right, Xavier?'

'Yes, yes,' confirmed the adviser in earnest.

'Hem,' said Lupe looking at Medina, 'I don't like that smirk on your face.'

'*No te preocupes* Lupita...' began el Jefe but was interrupted by the driver. He explained that there was a detour and that to avoid the congestion they were forced to take Hans Crescent where they came up against a crowd of protesters who obstructed the traffic. It was no more than a

95

couple of dozen people who were surrounded by another dozen policemen and all standing in front of a red brick building. From one of the building's balconies flew a flag. The protesters carried placards, chanted slogans and beat drums. As the vehicle came to a stop, Medina got out of the car to see what the fuss was about. Pachenga and Ituribe followed suit while Guadalupe declared it was way too cold.

Medina stood in his white suit next to the white limo attracting the attention of many protesters. His own attention however, was directed towards one of the balconies of the red brick building where a tall, white haired man held a microphone and addressed the cheering crowd.

'Who is the guy?' Medina asked Ituribe, 'is this the famous Hyde Park where people can say anything they want?'

'No,' said Ituribe, 'I don't think so. I think this is the Ecuadorian Embassy and that is Julian Assange.'

'French,' concluded El Guapo, 'what's he doing here, in the Embassy?'

'He can't get out as they would arrest him,' said Ituribe and pointed a finger at the policemen. 'He's been in here a couple of years now.'

'What did he do?'

'He revealed some compromising documents that belong to the United States of America.'

'Ha, ha,' laughed El Guapo Medina wholeheartedly, 'So he cannot say everything he wants, right?' And then, 'Who does he work for? For that Wiki crime syndicate thing?'

'No-one, he doesn't work for anyone' said Ituribe, 'WikiLeaks is an independent organisation, or so they say.'

'Independent? Ha, ha, that's a good one... is this the guy that intercepts communications?'

'No, that's the government,' explained Ituribe, 'they have a surveillance project.'

'So, why did this guy reveal secret documents?'

'Idealist, believes that he is doing the right thing!'

'Idealist,' said El Guapo, 'I am an idealist too! I was born an idealist. I was the greatest idealist this world has ever seen. Pancho Villa, Emiliano Zapata and I. But I, José Saldero El Guapo, am a free man. I don't live in a stupid Embassy and don't sing from a balcony like a canary, do I?'

'Of course not, jefe,' said Ituribe while Pachenga nodded. The hard man couldn't stand crowds or people expressing opinions. He couldn't stand opinions full stop.

'Hello, whitey,' yelled Medina while jumping up and down and waving his hands in the middle of the street. 'You should come and work for me. I'll pay you well to do the same job, no problem. And you can say anything you like,ha,ha...'

11

The widow - Milla Ivanovna

Senka Golovkin switched his mobile phone off and put it back in his pocket.

'He's coming,' he said.

'Is he bringing the jewel?' said Milla Ivanovna.

'Yes, he agreed to bring it,' said Senka and leaned back into the large seat. 'We will send Sergey tonight to pick them up and bring them to Cambridge.'

In the meantime, the driver was fully focused on the traffic and on reading the relevant information from a laptop-size touch screen. The destination was Canary Wharf and Number One Canada Square building, one of the tallest skyscrapers in London and home to many a multinational company including at least half a dozen that belonged to Aleksey Kaganov's global empire.

Milla Ivanovna was a child of ambitious middle-class parents determined to see their daughter perform at the Mariinsky and Bolshoi theatres. However, after graduation from the prestigious Vaganova ballet school, the girl met Aleksey Kaganov. The attraction was immediate and mutual and she decided to move with Aleksey to London. When a couple of years later Milla announced that she was expecting a baby, the couple found a new home in Saffron Walden, a town between London and Cambridge. This mansion, Alden House, was not for sale so the Boss had to resort to his political channels to locate the owner. He informed the man that his wife liked the estate.

'I am terribly sorry,' said Lord Alden, 'But the house is not for sale, you see. My late father left a provision in his will that...'

'I am terribly sorry,' interrupted the Boss, 'I didn't make myself sufficiently clear. My wife likes the house and money is no object. So, there are no problems. This is Senka Golovkin, my secretary. You tell him a figure and he will transfer the money into your account. It is very simple, really.'

'But I...'.

'I don't need to know the figure,' said the Boss, 'actually, I don't want to know the figure, you see. Money is no object, this is now my family home.'

So, Oleg was born in Alden House. A vivacious child, he liked horses, quad bikes and hunting.

'A hunter by birth,' Milla Ivanovna would explain, 'like grandfather like grandson.'

Now in her mid-thirties, her presence still commanded attention and respect. Her posture was firmly upright, her movements graceful and her Russian accent most often described as charming. Milla Ivanovna's secret weapon though, was the penetrating gaze of her green eyes and the ability to scan with a minimal margin of error any man, woman or child who would find themselves crossing her path. As a Georgian businessman once put it, 'her gaze has the same effect on men as the headlights of a car have on a rabbit standing in the middle of the road – admiration, terror and ultimately, destruction.'

Unlike the average BMW, Milla Ivanovna knew how to choose her rabbits.

She was now seated in the back of a car carefully scrutinising Semyon Fomich Golovkin with her thoughts running wild through an altogether different domain.

'Senka,' she said and switched the interphone communication with the driver off. 'You are my closest aide, aren't you?'

'Yes...?'

'Always been, right?'

'Sure...' said Golovkin and shuffled in his seat. He never enjoyed talking to Milla Ivanovna. He enjoyed it even less now that the Boss was gone.

'Senka,' she said, 'what do you really think of me?'

'Milla Ivanovna, you know that I...' said Senka raising his hands as if praying to the Almighty for help.

'Of course, of course, Senka...' she interjected.

Senka might have been a grandmaster in chess, a capable accountant and an astute adviser but he had little or no experience in urban warfare, terrorist tactics or hand-to-hand mortal combat, all arts that Milla Ivanovna was very fond of.

'I know how devoted you have always been to Aleksey Kaganov and that you two went through a lot together.' She didn't say 'before I had even met the Boss,' but that is what Senka correctly understood. He didn't say anything and Milla Ivanovna adjusted her scarf and wedding ring on her right hand before continuing: 'I know, I know that you always acted with the best interest of our family in mind and thank God for that, otherwise we wouldn't be sitting here and chatting, of course.'

Semyon Fomich grew up in Krasnoyarsk but upon his parents' premature death he was sent to stay with his father's relative in Voronezh. The relative was colonel Mikhail Borisovitch Gorsky, Alex Gorsky's father.

From a very young age, Senka excelled in the game of chess which earned him a scholarship for the Lomonosov University. He studied physics and upon graduation was offered employment in the Ministry of Finance where one day he met Aleksey Kaganov, a rising star of the vibrant Russian post-communist and proto-capitalist era of the early '90s. Kaganov spotted Senka's many talents and recruited him as his secretary. So, before one could say checkmate, Senka found himself in a country house, a dacha, surrounded by a couple of very young and gorgeous girls and near-industrial quantities of champagne, caviar and cocaine. As the Boss later explained to Senka, in their line of business, deals were sealed by a handshake. He also drew Senka's attention to the fact that he had just had sexual intercourse with two minors under the influence of drugs and that the prison sentence for such an offence was up to thirty-five years in jail. He didn't forget to stress, of course, that the whole evening was recorded by several cameras. Senka understood the subtle point the Boss was making and became Kaganov's man of trust. Reliable, assured, 'silent - like death,' was one of Boss's favourite expressions, 'ha, ha, ha...'.

Senka Golovkin wasn't used to dealing with women and Milla Ivanovna had never shown any interest in Kaganov's business activities so that the two never exchanged more than two or three words... Senka Golovkin didn't understand women and he was afraid of things he didn't understand. He feared Milla Ivanovna like one fears darkness, an earthquake, sickness or death.

'Milla Ivanovna,' said Senka Golovkin, 'if I may...'

'Yes, Senka,' she said and her face turned into a cold mask.

'I was wondering, now that Aleksey Dmitrovich is not with us...'

'Yes?'

'Now that Aleksey Dmitrovich is not with us, would you know about a certain tape, a VHS tape that the Boss kept for me...'

'What do you mean? The tape is yours?'

'I mean, the tape is not mine but...'

'But?'

'I'm on the tape so...'

'Ah, that tape,' said Milla Ivanovna with a broad smile, 'ha, ha, that tape.'

'So, you know?' said Senka who had still nurtured some outside hopes that she didn't know about the tape.

'The tape is in the safe in Aleksey's study. Fear not Senka, fear not!'

'Could I...'

'No, Senka,' said the woman in black, 'that was between you and Aleksey as I understand and it is going to stay like that!'

Slightly confused by Milla Ivanovna's line of thinking, Senka uttered, 'sure, sure, I just thought that...'

'I know Senka, I know. It's all very sad, isn't it? Anyway, let us talk about the future, shall we?'

'Yes, of course, the future...'

'What do we know about these people? This Lord, for instance?' she said pronouncing the title with a curious mixture of importance and irony.

'Lord Mintbatten is the president of the...'

'No, no Senka,' interrupted him Milla Ivanovna, 'I didn't make myself clear. I am not interested in the official side of the story. Give me some real information about real people, give me something tangible!'

'Tangible?'

'Yes, tangible, real people, like... Is the man on drugs, does he bet on horses, is he a womaniser, a paedophile? You know... That sort of stuff!'

At this point Senka had already opened his briefcase and started rummaging through his papers.

'So?' she said.

'His wife is the second daughter of Avram Rotsohn...'

'Not gay then!'

'I didn't say that!'

'What did you say?'

'That was his first wife, she was a wealthy heiress...'

'How many wives are we talking about?'

'According to my papers - five.'

'Not young then, and lucky to be alive... After five wives, I mean,' said Milla Ivanovna with the flair of a connoisseur. 'So, we have this English aristocratic playboy... and he is our main financial adviser?'

'He is President of the Rothson, Mintbatten & CEN, a major international bank.'

'How major?'

'They operate with Libyan and Iraq oil assets, for instance, that major.'

'I see.'

'The RM & CEN will take care of the cash and make it available for investment.'

'Are you telling me that the Mexican's drug cash will flow into their accounts and come out clean and ready to be invested in our operation?'

'Something like that,' said advisor Golovkin, 'the drilling, the extraction, the security and government bribes will be taken care of.'

'Fine, tell me more about Rothson, Mintbatten & CEN.'

'The Boss, Aleksey Dmitrovich, made initial contact last summer through our partners in Geneva. This was when we first learnt that the Kremlin decided to go public with the Khatanga diamond crater.'

'Why was that so important?' said Milla Ivanovna to the great relief of the advisor Golovkin who was glad to learn that the Boss didn't confide to his wife in everything. 'Well, the public announcement was a clear signal that the Kremlin was ready to take over the exploitation of the diamond mine,' said Senka. 'That also meant that the local gubernator, Aleksey Dmitrovich in this case, was being cast aside. The plan probably being to pay him off with some peanuts or...'

'Or?'

'Or worse,' said Golovkin. He then raised a hand to cover his mouth and coughed discreetly.

'Worse as in?'

'Life, Milla Ivanovna. The ultimate price is life,' explained Senka Golovkin. She shuffled in her seat and Senka Golovkin said: 'The Boss died in a car accident, didn't he? The police confirmed that there wasn't anything sinister about it, right?'

'No, no, of course not,' Milla Ivanovna reassured him. 'I identified the charred body by the ring, gold chain and diamond he wore all the time. There was a witness who saw the driver losing control and coming off the road.'

'Of course,' said Golovkin.

'Where will the Kremlin find the money for the exploitation of the crater? As far as I understand only one or two international companies in the world have the equipment and personnel to do that and they are expensive.'

'They don't have the necessary funds. The Popigai crater in Khatanga is hundred kilometres wide and the diamonds sit deep. The investment needed to reach them is going to be massive before there is any revenue to speak of. It might take several years before the first diamonds are extracted.'

'So, again, why did they announce its existence?'

'It's complex...'

'Don't give me that complex thing, Senka,' Milla Ivanovna cut him short.

'Right... the Boss is... sorry, was tipped by the Western powers to run for the Presidential office next year. From the point of view of the Kremlin, taking away his resources is a good move. Hence, they present these resources as a public, national treasure and seize them. Furthermore, by going public they are opening the bidding process. They need investors. And, perhaps most importantly, a great strategic move.'

'Why strategic?'

'Because, they are telling the world two things, firstly we can flood the world with precious stones any time we want. The market turns unstable and is in their hands. Secondly, and this is the biggest catch, they can establish the diamond as the reserve currency. The US treasury does not have anything like the necessary gold to support its currency. A diamond Rouble would be a serious contender, especially when combined with a nuclear capability.'

'A diamond Rouble?'

'Yes. A Rouble supported by the Chinese Yuan and convertible in diamonds. No financial speculations, no derivatives or hedge-funds, no money printing and quantitative easing, just diamonds!'

Milla Ivanovna was now looking through the dark car window at the passers-by, shoppers who all seemed to be in a terrible hurry. They carried plastic bags and protected themselves from the rain with colourful umbrellas. After a while the car stopped in the middle of a traffic jam and stood stationary for a couple of minutes. She pressed the interphone button and said, 'what's going on, Sergey?'

Sergey took off his safety belt and got out in the street to find out the cause of the congestion. He came back shortly afterwards.

'Strange,' he said, 'there is a crowd of protesters ahead of us blocking the traffic. That fellow Assange is talking from the balcony while there is another man in the middle of the street gesticulating and yelling in Spanish. Next to him there is another man with an oversized cowboy hat and huge moustache. Funny people!'

'By the way, this Mexican, what is he like?' said Milla Ivanovna who always imagined Mexico as a mythical destination populated by Aztec and Maya demigods.

'An animal, they say,' said Golovkin, 'that's what they say.'

'An animal? Is that's what they say, an animal?'

'Yes, that's what they say,' said Senka. 'But what about the jewel? Do we still need the jewel now, that the Boss is gone?'

Milla Ivanovna switched the interphone off and turned to him with an expression of amazement.

'Yes, we must have the Russian Soul, my dear Senka,' she said. 'And we better get it, right? I hold you personally responsible for the fate of that jewel. You understand?'

'I do,' said Senka Golovkin with a nod. His chess-player's mind started racing in several directions at once. 'There is always a solution,' was his motto and all he needed to do now was to find it.

12

The Fravashis

In less than five minutes Niusha and Gorsky found themselves in front of house number 17 in the quiet surroundings of Willis Road. The row of houses was built in Edwardian style and each two-storey dwelling featured a pastel coloured front door and a bay window on the ground floor, another bay window on the first floor and a couple of smaller windows just below the roof. Niusha opened the tiny iron gate and entered the small fenced concrete area that hosted a bunch of old, rusty bicycles chained together. She then took a set of keys out of her pocket and opened the door.

'It's me,' she shouted.

Gorsky came in and was shown to a living room. It featured a couple of ancient leather armchairs, a large couch, a tea table and a flat screen TV set. The walls were dark green and the floor covered by a worn out dark grey fitted carpet. As the guest sat in one of the armchairs he noticed two framed pictures.

'It smells like rental property,' he thought. Having been through a fair number of those himself he knew how to tell a good from a bad landlord and a well-maintained flat from a run-down one.

'Take your coat off, make yourself at home,' said Niusha.

'I'll keep the coat on, thanks,' said Gorsky.

'Back in a minute,' she said and vanished through the door and into the corridor that led to the kitchen. Passing by the bottom of the stairs she yelled something upstairs and a man's voice replied.

'Come down,' she said so that Gorsky could hear her too, 'I want you to meet a good friend of mine. He just saved my life!'

She then turned towards Gorsky and said in a low, barely audible voice: 'Don't mention my business or I'll have to kill you!'

Gorsky nodded and the two exchanged glances.

'Saved your life? Did you just say he saved your life?' said a young man coming down the stairs. He was in his early thirties, not very tall and had short dark hair and dark eyes much like Niusha's.

'Aptin, Niusha's brother,' he said extending his right hand for a handshake. Gorsky got up from his seat and shook hands. He couldn't help noticing that Aptin's hand was no bigger than a child's.

'Not the hand of a brick layer or a soldier,' crossed Gorsky's mind, 'more that of an artist.'

'I took the dog to the playground around the corner,' explained Niusha, 'and a gang of local hoodlums started pushing me around.'

'The usual bunch that hangs around there?' said Aptin with a worried expression on his face.

'Yeah, it was the usual bunch. Give or take. There was one new face but the routine was normal: insults, racial slurs, threats, you know...' said Niusha. She explained how this stranger, Gorsky was his name, came to rescue her from the claws of five or perhaps six hoodlums who then attacked him with broken bottles, knives and baseball bats but how the stranger repelled all the attackers and made them flee. For his trouble, Gorsky was hit in the head with the bat that left him with a very bad cut and a bruise that she managed to treat. There was no need to see a doctor but a period of rest was required.

'Right,' said Aptin interrupting Niusha and turning towards Gorsky, 'thank you for protecting my sister. Thank you so much.'

'That's fine,' said Gorsky, 'It wasn't as dramatic as Niusha would like you to believe.'

'It was, it was dramatic. He got bumped in the head too,' she said and pointed at his head.

As soon as Aptin took a seat on the couch and started chatting to the guest, the doorbell rang. 'I am waiting for some friends,' he excused himself and went to open the door. Gorsky heard clamour at the door and the two newcomers appeared in the living room. One was short and chubby, had short, dark red hair, a nose ring and a couple of hoops in her ear lobe. The other was skinny and probably two metres tall, with long blond hair, a shirt with flowery motifs and an ancient, bleached denim jacket. 'These are Aptin's colleagues,' said Niusha who had rushed in from the kitchen to do the introductions. She then told an even more enhanced version of that morning's events adding a mild concussion suffered by her saviour. The attackers were six, possibly seven. The newcomers clapped their hands in awe, hugged Niusha and expressed their gratitude to Gorsky.

'This is Terry,' said Niusha eventually, pointing at the person with short, red hair, 'and this is Jan.' They shook hands and set down, Terry and Jan on the couch and Aptin on the other armchair.

'You're not from 'round here.' asked Terry.

'I live here but I am Russian,' said Gorsky.

'I thought so. Russian, ha? Cool, that's very much 'not from here,' ha? I'm from the States myself,' she said, 'you call me TK, everyone else does.'

'What does the K stand for?' said Gorsky.

109

'I don't remember,' said Terry and giggled. 'A kind of joke it was, really. Names are just arbitrary, a joke anyway.'

'And I am just another bloody foreigner,' said Jan with a broad smile, 'Austrian, in temporary employment of the Crown.'

Niusha brought in teas and coffees and they continued with the introductions. Gorsky listened carefully. These people were not the usual mafia-style associates, soldiers or martial artists. There was something disjointed about them, different.

TK told Gorsky how she ran away from her parents' Mid-Western home and went to California. A girl who knew she wasn't quite a girl. She had to find out. Once she did find out, she left for New York. Life was good in Brooklyn. She had friends, a studio. There was a handful of galleries that would commission her work. At some point, she made a short film about a famous Chinese artist and made some money. It was all fine until a couple of years ago.

'I was on my way back from a rubbish dump. I picked up a couple of car tyres that I needed for an installation. A TV crew stopped me and asked about the murder of a Puerto Rican girl whose body was found near the dump. I said I didn't know anything about it. As I didn't. But the interview was aired and I was referred to as a witness! They had to fill some TV time, you see?

As it happens, the girl was a Puerto Rican prostitute killed by some Russian psycho associated with their mafia. So, suddenly I was wanted by the NYPD to provide information, by the Russians to keep me quiet, and by the Puerto Ricans for I witnessed the murder!'

TK left in a hurry. She boarded a plane to Brazil and hid there for a couple of months before coming to London. She worked in a pub now, pulling pints of beer.

'I never had a drop of the stuff in my life,' she said.

'My life is not that dramatic,' said Jan. 'I came here to study and now sell LPs, vinyl, you know? Work in a shop.'

'Jan is very important to our cause,' said Aptin, 'he is our ears and eyes. He eavesdrops on police communication in the area and is writing a book about the abuse of the rights of minorities.'

'Yes, all kind of minorities, disenfranchised people in general. Could be gay or black, Eastern European or Pakistani... you know.'

'And you, Aptin,' Gorsky turned to the host. 'What do you do?'

'I am a chemist, a researcher at the University, carbon allotropes,' said Aptin. 'Not that it means anything to most people.'

'Sounds interesting, anyway,' said Gorsky who didn't have the faintest idea what these allotropes might be.

'Aptin is very humble,' jumped in Niusha, 'and the allotropes are his hobby now. He is a senior lecturer and his group carries out important, EU funded research on diamond carbonate structures in Nano technological applications. Did I get this right, Aptin?'

'Spot on, you're getting good at it,' said Aptin.

'And me, yes,' said Niusha, 'I work at the homeless people hospice around the corner.'

'And you, Alex Gorsky?' said TK. 'How about you? What's your sin in this town?'

'I am a gymnastics teacher,' said Gorsky with a straight face. 'I work at the Chesterton gym part time and part time as a security guard for a wealthy Russian family. They have a house near Saffron Walden and the son attends school here in Cambridge so I often take him to school and back, stuff like that.'

'You were in the army or something?' asked TK.

Gorsky hesitated with the reply. He looked at the faces around him.

'Yes,' he said eventually making his mind up, 'I was in military service for a number for years.'

'Been in a war?' asked Jan enthusiastically, 'Afghanistan, Chechnya, you know, one of those places?'

'Yes, Chechnya,' said Gorsky. 'I've been in Chechnya.'

At that point the doorbell rang again; Aptin excused himself and went to answer it.

'We are meeting this morning,' said TK, 'I don't know if Niusha or Aptin mentioned our charming activities to you...'

'No, we didn't,' said Niusha at which point Aptin came back in with the new arrival. 'This is Steve,' he said, 'Steve the Drummer.'

'Nice to meet you... Drummer,' said Gorsky and nodded his head. He was beginning to like this motley crew of oddballs.

'Steve is a musician,' said Aptin.

'You bet I am,' said Steve showing a toothless grin. He had long, greasy hair, unkempt beard and traces of rough life on the streets all over his outfit. He could have been in his late thirties or early fifties and no one knew his exact or even approximate age.

'We are part of an anti-imperialist movement,' TK said to Gorsky while the others starting chatting about a different matter. 'There are different factions like the Greens, the Anti-Globalists, and the Anti-Capitalists, but on one thing we all agree, we oppose the international financial institutions and their close ties with politics and the arms industry and trade, war, drugs, slavery...'

'Marx was right,' said Jan.

'Sure, mate, sure,' added Steve, 'good old Karl was spot on!'

'Gorsky, sorry to bother you with this stuff. I think it is better if we proceeded with our business. Let's go upstairs!' said Aptin and everyone stood up ready to move. Everyone except Steve the Drummer who planted himself in the armchair and crossed his arms with a disdainful expression on his face.

'Steve,' said Aptin, 'will you, please, stop acting for once and just behave like everyone else does?'

'I'm coming, I'm coming,' said Steve. 'You kick off the meet and I'll be on my way!'

'Let me tell you, my friend,' said Jan to Gorsky as Aptin vanished up the stairs. 'They might be laughing at the mention of Marx,' he said and pointed his finger towards the upper floor. 'But countries as we know them today are but a relic of the romantic idea and an invention of the colonial European past. Flags, national anthems, football teams, borders, languages... All rubbish, smoke screens to hide the totalitarian, oppressive, undemocratic nature of the system and the rapacious nature of ruling class that protects itself with the police and army where we are just the cannon fodder or, at best, a screw in their big engine. Did you see the Matrix?'

'The Matrix?' said Gorsky not without surprise.

'The movie!'

'No, I didn't,' he said, 'I tried three times but failed and fell asleep all three times.'

'You fell asleep watching the Matrix?' said Jan. 'Wooow! Shame, anyway, I'll tell you, we are all prisoners of the matrix. Life is not life, reality is not reality. It's all fake of the fake, mirror images, not people, binary functions only, tax codes, shares... you understand?'

'Yes,' said Gorsky but was saved by Aptin's appearance.

'He's always like that, sorry,' the host said before calling on everyone. 'Let's go, plenty of stuff to go through.'

'Sure,' said Jan and once he reached the doorway he turned and pointed a finger at Gorsky. 'The matrix, remember! Anarchy is the solution to global oppression. Anarchy as disorder, lawlessness, a state of freedom of the individual to express themselves in a creative way, to... we 're all in the matrix!'

'Of course,' said Gorsky, 'we're in the matrix.'

'Jan!' Aptin's voice was heard from the upper floor.

'Right,' said Jan, 'We are against corporate greed, corporate globalisation and the plundering of natural resources.'

'Jan!' came a shout from upstairs.

'OK, fine, I am coming...' said Jan, 'See you next time.'

'Good bye,' said Gorsky trying to produce a smile.

There was a knock on the front door, then another one. 'This must be Nick,' said Niusha and went to let the newest comer in.

She came back followed by a man with short brown hair and black rimmed glasses. He wore a dark green jacket, white trousers and was probably in his mid-thirties.

'Let me introduce you to my friend, Gorsky,' said Niusha. 'This is Nick...'

'Nice to meet you,' said Gorsky getting up from the armchair.

'He's Russian,' added Niusha trying to be helpful as Nick extended his hand.

'What do you make of your president?' said Nick, 'Myshkin?'

'Nothing,' said Gorsky and sat back in the chair.

'I was hoping not to see you today,' added Steve from the comfort of his armchair.

'Alex saved me this morning from a group of maniacs... in the park next to the church, you know?' said Niusha.

'It would have been too good,' said Steve, 'too good.'

'Thanks for saving our brightest star,' said Nick while trying not to pay attention at Steve's interjections and gesticulations. 'What do you do here in Cambridge?'

'A driver,' said Gorsky.

'As in taxi driver?' said Nick with a grin.

'No, I work for a Russian family, drive kids around,' said Gorsky who somehow didn't feel like expanding his account to his martial arts activities. Because he was already tired of explaining things or because... He didn't know why himself. 'I'm a driver,' he concluded.

'You could join us,' Nick offered before turning to the others. 'Niusha, have you recruited your friend for our cause?'

'No, not yet. It's still too early for that. Let's give him a couple of days of freedom.'

'But we need people for our protests in London. That's in two days!' said Nick.

As Gorsky opened his mouth to say something, Niusha interrupted him: 'I'll tell you about it if you're interested.'

'You couldn't organise a piss up in brewery,' said Steve in a voice that was turning more and more raucous and threatening.

'Go away,' said Nick waving his hand as if he were defending himself from a swarm of flies, 'and shut up!'

'Don't you dare give me that kind of shit, pretty boy!' said Steve closing his hands into fists. 'Save the attitude for your posh London mates. You don't tell me what to do!'

At which point Niusha felt necessary to intervene and ask both to proceed to the upper floor where the meeting was about to begin.

'They cannot start without me,' said Nick, 'I'm the chair.'

'We can start without you,' said Steve, '... and we can also finish without you. Without you is actually a good idea!'

As the two walked up the stairs still quarrelling, Gorsky stood up from his chair getting ready to go when, through the open kitchen door, he noticed a poster featuring a large bird of some sort.

'What's that?' he said entering the kitchen.

'That is a Fravashi,' said Niusha passing him a mug, 'and this is your tea.'

'Thanks. What's a Fravashi?'

'The Fravashi is God's messenger, an almighty being and a spirit protector that helps us in the fight between good and evil, between spirituality and materialism. It's Zoroastrianism, an ancient, traditionally Persian religion and philosophy. It still exists in Iran and has followers around the world, even here, in this country.'

'You're Iranian?'

'Yes and no,' said Niusha. 'Our father left Iran in the late seventies. Aptin and I were born here, we're British. I visited family back in Iran only once though Aptin has been there several times. We both speak the language. Our parents taught us. It was considered disrespectful to address an elder in English.'

'A Fravashi,' said Gorsky observing the poster.

'We are Muslims though,' said Niusha. 'Not really that devout and practising but still, of Muslim religion. We do respect both our traditions though, the Zoroastrian and the Muslim one. They can coexist in one and same person if the mind and spirit are at peace.'

Gorsky drank his tea and placed his mug next to the kitchen sink. 'I have to go now, thanks.'

'Thank you,' she said, 'I'll get you your friend... What was his name?'

'Knyaz. It's Russian for Duke or Prince, something like that.'

'Knyaz, nice name,' she said, opened the kitchen door and waved for the dog to come.

'Do they always talk to each other like that?' Gorsky asked.

'Who do you mean?'

'The two of them,' said Gorsky pointing a finger to the upper floor.

'Oh, yes,' she said, 'Steve doesn't like Nick for some reason and won't let go. Nick is the coordinator of the protests. He was sent from London to organise the cell's activities in line with the other cells around the country and the group meets here. Steve just can't get his head around the fact that someone from the outside, as he sees it, is in charge. Apart from that it seems to be personal too. He just can't stomach the man.'

13

Milla Ivanovna has visitors

It turned out to be a calm and starry December night. No wind, clouds or moon, thought Milla Ivanovna while looking through the window of the lavishly appointed Alden House library.

'A good night for crime,' she mused as a smile appeared in the corner of her lips. Since her teenage days, Milla Ivanovna had been an avid reader of Agatha Christie. She developed a strong preference for the flamboyant appearance and the stern logic of the Belgian sleuth Poirot rather than for the mild mannered, unassuming Miss Marple. Milla Ivanovna was fond of secrets, riddles and mysteries too. She read horoscopes regularly, consulted fortune-tellers and palm-readers, attended spiritual sessions and on one occasion was spoken to by the ghost of Rasputin, the legendary yurodivy mystic who told her that she should live in a proper royal court. 'Life is a secret, isn't it,' she liked to add in conversations, like one adds salt to a meal, *'Vsya zhizn'... yest' divnaya tayna.'*

Lord Mintbatten was to be the first of two visitors that evening. It was important to meet people informally before the official, procedural meeting on Friday.

'Talk to them beforehand,' the Boss used to say. 'Get a feel for these people. They have weak spots, they have buttons you need to learn how to press.'

She had a head start and was going to make the most of it. The Lord would come earlier in the evening to introduce himself and outline his vision of their future business association. He would then be joined by the Mexican who was supposed to bring the jewel. She wanted to see it, touch it and hold it. She wanted to feel this majestic firebird, this mythical precious ornament that transcended history.

Then, there was the Moscow connection. Sailgood and Deutsch pledged full support for Aleksey Kaganov's presidential campaign.

'Valuable partners, very valuable indeed,' is how Kaganov used to describe them.

The scene was set and the show was about to begin. Milla Ivanovna decided to wear a long black dress despite a pronounced aversion for dark colours. They made her look a touch too pale. She was in mourning though, wasn't she? It was out of the question not to wear black. She couldn't resists adding a discreet white gold and red ruby necklace and a brooch in the form of an orchid - a very nice touch, for connoisseurs only.

'Let's see if this Lord has any finesse or it's just the title,' she thought as she noticed the lights of a car entering through the main gate.

'Mintbatten,' she said and turned to face Senka Golovkin who was seated on a sofa and going through the contents of a large black folder. 'Let's see what these lords are made of. Go and get him, Senka.'

Golovkin closed the folder and put it on the table in front of the couch. He didn't like Milla Ivanovna's tone. But then again, he never liked the woman in the first place. He stood up, straightened his dark blue tie and walked out of the library and into the corridor towards the entrance. As he left the room, Milla Ivanovna turned to the wall-mounted mirror to make sure that her black dress followed the curves of her body and that the jewellery she was wearing matched the colour of her eye shadow and lipstick. The orchid was reassuring, she thought as she adjusted the brooch, for a poor, recently widowed woman facing a pack of rampant, roaring lions.

'Lord Mintbatten, Ma'm,' announced the maid standing in the doorway of the library. Milla Ivanovna turned around and nodded for the visitor to be let in.

A tall white-haired man in his seventies marched into the room followed by Golovkin. 'My dear Madame Kaganova,' he said placing his left hand on the side of his dark blue striped suit where the heart should be. 'Please, accept my deepest and sincerest condolences!'

Milla Ivanovna stood immobile and solemn. A caryatid of sorts.

'Thank you,' she said in a tone that stopped the visitor in his stride some six feet in front of her. 'Lyudmila Ivanovna, please. You may call me Milla Ivanovna.'

'Of course, of course,' said the visitor, 'Call me David, please. Pronounced the French way, Da-vid. My mother was French, you see, and I was given the name after my great-grandfather, a renowned architect who planned the reconstruction of the Palais de Justice in Paris. Otherwise, my full name is David Nathaniel Francis Mintbatten, Lord of Bloomsberry.'

'I see. Take a seat please,' said Milla Ivanovna and walked to the large sofa. Lord Mintbatten settled a little bit further away from the lady of the house.

'May I offer you tea or coffee?' said the hostess.

'Tea, of course,' said the visitor with a broad smile and sat on the couch opposite. Golovkin sat in an armchair not very far from his black folder.

'English tea or... Russian tea?' she asked.

'I shall try your Russian tea,' said the lord.

Milla Ivanovna raised an eyebrow, summoned the housekeeper and gave instructions for the tea and biscuits to be brought in.

'It is a great tragedy, what happened to Mr Kaganov. When I heard the terrible news, I felt devastated as we spoke so many times over the phone...'

'Twice,' said Milla Ivanovna who didn't fail to notice the slightly wrong pronunciation of her surname.

'I beg your pardon?' said the lord.

'You spoke twice over the phone with Mr Kaganov.'

'Right, yes of course but we exchanged e-mails and documents and our project was coming together very nicely you see...'

'I know, I know, dear Lord,' said Milla Ivanovna lowering her gaze in a display of modesty and affection, 'Mr Kaganov always kept me very well informed about business matters, almost as if he had expected something to happen to him.'

It didn't take much in terms of time and resources for Milla Ivanovna to figure men out and put them in little multi-coloured boxes, all labelled and with clear instructions for dosage and general use. Longish white hair, pronounced Greek nose, tall but not too tall, slender, with an agile, light step, a man who took care of himself, probably into sports, fresh air, horse riding and the French Riviera. A man who obviously chose his own food, wine and company carefully, read the label that she stuck on Lord Mintbatten. Always thought of himself as attractive, probably attended a public school, survived the '60s and '70s, adventurous, promiscuous, paedophile? Hem, not sure about that one... It would be a useful weakness though, very useful, thought Milla Ivanovna and filed Lord's profile.

'Tragic, that is all very tragic, indeed,' said the Lord. 'However, I am immensely grateful for this opportunity to meet outside the official business framework. It is always useful to acquaint oneself more intimately with business partners before we get bogged down in the dreary details of our operation.'

Milla Ivanovna smiled her best formal smile just as the maid entered the room carrying a silver samovar. She was followed by another maid with a large tray with cups, a bowl of sugar and a saucer with cookies. They placed the samovar on a small side table and the cups, the bowl and the cookies on the table in front of Milla Ivanovna and her guest. Lord Mintbatten found the spectacle fascinating. He smiled and clapped his hands.

'What a charming ceremony!' he exclaimed.

'The samovar?' inquired Milla Ivanovna.

'Yes, you see,' continued the Lord clapping his hands one more time, 'After the Great War and the revolution in Russia, my family was in Geneva and my grandfather offered sanctuary to our Moscow cousins. These cousins, you see, they brought with them, among all the other things, a silver samovar quite like this one. They claimed they bought it in Yasnaya Polyana where it belonged to Leo Tolstoy, the great author.'

'Lev Nikolayevich,' said Milla Ivanovna.

'I beg your pardon?'

'Lev Nikolayevich Tolstoy,' she said giving emphasis to the Russian pronunciation of the name.

'Of course, quite... you see, and the tea from that samovar is different, much better than anything else I have ever tasted. Different,' he said and chuckled. 'Whenever I find myself in Geneva I go to our house to have a cup of tea.'

Milla Ivanovna began pouring the tea.

'Do you take sugar or milk?' she asked.

'Nothing, thank you. I want to taste the real Russian tea,' he said shaking his head and accepting the cup.

Adviser Golovkin took his cup from Milla Ivanovna's hands and leaned back in his seat. He sipped the tea. He observed, he listened and waited.

'Beautiful porcelain,' said the Lord raising the cup to his eyes and inspecting the flowery motif, 'Russian, I trust.'

'Of course, it is a Vorobyevsky pattern from the Lomonosov Imperial porcelain factory,' she said looking at the guest through her eyelashes. 'But tell me, Lord Mintbatten, please, you have met Aleksey Kaganov. What did you talk about, what kind of impression did he make on you?'

'Oh, my dearest Milla Ivanovna,' began the Lord and proceeded to give a prolonged, winding and detailed account of his positive impressions of the late Mr Kaganov... 'a most excellent man of impeccable integrity, a patriot and benefactor, an exemplary humanist and man of the world of a calibre that is nowadays sadly so rare.'

This, for some reason, reminded the Lord of the time when he met the Dalai Lama at a garden tea party in Connecticut. It was in the home of a tycoon who later jumped out of the window of his Wall Street office. The Lord was, of course, most impressed by Mr Kaganov's vibrant personality and the decisive, uncompromising stand he always took in business and politics. The man had an ardent desire to safeguard the interests of his motherland, Russia, and help the proud but sadly, oppressed people by agreeing for his name to be put forward in next year's presidential election. He was to be the candidate of the pro-democracy Druzhba party.

While the Lord was searching for the most adequate adjectives to express the highest esteem he held Mr Kaganov in, Senka Golovkin sipped his tea absorbed in his thoughts and trying to connect the Boss with words such as acumen, benefactor, philanthropy... It all reminded him of at least a dozen Boss's business partners and associates who met bitter ends in bizarre car accidents, exploding airplanes, in bath tubs connected to electricity or who were sent to prison on charges ranging from high treason, tax evasion, drugs and arms trafficking, to child pornography. Others were shot, like Vatayev and his wife. Yes, quite like that, crossed Senka's mind, just like the Vatayevs. He was too sentimental. It was as if he already missed the old days when the Boss was in charge and the world had a structured, recognisable shape. He switched off his reflective mode and returned to the room just in time to savour the following exchange.

'Well, for instance,' the Lord was saying, 'This mania for political correctness is leading us down the path of self-obliteration. Our very identity is at stake today. Foreign languages! Can you imagine the lack of intelligence behind the decision to teach languages to children in state schools? What do they need languages for? Working class kids will stay working class. You don't need languages or university degrees to operate a tractor, to run a barber shop, drive a lorry or fill in a spread sheet, do you? Complete nonsense. Foreign languages are for children blessed with a privileged upbringing and educated in excellent boarding schools. They will go on to study at Oxford or Cambridge, grow in stature and lead this country to even greater heights.'

At this point, Golovkin observed that the Lord was already red in the face and gesticulating considerably more than before. He can't even breathe properly, thought Golovkin and considered the possibility of the visitor having a heart attack or a stroke. Unlike Lord Mintbatten though, Milla Ivanovna sat on the couch with her back upright and her chin raised with her hands in the lap. She smiled, nodded and even sighed from time to time.

'Every society must respect order! Social order is a sure sign of achievement, the maturity of a civilisation and the more rigid, robust and firm the order, the more vital the society! Just look at the Greeks and Alexander the Great, Rome under Caesar, France under Napoleon, the British Empire at the time of Queen Victoria, the Americans today!' said Lord Mintbatten and made a pause obviously gasping for breath. A pause, that Senka Golovkin used to try to imagine Genghis Kahn wielding his sabre on horse-back, Hitler having tea on the peaceful terrace of the Berghof, and Koba Stalin visiting a Siberian gulag in mid-winter.

'A society that fails to enforce a firm structure is doomed. Social upheaval leads to chaos in the streets or worse, as in the case of your own country!' concluded the Lord and Senka Golovkin thought he saw a shadow in Milla Ivanovna's gaze.

But Lord Mintbatten wasn't finished. Encouraged by his interlocutor's silence he felt strongly encouraged to put on display his deep understanding of world history and exemplary locution. He went on to assert that what happened in Russia in 1917 was inexcusable and terrifying. Those communist animals bit the whole country off in a single go. They chewed it and spit out. They killed the Tsar, his family, wife, children, servants, dogs, cats and horses! They pillaged, raped, destroyed, murdered... The least they could do was to let the noble sovereign, Nikolay II, and his family leave and find sanctuary in England. Indeed, King George was waiting to offer sanctuary to his Russian cousin. Those two men were so sensitive, so gifted. They even looked alike! Milla Ivanovna felt obliged to draw the Lord's attention to the simple fact that, from her point of view, of course, George V was a miserable, cowardly, exemplar of low life that denied sanctuary to the Romanovs at the very moment when the Soviet government in Moscow was trying to get rid of them by dispatching them abroad. She returned the hand to her lap and took another deep breath looking the Lord straight in his, by now, somewhat worried, blue eyes. She continued by explaining how her father, the General Porphyry Mikhailovich Yepanchin used to say that English hypocrisy was as guilty of the Romanovs' deaths as were the Communists. Treason and especially betrayal against one's own family members, she concluded, must be the lowest point on any ethical scale!'

'*Mon Dieu!* But of course, *ma chère* Milla Ivanovná,' said Lord Mintbatten and decided to change the topic. He expressed his utter delight that Mr Kaganov brought such valuable business to his bank. He was sure, of course, that they were best placed to safeguard such a complex portfolio of interests for their firm had two centuries of experience in protecting the investments of major imperial houses across the globe. They even managed to safeguard the interests of clients in times of world upheavals such as the Boer War in South Africa, the crisis in the Congo, the Great War, Chile during Pinochet, and Argentina during Perón, just to mention a few, then, of course, the post-Soviet Russia in the '90s.

'My Lord,' interrupted Milla Ivanovna, 'our adviser, Mr Golovkin here, has prepared all the relevant materials for you and is waiting to go through them in detail.' At which point Senka Golovkin picked up the black folder from the table with both hands.

'*Naturellement, naturellement,*' said Mintbatten and turned towards Senka.

'Mr Golovkin is the administrative and financial brain behind our operations and he will be able to answer all your questions and work out the details of our cooperation. What I wanted to say is that we are dealing here with a business proposition that was very important to the late Mr Kaganov.

We own the biggest diamond mine in the world. It is situated at the bottom of a hundred kilometres wide Siberian meteor crater, as you probably know. It is in our interest to start the exploitation of this mine sooner rather than later. Our partners are the Garriburton Global and Mr Medina of Mexico. We also have strong support in parts of the Russian government and business community. Mr Kaganov was the Democratic Front's candidate for next year's presidential elections and his nomination was hailed by the Western international community as an important step towards the advancement of democracy and civil rights in Russia as well as towards the country's full inclusion in the global financial system. Your role is to give a legal structure to our little venture and to secure the flow of financial assets,' said Milla Ivanovna who obviously did pay attention during Boss' business meetings.

'You will transfer the monies coming from Mexico through your channels, dissociate the funds from their origin and prepare them for further investment in the Khatanga operation.'

'Of course, I...' said the Lord.

'I personally don't want to have anything to do with local institutions,' said Milla Ivanovna in a firm manner that didn't allow objections. 'This comprises the government, banks, multinational companies or any other agent inclusive of the Queen and the Archbishop of Canterbury. That will be your job and you will be handsomely rewarded. *N'est-ce pas,* my dear Lord?'

'Oui, oui, certainement, Madame. Britain is the ideal country for unimpeded investment, free of unnecessary regulations and burdensome scrutiny.'

'My dearest, that's all fine. But let us not be seduced by pretences. Mr Kaganov himself used to say that this country is a colony that sees itself as an empire. That's all,' said Milla

Ivanovna before explaining that the foreigners obviously find such a case of institutionalised schizophrenia charming. Freud and Jung would do wonders here. You have the Queen, the Princes, Buckingham Palace and then... Coke, hot dogs and the American president on television every day. Charming. To which assertion the visitor drew Milla Ivanovna's attention to the fact that Britain was widely recognised as a dynamic international business and financial hub that held a pivotal diplomatic and military role in global affairs!

'Is that so?' said the lady of the house and sipped the tea. Calm and composed, she sat upright with her neck extended and chin raised. After all, she did train to be a prima ballerina and to perform on the greatest stages.

'Well, yes,' said the visitor.

'Britain used to be great,' Milla Ivanovna said and raised the little finger of the hand that held the cup. 'It is now just another American colony and Mr Golovkin explained that to me very nicely.'

Senka Golovkin squeezed his black folder just a little bit harder.

'The only really great and important world powers are the Americans, Russia and China and there is nothing to debate about it. A colony, a colony!' she said and stamped the floor with a foot. 'And... This country of yours, Britain, missed the greatest opportunity to retain the status of empire.'

'I beg your pardon?' said the Lord who had given up the tea and returned the cup and saucer to the table. He was sitting like a school boy, with his hands firmly planted on his knees. 'What do you mean?'

'Nikolay II appealed for sanctuary to dear King George, didn't he? But no, the dear English cousin knew better and followed the advice of his short-sighted, back-stabbing ministers!'

'Ma chère Milla...'

'My dear Da-vid,' said Milla switching suddenly to the guest's first name. 'If only Queen Victoria were still alive. A woman, especially a woman of that stature would never have missed such an opportunity and the world would be a very different place today, wouldn't it?'

'If Queen Victoria were alive today?'

'No, if she were alive back in 1917 and granted sanctuary to the Romanovs.'

By this stage of the conversation, Lord Mintbatten had given up any hope of agreeing about historical events with Milla Ivanovna and resigned himself to nodding and glancing, from time to time, at Golovkin in the hope of deciphering clues from his facial expressions. Unfortunately for the Lord, Senka Golovkin observed this spectacle the way he followed chess tournaments, like a Sphinx, in a rational and expressionless mode.

'In which case, of course, at the demise of the Soviet Union, the heirs of Romanovs would have returned to Russia as British citizens and strengthened the ties between the two countries,' said Milla Ivanovna and spreading her arms as if to suggest the obvious - can't you see that?

'But no,' she continued, 'You chose to remain just a small island, an irrelevant colony on the outskirts of Europe.'

'But, Milla Ivanovna...' protested the Lord, 'Britain is an important factor...'

'Is it?' she interrupted him again, 'An important factor in international relations... I presume. My dear David, had the people of this island known anything about their own interests, they would have carried out a proper revolution just like other civilised countries in Europe and the world did! Russia and France did, and even America!'

Pleased with such an articulated and forceful exposition of her obviously very strong political views, Milla Ivanovna picked the cup from the table and sipped her tea. 'It's cold,' she said, 'What a shame.'

'Well of course, Madame Milla Ivanovna,' said Lord Mintbatten, 'I do understand your very subtle point of view. The British, however, are steeped in tradition...'

'The British? Aleksey used to say that there was no such thing as the British. You see, Da-vid, when you peel the first layer of the onion, you find that the Scots are Scots, the Irish are Irish and the Welsh are Welsh. Only the English keep on banging on about being British!'

'I see,' said the Lord who felt like he did on one occasion many years ago as an amateur boxer after having received a couple of blows to the head too many. Milla Ivanovna returned the cup to the table and got up from her seat. The visitor and Golovkin followed suit. She excused herself as she had a pressing commitment. Something about the late Kaganov's estate and inheritance, she said, most boring formalities. Lord Mintbatten nodded and Milla Ivanovna walked out of the room. As she disappeared, Golovkin invited the visitor to take his seat again and they both sat on the couch and started to go through the pile of documents. Golovkin explained that Khatanganeft owned a considerable chunk of the northern Siberian territories that are very rich in water, coal, oil, gas, diamonds and minerals of considerable strategic importance. While these resources are sought on the world market, their mining cost is considerable. Given the latest and precipitous developments in international politics, it was advisable to begin this process in earnest while Russia was still under international sanctions. Such a position allowed traders to lower the selling prices and to gain insight and access to well-guarded areas. The Kremlin needed hard cash. The finances are in place, courtesy of the Mexican tycoon and the role of RM & CEN is to ensure the smooth running of the monetary transactions. All smooth, safe and discrete.'

'Discrete, of course,' said the Lord pointing his finger at the documents. 'May I?'

'Please do,' said Senka. 'As you can see, Khatanganeft owns the land and we have established sound business contacts with both a good investor and Garriburton a subsidiary of Blackwater, a reputable mining and distribution company that is moving its business out of Zimbabwe and is happy to enter Russia. I must add at this point that our esteemed investor operates in cash only!'

'Cash?' said Mintbatten raising an eyebrow.

'US dollars.'

'What kind of money are we talking about?'

'Billions.'

'?'

'Six billion.'

'Six billion in cash?'

'The first year, and to be increased by ten to fifteen percent every year.'

'Six billion a year... Over how many years?'

'Five is a good number, we thought.'

'I see,' said the Mintbatten. 'And the cash comes from?'

'Mexico,' said Golovkin, 'We would like this money moved to London via the usual routes, Abu Dhabi and Hong Kong. Despite what Milla Ivanovna was saying, with due respect, we do trust the British financial system.'

'Oh, my goodness, I can assure you that you are right about that,' said Lord Mintbatten lowering his voice as if to confiding in Golovkin. 'Milla Ivanovna, is she always so outspoken or is it because of this unfortunate accident?'

'Because of the accident, you see,' said Golovkin who, as a matter of principle, didn't like telling lies but felt his duty to salvage the deal. 'It was a very hard blow for Milla Ivanovna and she is finding it difficult to deal with it.'

'I see. Terrible occurrence, utterly terrible!' said the Lord.

'We have our connections in the Russian establishment,' said Golovkin. 'The new regime will be friendly, they say. They will need the money to survive the winter.'

'Winter?'

'Yes, it's a Russian metaphor for... Trouble, in general!'

'I must tell you, Mr Golovkin, that given the risks involved in dealing with cash, our provision will have to be somewhat higher.'

'We understand and appreciate that.'

'The notes might be marked, you see.'

'Sure,' said Golovkin and stopped in mid-sentence as he heard a gentle knocking on the open door of the study. He raised his eyes and saw the maid standing in the doorway.

'Mr Medina is here,' she said and gestured towards the lobby.

14

Senka Golovkin, a man of action

'Very well,' said Golovkin to the maid, 'give us a minute.'

He collected the papers and put them back into the folder that he closed with an elastic band.

'Our investor is here,' he said and stood up from the couch. Lord Mintbatten followed suit with an expression of marked curiosity.

The sound of heavy and quick steps approached the study and the stocky frame of El Guapo Medina appeared in the doorway. He stopped for a moment and scanned the two men standing in the middle of the room the way wild animals sniff the air of an unfamiliar patch. He then smiled and walked in, followed by abogado Ituribe and his obligatory sombre facial expression. Golovkin made two steps to meet him and the two men shook hands.

'Senka Golovkin,' said he, 'secretary of the late Mr Kaganov and now at the service of Milla Ivanovna.'

'Wonderful!' exclaimed the Mexican shaking the hand with all his might. 'And this one?'

'This is Lord Mintbatten,' said Golovkin who managed to extract his hand from the deadly grip.

'Of the renowned ... I believe?' said Medina and shook the Lord's hand.

'Indeed,' said the financier trying to pull his hand back with a smile, 'Mr Medina.'

'El Guapo,' said the Mexican. 'Call me El Guapo. So, you are the financial genius that we owe our wellbeing to?'

'Well, I come from a long line of bankers...'

'Ha, ha, bankers,' said Medina putting one hand on Golovkin's shoulder. 'I come from a long line of buccaneers and peones, you know? Zapata y Pancho Villa!'

'Great Mexican revolutionaries,' explained Golovkin.

'Of course,' agreed Lord Mintbatten who had already had his yearly dose of historical revisionism.

'And where is that worldwide renowned beauty, the flower of the desert of London, ha, ha. You know, the most beautiful flowers grow in the desert of Sonora, among the hot rocks, snakes and rats. They grow despite having too much sun and not enough water, it's a miracle. Beauty is a miracle. Where is that woman whose touch can thaw the glaciers of Siberia and ...

'Also sign the documents we need, perhaps?' said Mintbatten coldly. He detested the petits playboys who could turn into a real nuisance and disrupt the ethereal art of seduction that he thought he was a master of.

While the introductions and the exchange of pleasantries took place in the middle of the study, abogado Ituribe walked into the room completely undetected, and took a seat in one of the armchairs. He placed the leather briefcase on his knees and then managed to fall back and sink into the cushions.

In the middle of this somewhat awkward conversation, it dawned on the Lord that this son of buccaneers, peones, zapatistas etc. was at the same time arguably the richest man in the world and that the business prospects of this encounter out-weighed by several orders of magnitude the range of concerns his vanity was trying to impose on him. The Mexican wearing the obligatory moustache, red shirt and rattle snake boots had cash to burn and Lord

Mintbatten could surely smell an opportunity from the distance of at least a hundred nautical miles.

'Take a seat, please,' said Golovkin. 'Mrs Kaganov will be with us shortly. I will go to inform her of your presence.'

When Golovkin left the room, Medina sat in an armchair and Mintbatten back on the couch. 'This is my consigliere,' said Medina making a gesture towards Ituribe who was barely visible among the large cushions and who was in the act of taking out of a pocket a silver cigarette holder. Abogado nodded, lifted the lid of the holder and offered its content to Lord Mintbatten who was sitting on the couch. 'Thank you,' declined the Lord politely. It did cross his mind that these Mexicans must have the real stuff though, but the circumstances called for self-restraint.

'Lord, you said?' said El Guapo while scrutinizing the financier from the tip of his shoes to the parting in the white hair.

'Yes,' confirmed Mintbatten.

'So, you inherited the title?'

'Of course, I did.'

'How many generations?'

'Fifth!' said the Lord with a touch of humility.

'And... how did your ancestor get it?' El Guapo was relentless.

'For financial services to the Crown, you see. My great-grand-father, Adalbert Bethmann was a renowned banker in Frankfurt and a renowned philanthropist for which services Queen Victoria bestowed upon him the peerage.'

'The Queen bestowed the peerage... Upon him,' repeated Medina tentatively. He was of course, more accustomed to the El Paso variety of Spanglish than Mintbatten's polished English.

'But he was German?' asked El Guapo.

'Yes, he was German but later in life he transferred his assets to England.'

'Victoria is not alive anymore?'

'No, she died more than hundred years ago,' explained Mintbatten.

'And who's the new one?'

'Elizabeth II,' said Mintbatten dryly for he found it hard to accept that there were people on the planet who haven't heard of the Queen. Or, was the visitor to the United Kingdom just having fun?

Ituribe caught the opportunity created by the sheer intensity of that conversation to swallow one of the pills from his cigarette holder. He was cool. He was relaxed. Working for señor Medina never came easy, true. On the other hand, the dull moments he cared to remember could be counted on the fingers of one hand. He was relaxed.

'And who was the first?' asked the king of drugs.

'Elizabeth the First... Daughter of Henry VIII.'

'Lots of Henrys, I see,' said the Mexican. 'And how do I become a Lord?'

'You?'

'Yes,' said El Guapo jumping from his seat and landing on the couch next to Mintbatten. 'How do I become Lord Saldero? José Saldero Medina de la Sonora. How much money do they want for that?'

'Well,' said the Lord who took a white handkerchief out of his pocket, placed it in front of his mouth and coughed twice - gently. 'You need to make a significant contribution to the Crown and country. I can see what I can do, of course. I have some connections, you see...'

'Crown and country? You're joking? I don't really care about those folks. Just tell me how much money, I pay and you then contribute as much as you like! Comprende?' he said and extended a hand to seal the said deal.

'I am sure that something can be arranged.'

Fortunately for the beleaguered aristocrat, short, brisk steps were heard and Milla Ivanovna appeared in the doorway. She cast a prima donna-like glance over the stage and audience, commanding silence, attention and adulation. She then made her first well-choreographed step on the stage of global finance, politics and deception. The great ballerinas Anna Pavlovna and Tamara Karsavina walked hand in hand with Milla Ivonovna. The greatest ballerinas carried the skinny Sankt Petersburg girl several feet over the study room carpet and towards her faithful admirers. The dream never left her for good. It just got mixed up with other ingredients to form a most peculiar brew. El Guapo Medina stopped listening and Lord Mintbatten stopped talking. Abogado Ituribe, who was in a state of self-induced stupor, appeared incapable of detecting a siren approaching and stayed put, in mortal danger.

'Que preciosa!' said El Guapo and jumped from his seat. Lord Mintbatten emitted two tiny coughs and followed suit while Senka Golovkin entered the room undetected, the way he preferred to do things.

'Encantado señora Kara...' continued the Mexican while extending both his hands towards Milla Ivonovna in an obvious attempt to kiss her.

'Kaganov,' interjected Lord Mintbatten with the sweetest smile while at the same time asserting his newly acquired and hard-earned authority in all things Russian. 'It is pronounced Kaganov!'

'Yes, indeed. Kaganov...' said Milla Ivonovna. 'But you may call me Milla Ivonovna,' she concluded offering her right hand to El Guapo for a kiss.

'Encantado, Milla Ivonovna,' said the Mexican, 'José Saldero Medina, El Guapo for friends of course.'

'El Guapo?' she said.

'Yes, the Handsome,' he said not without modesty. 'It runs in the family, you see. My father's line, of course.'

'Take a seat, please,' said Milla Ivanovna and she herself took a seat in one of the large armchairs.

'And that is,' said El Guapo while taking a seat himself on the sofa not very far from the lady of the house. 'My trusted consigliere Ituribe.'

Ituribe, who had managed to get up on his feet, sat back again in his chair, produced something like a smile and nodded. Milla Ivanovna scanned him. She then dropped him in one of the bottom drawers of her scotch chest. She sighed and expressed her sorrow and desolation because the late Aleksey Kaganov wasn't there in person to greet such fine gentlemen and discuss these most promising business propositions. However, she concluded, life must go on as the fate of her beloved country, Russia, and of the rest of the world, of course, depended on this very complex and ambitious political, business and financial proposition. She then explained how Mr Kaganov was the man with perfect qualities, credentials and contacts to hammer this deal.

'If he were still alive,' she said with tears in her eyes, 'The fate of Russia and her relationship with the international community would be in safe hands. Aleksey Dmitrovich has... had, that is, the level of political and practical sophistication required to win the Russian elections and replace that odious dictator, Myshkin!' she sighed again and used a tiny embroidered handkerchief to wipe a tear from the corner of her eye.

'They did it,' she continued. 'I am sure they did it!'

'The Russians?' said Mintbatten.

'He's dead?' said El Guapo. '*Muerto, matado?*'

The conversation was taking an interesting turn, thought Golovkin. He did expect the Boss's sudden disappearance to foment a range of theories including the Sicilian Mafia, a possible FSB organised execution or an MI6 sponsored assassination. The one single person Senka knew he could not afford to underestimate was the grieving widow, Milla Ivanovna. She was the non-professional link in a chain of deception, lies, ever changing alliances and shifting priorities.

'Definitely,' said Milla Ivanovna. 'I am absolutely sure that Myshkin personally stands behind my husband's murder. The brute!'

'Because of this deal?' inquired Mintbatten.

'No,' said Milla Ivanovna. 'Because of Aleksey's political ambitions.'

'I see,' said the Lord.

'Money is everything,' concluded El Guapo with a cunning shine coming from his dark brown eyes. 'Money is politics, politics is money!'

Milla Ivanovna then proceeded to explain that the Boss's death was a tragic event but that the legacy of the late Kaganov must be preserved and that no greater sin could be committed than to yield to the sinister, dark forces behind his death. She then sobbed and used the handkerchief to wipe the tears.

'Are you sure you will be able to negotiate and do business with the very people responsible for your husband's death?' asked Mintbatten.

'Good question, Mint,' El Guapo congratulated him. 'Will this not be too much strain for you, *querida?*'

'Thank you, gentlemen,' said Milla Ivanovna. 'I shall be fine. I want to bring my husband's work to fruition.'

Business is fine, concluded Senka Golovkin quietly sitting in his corner and mumbling to himself. And you, Abogado Ituribe, you understand either everything or nothing. A Harvard graduate, someone said. Well done, doped to the core, poor thing. Must be hard to work for a mass murderer. Nice piece of work, our business partner, isn't he?

'Mr Golovkin here,' Milla Ivanovna said summoning the adviser's attention back. 'Worked with my husband over a number of years and he is best placed to explain the strategy and discuss the details of our enterprise. But before I leave you to prepare the ground for our meeting this Friday, I want to make sure one thing,' she said and turned her attention to El Guapo Medina.

'Sí?' he said.

'The diamond, El Guapo. The *Russkaya Dusha*, where is the Russian Soul?'

'The diamond,' said the Mexican baring his snow-white teeth in a smile, 'is... Here!'

'Here?' repeated a chorus of voices.

'Yes, here,' said El Guapo kicking Ituribe in the shin. 'Give me the briefcase!'

The consigliere obliged and Medina placed the leather briefcase in the middle of the coffee table, a signal for everyone to jump from their seats and gather around. Medina lifted the lid and took out of the briefcase a dark green box. He pressed a barely visible lever and opened the box.

'The Russian Soul,' cried Milla Ivanovna.

'The jewel,' said Lord Mintbatten while even Ituribe showed interest and viewed this object over his Boss' shoulders.

'The Russian Soul... In my possession,' said Milla Ivanovna whose eyes seemed to have grown in size. Her hands were shaking as she knelt next to the table to caress the jewel.

'It looks as the legend has it,' she said, 'exactly as the legend has it.'

'Where did you find it?' inquired Senka Golovkin.

'Ha, ha,' said El Guapo, 'we Mexicans do know things, you know.'

'Like, where to find precious jewels?' interjected the Lord.

'I found this beauty in the monkey's cage of Frida Kahlo's Blue House in Mexico City,' exclaimed El Guapo with a large theatrical gesture. 'It was guarded by a rattlesnake, a scorpion and a one-eyed eagle, travel companions of lost souls in search for immortality!'

'Is that for real?' said Milla Ivanovna.

Ituribe sat back into his chair as though he recognised a well-rehearsed drill.

'Of course, it's real,' said El Guapo. 'As real as the cold, bright stars in a Sonora desert winter night.'

Milla Ivanovna took the jewel and lifted it above her head. She sighed in admiration. The jewel seemed to explode in a galaxy of magical colours. She pressed a little button on the side and released the lid that smoothly opened, leaving on display a diamond composition representing a family, the Romanov family, a father, four daughters and a baby in mother's arms - The Russian Soul.

'And where is the surprise?' said Milla Ivanovna with a shade of disappointment detectable in her voice.

'The Orlov?' said El Guapo.

'Yes, the great diamond!' she said.

'I don't know,' said El Guapo, 'that's the jewel you wanted, that's it!'

'There's another little lever here,' said Golovkin pointing with a finger. Milla Ivanovna found the lever and pressed it.

The Romanov family rotated and sprung up revealing another compartment underneath. They all looked inside and there it was - the legendary diamond, the Orlov!

'Catherine the Great and now... me!' said Milla Ivanovna and launched herself with both hands towards the diamond.

'Power and beauty!' she cried as her eyes glowed.

Everyone hailed the splendour of the diamond and eventually decided to place it back in its natural dwelling, as Milla Ivanovna put it. So, they returned the precious stone to the lower compartment of the Easter egg and placed the half with the Romanov family on top. The Russian Soul was there, in the house of the late Aleksey Kaganov, in the hands of his widow and before the eyes of the business partners.

'Once repatriated,' said Milla Ivanovna, 'this jewel will open the gates to the heart of Russia!'

'Well said,' commented Lord Mintbatten.

'However,' said Medina, 'Without wishing to rain on your parade, as they say in this country, what makes you so sure that this specific egg is so different from the others? Maybe other eggs display similar qualities and command a comparable degree of respect?'

'Well, my dear El Guapo,' said Milla Ivanovna. 'Documentation is available that confirms the standing of the Russian Soul in the hierarchy of jewels and esoteric symbols. On the other hand, as you might as well know, I do have in my possession six other Fabergé Easter Eggs from the Romanov collection and a dozen others sold mostly in Europe.'

'Your beauty deserves no less,' observed El Guapo.

'And you keep all these jewels here, in the house?' inquired Lord Mintbatten.

'Yes, I keep them in the drawing room safe. It's next door. Come, I will show you,' said Milla Ivanovna and made a gesture for the party to follow her. Even *abogado* Ituribe jumped on his feet and followed the party through a double door and out of the main study.

Only Senka Golovkin stayed behind and as the chatter died out he sat on the couch staring at the Russian Soul. During his chess career, he never sacrificed a piece more valuable than a knight. Sacrifices required elaborate and robust retaliation plans. The clock was running though, and the pressure in his head and heart grew by the minute. Things didn't add up. He couldn't put his finger on the offending spot but something wasn't right. Golovkin detested rushed decisions and despised illogical conclusions. He feared irrational behaviour and tried to stay away from feelings. And yet, in a moment of complete abandonment, he jumped from the couch, shut the lid of the jewel and put it back into its green velvet coated box. He picked the box up and stormed out of the house.

Minutes later he was driving through the rain among the hills of the Uttlesford countryside. He switched the radio off, turned the wipers onto maximum speed, the headlights onto high beam and put his foot down on the accelerator.

15

Water, air, diamonds

On a typically grey and sombre English morning, some serious people were having breakfast while browsing their trusted online news outlets.

Jack Sailgood sat at the breakfast table with Sarah, his wife of thirty-five years. Lady Sarah was a passionate home improver and gardener with many great ideas and a handful of professionally drafted plans. Due to the Ukrainian crisis, though, Jack was rarely in England. Sarah stayed behind. The one single thing that she wanted more than anything else in the world was that new extension to their Sussex home. She dreamed of having a house big and comfortable enough for their three daughters and grandchildren to come over Christmas and to stay with them in summer.

While Sarah went on detailing her plans, Sir Jack sipped his English Breakfast tea and nodded. He had his tablet on the table and would touch the screen with his left index finger. One article caught his attention:

Alvosa recently signed a deal to supply the auction house Sotheby's with large diamonds to market through its retail diamond division. Alvosa provided two diamonds weighing between 50 and 70 ct in the first sale of this agreement. The diamonds carry GIA grading reports... The local press noted an increasing problem with undisclosed synthetic or imitation gemstones, diamonds and pearls being passed as natural.

Alvosa was the biggest Russian diamond producer but its credibility was dented by the production and sale of synthetic diamonds passed off as natural. Right, thought Sir Jack, the market wants diamonds and Khatanga can provide them!

* * *

'They must manufacture these clouds and the rain. Not to disappoint the overseas visitors, I guess,' thought Tom Deutsch while sitting at the breakfast table of his twenty-fifth-floor Pimlico apartment overlooking the Thames and the MI6 Vauxhall headquarters. 'I can barely see the river, never mind the spy centre!' he mumbled between two mouthfuls of black pudding.

Deutsch had a full English breakfast that consisted of a fried egg, half a tomato, a sausage, a rasher of bacon, two slices of black pudding and two slices of toast with unsalted butter, more than he would eat during a whole day back in Washington DC. He managed to persuade the chef to serve him black coffee. That counted as a success. After breakfast, though, he felt like returning to bed.

'Anyway, let me see the news before I make a move,' he thought and lifted the lid of his laptop computer. After a couple of clicks he found an article that caught his eye:

Before the Mirny pipe began producing diamonds, Russian engineers in Siberia had to find ways of overcoming the incredibly harsh conditions at the mine site. During the eight winter months in Yakutia, they found that steel tools became so brittle that they broke easily, like matchsticks, oil froze into solid blocks, and rubber tires shattered like fragile crockery in sub-zero temperatures. Furthermore, when summer came, the top layer of permafrost melted into a swamp of uncontrollable mud. Despite these natural impediments, engineers turned Mirny into an open-pit mine. Jet engines were used to blast holes in the permafrost, and enormous charges of dynamite were used to excavate the surface rock and loosen the underlying kimberlite ore. The entire mine had to be covered at night to prevent the machinery from freezing.

'Right,' mumbled Deutsch. 'Goodbye sunny Africa and welcome Siberia! The article fails to mention the political establishment, the Red Army, the nuclear deterrent and the gentlemen from various organised crime syndicates.'

* * *

Lord Mintbatten had just completed his morning routine and joined his partner Antonio at the breakfast table. Antonio was Sicilian and in his early forties, a self-declared expert in life-style choices and healthy living. He kept himself busy writing a blog named Antonio La Vita and keeping Davide in fine physical and spiritual shape with a complex routine of gymnastics, Californian Vayananda yoga, healthy food consumption, frequent exotic travel and *molto amore.*

'We will live forever,' said Antonio and put another slice of mango next to the feijoa in his plate.

'You might, Tonio,' said Davide while playing around with his laptop. 'What about me? I will have to deal with that ghastly, abominable woman, her primitive taste and intolerable arrogance... And then, if that weren't enough, there comes the macho Mexican gangster. Unbelievable! I am speechless, speechless!'

'I think that you get upset too easily,' said Tonio, 'You need to keep your Karma in the right balance. It's just a job, after all, *pazienza!*'

'Just a job, easy for you to say...'

'We need the money, I know'

'How did these people make their money? It's one of the greatest mysteries of the universe, Tonio.'

'Yes, it must be,' agreed Tonio while attending to his fingernails as Davide began reading an interesting piece in the Asian Market Daily:

Exports from Russian state diamond mine industry are set to get a huge boost as President Myshkin inks a long-sought deal with India's Prime Minister Rhandi during his visit to the Asian country next month. The potential long-term contract with Indian traders is a way for Russia to bypass imposed sanctions over its actions in The Ukraine, the Economic Times reports. It would make India a key hub for the trade of precious stones until now dominated by Belgium, Dubai, Israel, London, New York and Hong Kong. Furthermore, there is speculation that Russia is proposing the establishment of a Sino-Russian common currency with diamond standard that could seriously jeopardise the so far indisputable position of the US dollar as the world's reserve currency.

'A diamond Rouble?' exclaimed David.

'Diamond what?'

'I just hope we have a back-up man to replace Kaganov and win the next elections in bear-land.'

'Bear... Land?'

'Yes, in Moscovia,' said the financial guru and continued to read:

The Russian leader is also expected to address a joint session of parliament, an honour that is reserved for only a few foreign dignitaries. This, according to several media reports, may happen during the 15th India-Russia Annual Summit, to be held next Thursday in New Delhi. In April both countries signed a memorandum of understanding to share diamond trade data. India, the world's largest diamond processor, accounts for roughly 60% of global polished diamond output in value terms. Last year alone it imported $18 billion worth of rough diamonds and exported $25 billion in polished precious rocks. Avrosa generates around 30% of the world's rough diamonds. Last year it produced a total of 45 million carats, or about 98% of Russia's total output.

'Good grief,' cried Lord Mintbatten. 'That vile woman is to inherit a diamond mine and to control the world production of precious stones!'

'Magnifico!' said Tonio.

* * *

Abogado Ituribe was up early. Having managed to avoid Maria Guadalupe's morning tantrums he was calm and relaxed. He found a small Anatolian parlour around the corner where he had a spinach börek with yoghurt followed by a cup of kahva and rose-petal Turkish delight. He had his laptop open on the table and managed to hook it up to the Dorchester wireless service. He read the Jewish Business News:

Russian tycoon Viktor Goldberg, who has just bought a Fabergé jewellery collection from the Zerbos family, says he will put his acquisitions on public display across Russia. Yekaterinburg, in the Urals region, will be the first exhibition venue for the collection, which includes nine Easter eggs commissioned from Peter Carl Fabergé by Russian Emperor Nicholas II. According to the Yekaterinburg Bishopric's press service, Goldberg has chosen the city as the first destination for his travelling exhibition because it was here that the Emperor and his family died a martyr's death, an event commemorated by the local Cathedral of All Saints. The Fabergé exhibition in Yekaterinburg is expected to open some-time during the Orthodox Easter season. Its centrepiece will be what is known as the Coronation Egg, the one that Nicholas II offered to his spouse Alexandra Fyodorovna in 1897 to mark his ascent to the throne. The collection will then be shown to the public in other Russian cities, including Tyumen, Irkutsk, Moscow, and St. Petersburg.

* * *

Hours later, in an underground facility near Denver, Colorado, an old man sat at a desk reading a paper document several pages long. The man was known as Mr Hank. No one remembered his real name or where he came from. What everybody in the underground world he inhabited knew was that Mr Hank was in charge. He didn't have a uniform or an official title. He didn't need one. His organisation didn't have a name or a letterhead and his name never appeared in the newspapers or on television. His signature never adorned an official document. He was over a hundred years old and always young.

Mr Hank interrupted his reading and picked up two pills from a small white saucer. One pill was red and the other one green. They were designed and produced for him by a team of nutritionists working at the New York Rockefeller Medical Research Unit. He swallowed the pills and washed them down with a glass of water.

There was a knock on the door. At the second, timid, knock Mr Hank said, 'Come in.'

A young black man in a white uniform came in. He carried a tray with a glass on it.

'I brought you your carrot juice, Mr Hank,' he said.

'Thank you, Augustus, you can leave it here on my desk.'

'Yes, Sir,' said the young man and placed a tall glass on the table.

'Any news from Istanbul?' said the old man.

'Yes, Mr Hank, doctor Sönmez is personally taking care of the organs and will be transporting them here in the next two days.'

'All according to the given specification?'

'Yes.'

'The transplant team is ready?'

'Yes, they are waiting for your instructions.'

'Thank you, Augustus,' said Mr Hank. 'Being old is painful, you see. There is science, thankfully, to alleviate old age.'

'Certainly.'

'How is your family, Augustus?'

'Fine, Mr Hank, they are fine. My wife is having some respiratory problems. The asthma, you know.'

'Take a holiday, Augustus,' said Mr Hank. 'Take the family to Florida. Get out of the cold. Will you do that for me?'

'I sure will, Mr Hank. Thank you very much!'

'The Company will pay for your trip. Don't worry, just go.'

'Thank you, Mr Hank,' said the young man. 'Thank you from the bottom of my heart.'

'Don't mention it,' said the old man, taking a sip of the carrot juice and continuing to read his papers. Augustus left the room without making a sound.

Mr Hank glanced at the first page of a document entitled 'The World Water report.' He then turned to page three:

Appropriate legal and institutional frameworks are required to guarantee that water resources are managed and used sustainably. These include laws and regulations whose enforcement ensures a balance between water availability and use. They also protect the resource against pollution and over-abstraction. Managing water across competing developmental sectors is required to ensure that benefits created for one group of stakeholders do not put others at a disadvantage. Water needs to be at the centre of a multi-sectorial dialogue, which includes decision-making processes and mechanisms for conflict resolution within the context of national inter-ministerial bodies and multilateral agencies, and in the case of trans-boundary waters. Decisions that determine how water resources are used (or abused) are not made by water managers alone, but driven by various socio-economic development objectives and the operational decisions to achieve them. Progress towards sustainable development requires engaging a broad range of actors in government, civil society and business to assure that water is considered in their decision-making and to promote cooperation across disciplines, sectors and borders.

Mr Hank finished reading the Report and then drank the carrot juice in one mighty gulp. The United Nations is a useful organisation, very useful. Not a word about privatisation in the Report. Good work, good work. The legal framework is nearly ready. He picked up the next piece of paper that was sitting on the same pile. It was a print-out of a five- or six-lines long e-mail signed by Tom Deutsch. Mr Hank took another piece of the fruit and started to chew - slowly, patiently. He had read the message twice and still couldn't believe his eyes. He knew people could be untrustworthy or outright useless. But this man, Mr Hank thought, he was something else, in a league of his own. Was he trying to establish a new paradigm in incompetence? He was too upset to dwell on Deutsch's shortcomings and he picked up the next piece of paper and read the introductory summary:

London. Scientists agree that the fate of mankind is contingent on the availability of the most basic resources such as water and air. While the previous period in our history was characterised by a race for commodities such as petrol, gas, gold and diamonds, the future will depend on the basic resources necessary for the continuation of life on the planet. Amazon and Siberia are being widely recognised as of pivotal importance in the future race for these resources.

When he finished reading the paragraph, Mr Hank switched back to the message from Deutsch. He read it four times and he still could not believe his eyes: 'Unfortunate. Slight problem. Both the Russian candidate and the jewel missing. Am in London taking care of situation. Will report back ASAP - T. Deutsch.

'This must be,' mumbled Mr Hank in disgust, 'surely, the pinnacle of incompetence!'

16

The sword

Gorsky crossed the street with Knyaz on a tight leash. They were returning from their evening stroll. They walked past the Zionist Church playground and Gorsky looked around to check the benches. There was no one, all quiet. A lady walked a very small dog down the path. The puppy wore a tartan coat and she called him Oscar.

'That's fine, Knyaz,' said Gorsky. 'Let's move on.'

Minutes later, they entered their apartment block and took the stairs. On the first floor, in the middle of the corridor stood Mrs Moustakas.

'Good evening,' she said.

'Good evening, Mrs Moustakas,' said Gorsky and continued to walk as if to avoid the neighbour. Mrs Moustakas made a quick step towards him and grabbed him by the sleeve. The situation in Greece was dire! Her brother in law had to sell his firm and was now struggling to meet the payments for their apartment in Kolonaki. To be fair, they didn't need five rooms for they only have two children and the eldest of the two had left for Germany last year. But it was a matter of dignity for them. What was the world coming to? People need to meet their obligations, pay the rent! Gorsky nodded as he was paying his rent to the Moustakas and would have preferred to pay even more if that could only save him from Pelaskevi Moustakas's impromptu monologues. Greece was dying, she explained with a sigh while holding the sleeve even tighter. The Mediterranean was dying, the ancient civilizations... She then lowered her voice, the Turks were coming. One should never trust the Turks. Only stupid people trust the Turks. Her great-grand mother told her many times when she was a little girl. Never trust a Turk!

'Mrs Moustakas,' Gorsky managed to insert his question. 'Did your husband have the time to cast a glance at the item I gave him?'

'Ah, you mean the sword? Yes, I think so. Come in, come in... He is in front of the TV, as always.'

Gorsky entered the narrow corridor of the Moustakas' flat and followed the landlady to the very end and a wide room that featured an oversized TV set and Mr Moustakas sitting in a large armchair with a couple of beer cans and a full ashtray on the table in front of him. The pair exchanged a couple of Greek words that sounded like insults and Mrs Moustakas showed the visitor to a chair.

Before addressing Gorsky, Mr Moustakas made a sneering grimace.

'Go away, woman,' he said and waved his wife away. He then picked up the remote control and switched the sound off. Colourful footballers continued to run up and down the green pitch.

'Good evening, Mr Moustakas,' said Gorsky, 'sorry to interrupt you.'

'Hello,' said the host, getting up from his chair and leaving the room. He quickly came back carrying the red box.

'Your sword,' he said and sat back into the armchair.

'Well, it's not exactly mine,' said Gorsky, 'did you have the time to look at it?'

'I did, I did,' said Moustakas opening the box. 'It's a very well-made piece, very nice. But I don't think we can date it back to the 16th century, you see. The story that comes with the sword is good. This is certainly a product of a Lombard smith, that much is true. 18th century, I'd say. Late 18th.'

As the antiquarian delivered his verdict, Gorsky felt disappointed. Well, it was supposed to be the sword of the legendary painter, wasn't it? It didn't belong to him but still... It was a good story. Yes, it was a good story, that's all!

'It's not worthless, though,' said Moustakas. 'It's a nice item, comes with documentation and it can certainly attract buyers. I am willing to buy it. I can give you a nice, tidy little sum. As far as I understand, this belonged to the late Kaganov and now no one really wants it, right?'

'Sort of,' said Gorsky. 'Milla Ivanovna is not interested but she can change her mind, you know?'

'Sure. I can give you maybe two thousand for it? What do you think?'

'More, much more was paid for it!'

'Well, that's my offer. Up to you.'

'Thank you, Mr Moustakas,' said Gorsky and got up from the chair. 'I can't sell what is not mine.'

'Very well, if you change your mind, I'll be here,' said Moustakas and pressed the sound button on the remote. Arsenal had just scored the equaliser.

Gorsky picked up the box with the sword, said goodbye and left the flat. Knyaz was sitting in front of the door waiting.

'Let's go, old boy,' he said, 'the sword doesn't seem to be the sword!'

17

Brothers of tempests and rains

Gorsky went up the one flight of stairs in a couple of long strides that seemed to amuse Knyaz. They reached the apartment and Gorsky took the set of keys out of his pocket. He found the right key, inserted it in the lock and suddenly stopped. Something was different. He couldn't be sure what but something was different. Was the doormat not in the right place? Was the light in the corridor different? Was it the smell of Indian spices coming from the Punjabi Tandoor takeaway next door? He couldn't tell. Knyaz began snarling and puling.

Gorsky turned the key and opened the door. He stepped in and switched the light on. Knyaz wagged his tail and snarled some more, this time in one precise direction. At the opposite end of the living room there was a man sitting in the armchair. Mid-thirties, dark hair and eyes, medium built, he was one of those men that we often fail to register and classify as unremarkable like the average bloke in the pub, the bloke from the office next door. He held both his hands on the arms of the chair, clearly visible.

'*Privyet,* Rose,' said the newcomer.

Gorsky tapped the dog over the head, unleashed him and told him to sit in the corner. He then turned towards the visitor:

'*Privyet.* What's the occasion?'

'I hope you don't mind but I took the liberty to pour myself a drink,' said the visitor picking up a glass from the coffee table. 'Do you want one?'

'I don't drink,' said Gorsky. 'Where did you find the vodka? I don't keep any.'

'I know, I know... I mean, I knew that before coming so I brought some. My shout!'

Gorsky sat on the sofa and left the flute box on the coffee table. He looked at the visitor. Mark Hodayev. Many years later, but no mistake, Mark Hodayev.

'You look the same, Alex. Haven't changed much,' said the visitor and took a sip from the glass. 'I took a couple of rocks of ice from your fridge. Hope you don't mind, again. The bottle I brought was... Well, not cold.'

He recognised the visitor at once, but only now was he beginning to register the signs that the passage of time had left on the familiar face. The eyes were the same but sat deeper, barely visible through the narrow crack between eyelids. The face was longer, emaciated, the jaw stronger and the lips thinner. The visitor's hands were quick and steady, a tad too nervous perhaps.

'Ice is just about the only thing you will get from me,' said Gorsky. 'What do you want?'

'Ha, ha, the famous Russian hospitality,' said Hodayev. 'You wouldn't even offer me ice cubes!'

'If you asked me, the only thing you deserve is a piece of this steel,' said Gorsky nodding at the box on the table.

'What's that? May I?' said Hodayev and made a gesture as if to reach out for the box.

'Go ahead.'

Hodayev opened the box, took the sword out and started inspecting it. 'Nice,' he said. 'Must be old and valuable.'

'Not old enough and not valuable enough, it seems,' said Gorsky.

'Nec spe nec metu, says here,' said Hodayev.

'It was sold to Kaganov as the sword of a famous Italian artist.'

'Caravaggio, I presume,' said Hodayev rather casually.

'How do you know?' said Gorsky genuinely surprised by Mark's expertise.

'I recognise the motto, the Latin motto. It is associated with his days in the Roman taverns.'

'And what else do you know?'

'It's all propaganda,' said Hodayev in a self-assured manner.

'What's propaganda?' said Gorsky already irritated by this visit and the strange turn the conversation was taking.

'The man who wrote the history of late 16th and early 17th century Roman painting was Caravaggio's nemesis, a second tier, rather talentless painter whom our friend used to mock regularly. Hence, the story of Caravaggio as we know it was written by him and it's a fake.'

'You mean, that he killed a man and all of that?'

'Yes, he did kill a man in a duel. The man, Tommasoni, was the pimp of Caravaggio's favourite model. He deserved, oh yes, he so deserved, if you ask me, to be killed. That Tommasoni had a powerful family behind him, a sort of local mafia, you see. Our dear friend Caravaggio though, was brave or crazy enough to challenge him. And those were the days when duels were forbidden and the whole of the city of Rome afraid of standing up to bullies. There you go, the real and only truth about Michelangelo Merisi Caravaggio! Told to you by your most humble servant, Mark Davidovitch Hodayev,' he said and sliced the air with the sword. 'To me this sword seems good enough!'

'How do you know all of this?' said Gorsky.

'You forgot, my friend, that before meeting you in the beautiful and uplifting surroundings of the Caucasus I was a student of a great institution called the Art School of Voronezh!'

'You studied that at the university?' Gorsky was incredulous.

'No, I couldn't become an artist myself so I continued to be interested, let's say. And, of course, I spent some time in Rome where I had access to the archives.'

Gorsky stared at his long-lost friend. He tried to imagine Hodayev rummaging through the underground Vatican records, the 17th century police chronicles and civic libraries. But no, he couldn't imagine that. A dark shadow followed his friend now, a very long and very dark shadow.

'Private Mark Hodayev, sixth paratroopers regiment stationed in Chechnya, artist and traitor,' said Gorsky with a wry smile. 'What a nice career.'

They both remembered their first encounter, sitting around a campfire in the military outpost in Chechnya: New recruits, all eighteen or nineteen year olds. 'You're an artist?' said sergeant Perehovsky and pointed the finger at Hodayev, 'That's what we need here to fight the Chechens, girls and artists, ha, ha! Trapeze artists, clowns and jesters... Ha, ha!'

Hodayev jumped on his feet brandishing a knife.

'Say that again and I'll kill you,' he yelled at Perehovsky gnashing his teeth and picking a shovel up.

It was a bad night under the full moon and someone would have been cut to pieces if it weren't for corporal Gorsky who separated the two. More vodka and a bottle of Georgian brandy suddenly materialised.

'I am not a traitor, Alex,' said Hodayev calmly from the depth of his newly acquired shadow.

'Some people betray their country,' said Gorsky. 'Others betray their friends and brothers and that is worse, much worse. That turns them into Judases for an eternity and you burn in hell and in the memories of those that you betrayed. Did you not know that?'

After the campfire incident, Gorsky and Hodayev became best friends. Gorsky bigger and quieter, Hodayev louder and always ready for banter. During that year of military training in the Caucasus they became inseparable, in the cold snow and rivers and in the heat of the scorching mountain sun. It was only five days before their first combat mission. The brigade's intelligence officer, major Ivanov, summoned them both to separate interviews.

Gorsky remembered how he went to see Ivanov and was offered a seat. The major didn't sit down; he kept pacing the office from one wall to the other. With his hand behind the back he would take the cigarette out of his mouth and depose the ash in and around the ashtray.

'May I offer you a cup of tea? I know you are not a great coffee drinker,' said Ivanov carefully observing the expression of surprise on Gorsky's face. 'We have some English tea that you like, yes we do,' he said and ordered a cup of tea over the phone.

Ivanov made a point of demonstrating the full competence of the Russian intelligence services by mentioning that Ivan Borisovitch Gorsky, Gorsky's father, had some problems in the school where he taught maths and physics. The new director that came from Moscow was interested only in the advancement of her own career and didn't have any time for subtle local issues or staff with divergent opinions. And Ivan Borisovitch was one such man, said Ivanov. Irina Alexeyevna, Gorsky's mother, was doing fine in the post office, younger brother Sergey played ice hockey and wanted to turn pro some-day. The grand-grandfather was a prodigious sniper at Stalingrad, congratulations Gorsky. He served with Zaitsev, the legendary Zaitsev who registered two hundred twenty-five kills. Alexander Ivanovitch Gorsky registered one hundred fifty-seven kills and died himself in a German air raid. He might have overtaken the legendary Zaitsev, you see? You are obviously of good Russian stock. Ivanov was relentless. Your first love, Natasha Prokhorska married her university lecturer, Ivanov informed him. They have a daughter. Your friend Igor Vorontsevitch is a medical student in St. Petersburg and a very good one too. Tomorrow he will become a doctor. What will become of you, Gorsky? What is your mission in life?

Gorsky took a sip of the English tea. It was warm and it tasted nice, served in a porcelain cup the like of which he hadn't seen in a while.

'You're nineteen,' continued Ivanov, 'not married, no profession to speak of. You work in a tin factory, you spent half a year in Siberia, you like martial arts and foreign languages. Why foreign languages? why English? you like English music and want to understand the lyrics, right? You come from a musical family, Gorsky. Why no instruments? you had opportunities. You can play a couple of songs on the guitar, though. Correct?'

He made a brief pause, searched his pockets before continuing.

'Do you love your country?' he said. 'Do you love your country, Gorsky?'

Ivanov then went to a wooden cabinet and from a shelf took a tall, porcelain teacup and placed it in front of Gorsky. There was a red rose in the cup. A fresh, red rose. It smelt like spring, like the Caucasian plains on a sunny morning.

'Smell this rose, Gorsky. No poet has ever managed to do justice to the delicacy of its petals or the allure of its scent. Not Pushkin, not Yesenin or Mayakovski...' Ivanov then placed his hand over his heart and began to recite: I know a rock in a highland's ravine, on which only eagles might ever be seen, but a black wooden cross over the precipice reigns, it rots and it ages from tempests and rains..."

That's where Ivanov stopped reciting. He had a triumphant expression on his face.

'Oh, if I were able to rise there and stay,' Gorsky then continued, 'then how I'd cry there and how I'd pray; And then I would throw off real life's chains and live as a brother of tempests and rains!'

'Oh, we know our Lermontovs,' said Ivanov and clapped his hands in admiration... or mockery.

'Yes, major Ivanov, we know our Lermontovs,' said Gorsky.

'Lermontov, the great poet of the Caucasus,' said Ivanov pointing at the ceiling for some reason.

He then went on to say that there was a river to be crossed at some point in life. Great men know when, where and how to cross it. Great men lived meaningful lives. No bridges, no rafts or ferries, just the fast, cold water of the mountain river.

'Leave behind the smell of diesel and gun powder,' said Ivanov, 'ditch the wet and worn military uniforms. Forget the cold, iron touch of your AK-47, Corporal Gorsky. Your name was forwarded to me by your commanding officer. Best in the class, he said. The service I am here to offer is to the Fatherland - counter intelligence. You will undergo five years of specialist training and you will then be deployed in one of our Western posts.'

Ivanov went through his pockets as if he had lost something.

'You see this rose?' he said suddenly pointing at the flower, 'it's full of life and promise. Scent, can't you tell the scent? You will have a decent, renewable bank account, legitimate business interests and apartments in major cities...

in Rome, Berlin, London... you will collect information, establish networks... you know, that sort of stuff!'

Later that evening, Gorsky and Hodayev sat around a campfire and told each other about these interviews. They were both summoned and they were both presented with the same red rose. 'Was it really the same?' said Hodayev laughing. 'Pass me the vodka,' said Gorsky. 'Your name will be retrospectively erased from the roster of this military unit... Ha, ha,' laughed Hodayev. 'First thing in the morning, you will travel to Moscow for further assessment. You cannot tell anyone about this conversation or your future work. You will be an engineer in state employment...'

'And you will have a new name and new documents,' Gorsky completed the sentence, 'Ha, ha.'

They drank vodka, and then more vodka and gave an oath to each other not to accept Ivanov's offer. We will never betray our comrades, they said, four days before their first combat mission. It was January. The snows of the Caucasus touching the sky.

'Never, brother,' said Hodayev.

'Never,' said Gorsky and they hugged and kissed each other, rolled in the snow, drank more vodka, smoked more cigarettes and howled songs about love and friendship. The captain's rose is just a metaphor. It is a metaphor, said Mark. He jumped on his feet and pointed his finger towards the night sky. Do you understand metaphors? They laughed and they laughed.

'Oh, if I were able to rise there and stay,' announced Gorsky pointing at the sky, 'Then, how I'd cry there and how I'd pray; And then I would throw off real life's chains and live as a brother of tempests and rains.'

'Hell, we do know our Lermontovs, major Ivanov!' they cried.

Sitting in the little Cambridge apartment, they now laughed again. They laughed at the memory of the long lost, glory days.

Mark Hodayev sat in the armchair and Gorsky on the sofa. He was still wearing his dark grey coat.

'How did you get in?' said Gorsky.

'I am a professional,' said Hodayev. 'Give me some credit.'

'Professional...' echoed Gorsky, 'you received news that your mother was on her deathbed and you were granted permission to visit. Three days, to Moscow and back. Three days, but the sad truth is that you never came back. Now I learn why. You picked the rose and abandoned your comrades. You went along with the metaphor, shall I say?'

'I am sorry,' said Hodayev, 'I had to perform my patriotic duty.'

'Cowards don't have motherlands. Cowards don't deserve motherlands,' Gorsky concluded bitterly.

'I wanted to come back and tell you but wasn't allowed.'

'Tell? Tell to whom? Whom did you want to talk to, Mark? Save your words and breath for the underworld for that's where you and I are heading.'

Hodayev took out of his pocket a lighter and a pack of cigarettes. He offered one to Gorsky who shook his head.

'May I?'

'No,' came a dry response.

Hodayev returned the pack and the lighter into his pocket and shrugged his shoulders as if to say, 'right, I knew this would happen.' He then began his account.

'In March '99, during the war in Yugoslavia, the Serbs brought down an American B-2 Stealth bomber. The pilot was evacuated but the aircraft stayed behind on enemy territory. The Serbs offered the vital parts to us in exchange for an S-300 anti-aircraft system and we agreed. The samples and electronics were then put on board the Tupolev 204 that transported the Russian Belgrade embassy staff and family members to Moscow. The Americans suspected what the cargo would be but that plane simply could not be brought down. That would be too much even by their enviable standards. The plane landed at Domodedovo airport and the FSB officer in charge of the operation, let's call him Colonel K., reported mission accomplished and died in a car crash a couple of months later. The B-2 samples were passed to the Chinese and the Americans didn't like it. To express their deep gratitude, they bombed the Chinese embassy in Belgrade. When Myshkin came to power he became very interested in this operation. No need to tell you that all the money went into private pockets and that the Serbs never received the S-300. That was my first task. I was part of the team that carried out a covert, international investigation about this illicit transfer of technology and assets, as we officially called it.'

Hodayev picked his glass up and downed its content. He poured more vodka and sat in the armchair waiting. Alex Gorsky was there. He was the man who could tell the story of the 6th Parachute Company.

'Well,' Gorsky said with a sneer, 'we arrived there on 31 January. Ninety men, Rose, and only four lived to see the dawn of the next day. Up in the gorge of the Argul, our company met a two thousand strong Chechen force. The Chechens wanted to negotiate so that we bypass each other but Major Yevtuchin had orders to stop any enemy activity. He said no. No negotiations and no passage. The fight started in the early afternoon and went on for two days and two nights. In front of us the Mujahedeen, left and right the minefields where Yevtuchin lost both legs - retreat, not an option. General Lentsov couldn't send us reinforcements because of the minefields. We couldn't get any air support because of the fog. On the second night, just before dawn, Major Yevtuchin spoke to us on the radio. 'Russian heroes,' he said, and I can still hear his voice, 'We have no more than two dozen men left and are running low on ammunition. The enemy is approaching and the single shots you can hear are the Mujahedeen executing our wounded comrades. Come the dawn the final assault will begin. We don't have the means to repel them anymore. I gave Captain Makarenko our coordinates and requested that they open fire at our positions and the enemy around us. It was my privilege and honour to have served with you...'. The artillery fire interrupted the radio communication as the first round hit his position. All hell broke loose. The Mujahedeen were upon us and we fought with bayonets and shovels, bare hands and teeth. In the morning, I realised I was surrounded by piles of dead bodies. It was carnage. We lost eighty-six men, three were wounded and only one came out of it unscarred - me. Eighty-six. The enemy lost six hundred in close combat and through artillery fire. I killed many men that night and I don't know how many. I fired my AK-74 until the man operating the PK machine gun next to me was killed so I took over. I might have killed more than hundred bandits, Mark. At the end, we fought with knives, bayonets and shovels, flesh against flesh, blood against blood.

When the artillery opened fire, the night sky erupted and a curtain of fire came down. The woods and mountains trembled.'

When Gorsky finished his account, a coating of silence fell over the room. After a while, Hodayev got up from the chair and brought an empty glass from the kitchen. He put it on the coffee table in front of Gorsky and poured vodka. He then filled his own glass to the brim.

'I don't drink,' said Gorsky.

'You're Russian,' said Hodayev. "One last time, for the Sixth company!'

'One last time,' said Gorsky, 'for the Sixth,'

They both emptied their glasses and put them back on the table with a thud. It was an old tradition. Hodayev poured more vodka and raised his glass.

'For mother Russia!'

Gorsky sat immobile, staring at the glass full of vodka as if having other thoughts on his mind. 'For mother Russia,' cried Hodayev again raising the glass and getting up thumping his feet. The glass stood still on the dark, flat surface of the table. Gorsky jumped on his feet, picked the glass up and threw it with the full might of his swing against the opposite wall where it exploded in a million shards and drops that sped across the room as through an expanding universe.

'For mother Russia, private Hodayev,' said Gorsky. 'And all the spilt guts and brains!'

Hodayev raised and emptied his glass.

'The theatre of our lives,' said Gorsky who was now pacing the room from one wall to the other stepping on the shards and liquor with his heavy-duty boots. 'Tell me, Mark, do you believe in what you are doing? Do you believe that your actions will change the world for the better? Do you think that you are fulfilling your humble human mission? In the morning, when you see your face in the mirror with no one around, are you satisfied, proud of yourself?'

Hodayev sat back in his chair. He always suspected there was such a thing as the day of reckoning. He thought it would feel like hitting a wall, an impact of a powerful, superior external force. He didn't expect an inner volcano to erupt and start burning and twisting his gut savagely.

'The vodka, is it the vodka?' crossed his mind but he knew, he knew full well that this was the moment he dreaded all these years, the moment when the masks, costumes and pretences would come off.

'Let's drink more vodka, comrade Mark. Let's drink more vodka and feel righteous, eh? Let's drink and feel alive when everyone else is dead, how about that, eh? Wouldn't that be great, comrade Mark?' said Gorsky and went to the kitchen from where he brought a new glass.

'Pour more vodka, let's drink vodka and salute our past,' he said and put the glass on the table in front of the visitor who obliged and poured more liquor from the bottle.

'To mother Russia and her sons,' said Gorsky, downed the content of the glass that he then smashed against the wall in nearly the same place as the first one. Hodayev emptied his glass and held it in his hand.

'What are you afraid of?' yelled Gorsky. 'Are you afraid, comrade Mark?'

Hodayev threw the glass against the wall himself. It bounced off it, fell on the floor and rolled under the coffee table.

'My god, my god,' cried Gorsky. 'What did the FSB do to you? Ha, ha, comrade Mark Hodayev defeated by an empty glass. What a spectacle!'

He sat back on the sofa but his eyes seemed on fire, his hands restless as his mind spinning in many directions simultaneously only to retrieve images and sounds that belonged to the other world, the other life, the other, the old, Alex Gorsky.

'They gave me medals, you know,' continued Gorsky. 'I was alive and they gave me medals. There was no one left to evaluate my behaviour in battle but I was alive. The country needed heroes. As a token of gratitude, the High Command sent me to the Military. I came out as captain and was assigned to the 106th regiment of the 475th airborne division.'

Gorsky paused as if finding it difficult to remember the name. 'In Beslan, the School Number One in Beslan, North Ossetia. On 1ˢᵗ September, the first day of school, the Chechen took more than a thousand-people hostage, eight hundred of them children. They made people lie on the floor of the gymnasium with explosive ordinance on top of their heads hanging from the ceiling and walls. The siege lasted three days...'

Hodayev knew the story of School Number One in Beslan. Everyone knew the story that left scars on the Russian soul.

'... On the third day, conflicting orders were issued. The police opened fire. Shooting and explosions inside the school started and we stormed the building. Two hundred children died and many adult hostages too. We lost all three commanding officers and twelve soldiers. That evening, when the siege was over, Colonel Ivanov congratulated our unit and said we would all get the Medal for Courage. I asked about our fallen comrades. They would get medals too, said Colonel Ivanov. And what about the children and the teachers of School Number One, I asked. He said they were civilians and unfortunate victims but that we defended higher state interests with valour. You see, Rose, I wasn't brought up to live like that. I cannot thrive on such misery. I don't understand these allegedly higher state interests and I don't want to. They all pretend there is something very important and mystical. Rubbish! I faced enemies and death. There is no mystery. While still in the crib, I must have been touched by an angel. Got lucky. Gently, with his little finger he must have touched my forehead while I was asleep. No bullet, dagger or grenade can harm me, comrade Hodayev. It's a curse for I was harmed on the inside and I couldn't take it anymore. Colonel Ivanov, I said, you're a fool. You're a bloody fool. A drop of sweat or blood, a tear from any of these children is worth more than any of your stupid higher state interests. Oh, Colonel Ivanov, much more.'

'I see,' said Hodayev.

'No, you don't see, Mark. You have no idea what the void looks and feels like. You, with your state sponsored bank account and a top-secret list of duties. You are a mannequin with a time bomb, a commodity of the FSB programmed to shadow your own clone in a Manchester United or MI6 uniform. How can you from your cosmic altitudes see what the little ants on planet earth are up to?'

'I need your help,' said Hodayev holding his head with both hands and looking at the floor.

Gorsky stopped pacing the room. Like wild animals in the forest, he sensed the sway of tree branches and the sound and smell of predators and prey.

'Mark, the Rose Hodayev needs my help,' said Gorsky as if giving a statement and began to laugh. 'Ha, ha, they need my help... You don't need the help of the Argul hundred and the Beslan children... Ha, ha, you need the help of Alex Gorsky who had the misfortune to live long enough to learn about human nature and despise it. Private Hodayev, I do not care about your needs.'

'I personally need your help, Alex. We also need your help, assistance, collaboration... Call it what you wish,' said Hodayev and picked up a small, colourful canvas bag from the floor and placed it on his knees. He took a bunch of folders from it that he placed on the table.

'What's that?' said Gorsky.

'It's the Report on the Russian Soul.'

'Really? Say no more, a Report on the immortal Russian Soul. Written, I guess, by one of your FSB friends who must be an expert in the field.'

'Read it,' said Hodayev. 'That's all I'm asking.'

'I don't care about your interpretation of the Russian soul.'

'The British wrote it, not us,' said Hodayev getting up from his seat.

'I care even less about their interpretation.'

'Read it. Once you do, we must meet, as soon as possible. There is a Chagall exhibition at the Tate Modern in London. I'll be there tomorrow afternoon, four o'clock. It's an open public space, safe. We can meet there.'

'Go away,' said Gorsky through his teeth.

Mark Hodayev came to the door, grabbed the handle and turned around: 'Where is your boss?'

'My boss?'

'Yes. Where is Aleksey Kaganov?'

'Dead, I presume,' said Gorsky.

'Are you sure?' teased Hodayev.

'What do you mean?'

'See you tomorrow,' said Hodayev, left the room and closed the door.

As Hodayev left and the sound of his steps died out in the corridor, Knyaz howled and came to sit next to Gorsky's feet.

'You know,' he said, 'even you know.'

After a while he picked up the papers that Hodayev left. A couple of pages. In English. Report, Strictly Confidential read on the blue folder. He opened it. The title read:

Fabergé's Lost Jewel.

The last batch of documents released by WikiLeaks features e-mails and reports traded among embassies here in Moscow as well as e-mails sent by the diplomatic staff of Russia, the United States and United Kingdom to business entities that operate in the City of London and Dubai. The content of these documents supports our view on the activities for the acquisition of Siberian natural resources. Useful information was also provided by Mr Aleksey Kaganov.

These documents are related to the legacy of the Russian Imperial House with special reference to the jewels, the graceful Easter eggs that Nikolay II Romanov commissioned from the Fabergé House. This with special reference to the 1905 egg named Russkaya Dusha. Beyond its pecuniary value, this jewel possesses a mystical aspect that cannot be underestimated. It is a symbol of national and spiritual unity of Russia that also confirms the entitlement of the Romanovs to rule the country. The Russkaya Dusha might just be the key to the greatest reserves of natural resources on the planet. In the wrong hands, the jewel could cause a power struggle in the Kremlin thus jeopardizing the position of our partners in the current Government. If President Myshkin were to come into possession of the Russian Soul, his position would be significantly strengthened.

Rumours about the Jewel began appearing around the year 2000, which coincides with President Myshkin's accession to power. Such rumours attracted the attention of powerful Russian oligarchs, international intelligence and financial services and prominent criminal organisations.

There are many hypotheses about this jewel. Hard evidence is scarce. Did Agathon Fabergé exchange the jewel for safe passage out of the country? Did Leon Trotsky have the jewel in his possession? Did he use a representative of the International Communist Movement, the Mexican painter Diego Rivera, to smuggle it out of the USSR and was the jewel meant to finance his vision of 'Permanent Revolution' and the overthrow of the Stalinist regime? Did Rivera try to sell the jewel in New York to John Rockefeller? Did the jewel seal the fate of Trotsky? And finally, what was the jewel's fate? It was last seen in the possession of the artist Frida Kahlo. Did she receive it from her husband, Diego Rivera, or from her lover, Leon Trotsky? The jewel vanished. Why is it reappearing now?

The Russian government has recently rehabilitated the Imperial Family and reinstated all their moral and legal rights. The Russian Orthodox Church has sanctified the last Russian Tsar, Nikolay II Romanov, his wife, Tsarina Alexandra Fyodorovna, their daughters Olga, Tatiana, Maria, Anastasia, and the Tsarevich Aleksey.

Until recent times, it was generally believed that the Tsar did not place his usual Easter egg orders with Fabergé House during the 1904-1905 Russo-Japanese war. The Fabergé documentation is now accessible and it does confirm the existence of a commission for Easter 1905. The jewel was meant to celebrate the birth of the Tsarevich. The Russkaya Dusha is of exceptional value. Among all other gemstones and varieties of gold, the egg contains the legendary Orlov, the very diamond that Catherine the Great had built into her sceptre. The Director General of the Kremlin Museum, Elena Gagarina, summoned a group of leading world experts to examine the diamond in the sceptre held at the Museum. The verdict was unanimous. The diamond *was undoubtedly of exceptional value. However, it was not the Orlov!*

The Russian oil magnate Victor Dunstelberg has acquired, in a behind closed doors sale thought to be worth several hundred million US dollars, the largest collection of Fabergé Imperial eggs ever. He said in an interview to Russian television that it was his intention to build a church in Yekaterinburg dedicated to the Virgin Mary on the very site where once stood the house of the Ipatiev family where the Romanovs were executed in 1918. He also asserted that his aim is to restore the continuity of Russian statehood in all its pride and glory. Next to the said church, Dunstelberg is building a sumptuous mausoleum dedicated to Nikolay II and his family. The inauguration ceremony is planned for the spring of next year and the honour of officially opening this memorial complex has been bestowed upon President Myshkin.

If the Russkaya Dusha emerged on the market it would command a breath-taking price tag. Nonetheless, it is our view that this is not likely. The Jewel will most probably be bartered as part of a strategic financial or political deal. The geopolitical situation in the Ukraine, the Baltic countries, the Caucasus and the Middle East further deteriorates. Confrontations in the Arctic and Pacific rims seem inevitable. For these and other reasons the change of regime in the Kremlin is a priority and the Russian Soul could prove to have a decisive role in such an operation.

'Aleksey Kaganov,' said Gorsky and threw the folder back on the table where it landed with a thud. 'Kaganov found the letters...'

18

Tate Modern

It was a couple of minutes past noon when Gorsky opened the door of his flat and Knyaz happily stormed out into the corridor.

'Don't go too far,' Gorsky said. 'We're only going to the Moustakas. Zen will take you out today as I'll be out of town.' He shut the door and checked that it was firmly locked. The previous night's intrusion didn't leave any visible signs. 'Mark is good,' thought Gorsky. 'Should have been an artist, an artisan or a smith at least. What a waste of talent.'

Paraskevi Moustakas opened the door wearing her usual flowery robe.

'Can you imagine that these criminals have just raised the prices of gas and electricity again! And only last month they announced a seventy per cent increase in profit! Free market my fat arse!' she said in lieu of a greeting.

'Good day,' said Gorsky while Knyaz, who obviously liked the flamboyant act of Mrs Moustakas, wagged his tail and stuck out his tongue.

'Well, I hope that everyone has realised by now that the government in this country is totally corrupt and made up of thieves and criminals!'

'Yes... Could I please ask you...?'

'Fascist swine. Let me tell you that they are all fascist swine.' It seemed to Gorsky that she didn't breathe while swearing. 'My grandmother used to curse the Turks. The

Germans are worse, much worse. The bastards occupied and destroyed our country! Instead of paying the reparations they created this awful debt that decent working people cannot repay. Criminal, that is completely criminal!'

'Sorry to interrupt, Mrs Moustakas. I must go. I wanted to ask you to mind Knyaz this afternoon and ask your son to take him out for a walk. I know that Zenon likes taking Knyaz out and if that is not too much to...'

'The Fascists didn't allow free speech. Didn't allow any kind of speech, you know?'

'I'll be back later tonight. Not too late, I hope,' said Gorsky handing the leash to the Greek woman who was obviously so enthralled by the subject of daily politics and fascism.

'Yes, sure,' she finally said. 'Zenon is coming from school at five today. They can go out before dinner. We don't go to bed before midnight. Don't worry. By the time Stavros has watched all the football there is on television...'

When Gorsky turned around to leave, Mrs Moustakas grabbed the sleeve of his coat and said: 'Ah, forgot to tell you...'

'What?'

'There was a man in the street last night, here in front of the building. I think he was looking at your windows.'

'My age, medium built, dark hair, leather jacket with little bag...' said Gorsky describing Hodayev.

'No, not at all,' said Mrs Moustakas. 'This man was older, blond or white hair wearing a suit, had a tie... He came out of a big car that stopped at the beginning of the street and walked up and down. Stopped in front of our building and looked up at the windows.'

'Are you sure he was looking at my windows?'

'Mr Gorsky, maybe I don't know much about world politics but the one thing I know is our street.'

178

'Thank you,' said Gorsky and came down the stairs. He stepped out into the street and felt the cold wind on his face and hands. 'Straight from Siberia, as they say here,' he thought. 'They have no idea what the Siberian wind feels like, no idea.' He found his trusted, red '98 Volkswagen Golf, opened the door and sat in the car. 'Less than one hour to Redbridge, then tube to the city centre... I'm doing fine,' he thought and started the engine. The traffic wasn't heavy. He drove into East Road and at the Cambridge Royal Hotel roundabout turned left into Trumpington Road onto the M11 that would lead him straight to London.

* * *

An hour later, Gorsky got out at St. Paul's. He quickly emerged from the underground, went along Paternoster Row and then, meandering among several groups of tourists, reached Queen Anne's statue. He stopped in front of the monument and turned towards the Cathedral. He liked that spot. He thought it was an impressive symbol. Not as impressive as the one in Rome the other day but still, impressive.

Gorsky then continued and reached the pedestrian Peter's Hill walk that crossed Queen Victoria Street. He slowed his pace and raised his eyes. It was a quarter to four in the afternoon and he was looking at the old power plant that now housed Tate Modern. He turned around. No one followed him. Good. He saw the dome of the Cathedral and then looked down the Millennium Bridge. Across the Thames he saw the tall windows and red brick walls of the Tate. He then crossed the pedestrian bridge.

He was going to meet Mark Hodayev, after all. Why was he doing this? Why did he come to London? Was it patriotism, friendship or fate? Gorsky felt a curious mix of anxiety and annoyance. He found himself in the middle of an affair he couldn't make much sense of. There was a dreadful storm out there in the high seas breaking masts of valiant clippers and filling merchants and seamen alike with awe and terror. What would he tell Mark Hodayev? He had no idea, but what he did know was that he couldn't stand on the side-lines and pretend it was none of his business. He wasn't the type, he had a spine.

Gorsky reached the end of the bridge that passed between Shakespeare's Globe Theatre to the left and the green patches on the right and was just about to turn left and take the stairs when his attention was drawn by a figure standing in one of the tall, narrow windows on the second floor of the Tate Modern. The windows were at the same height as the bridge and the figure looked no more than metres away, behind the thick glass. Gorsky knew the window very well, he had stood there more than once admiring the way in which the bridge and the Peter's Hill passage visually connected the old power plant building and the museum with St. Paul's.

The figure in the window moved and it looked familiar: medium height, dark brown leather jacket and a colourful shoulder bag. Gorsky stopped and raised a hand. He saw Mark turning to cast a glance out of the window. As he did so, an arm came from behind and wrapped itself around his throat. Mark's body hit the glass as he tried to free himself with both of his hands. He then lifted his feet and pushed against the window only to slide down slowly leaving a red smear on the glass. Gorsky ran down the stairs of the footbridge, though the main entrance and up the escalator. The passage was crowded and as he struggled to get through by shouting and pushing people aside, he noticed a dark-haired young man in a green jacket coming down in the opposite direction. The man glanced at Gorsky and ran downstairs.

Mark lay in front of the tall window that framed the passage to the Cathedral. Gorsky knelt next to the body and turned him over. The shirt was soaked in blood. Gorsky checked the stab-wounds and then looked Mark in the eyes. Hodayev was trying to breathe while his eyes were turning glassy. Then a gurgling sound and blood came out of his mouth.

'Stay, Mark,' said Gorsky placing a hand under Hodayev's head.

He then turned around and shouted, 'a doctor, quickly!'

'I knew you would come...' said Hodayev.

'Of course, you did,' said Gorsky, 'don't go, we'll fix you.'

'You can't, Alex. You can't... fix...'

'Don't talk,' said Gorsky, trying to keep Hodayev's head upright and wipe his lips.

'Artist...' said Hodayev with a faint smile, '... or die in the high mountains... no good this way, no good...'.

Hodayev's eyes froze. Gorsky lowered his head to check for even the faintest trace of breathing. There was nothing. He closed Hodayev's eyelids and lowered his head. He checked Hodayev's pockets and the bag. Nothing. If there was anything it was gone. He jumped up on his feet and realised that a small crowd gathered around them.

'A doctor, a doctor, I am going to get a doctor!' he shouted and walked away leaving Mark Hodayev's body in a pool of blood. He ran down the escalator and out of the building. He walked briskly up the Bankside to the Blackfriars Bridge where he crossed the river and reached the tube station. In less than half an hour he was sitting in his car at Redbridge and within another hour he was parking the car near his apartment building in Cambridge.

Gorsky remembered the young man on the stairway, the green jacket, and the stare. He knew that face. He couldn't tie it to a time and a place but he knew the face. He was sure of that. He knew the face.

Gorsky switched the engine and the headlights off, undid his seat belt and pulled the key out of the ignition. He got out of the car, walked to his apartment block and entered the building. He ran up the stairs to his apartment and had already inserted the key in the lock when he suddenly remembered that he needed to collect the dog.

'Well,' he thought, 'better do it now than later.'

He returned downstairs and knocked at the Moustakas door. He looked at his wristwatch; it was a couple of minutes past seven. Mrs Moustakas opened the door and greeted him with another tirade about Greek people being independent and freedom loving while the European Union was corrupted and the Turks just about to conquer the Mediterranean and...

'The dog,' said Gorsky.

'Ah, Knyaz, of course!' she said and yelled for Zenon.

At that very moment, a powerful explosion shook the building. To avoid failing Mrs Moustakas held onto the doorway while Gorsky was thrown against the wall.

'What is this?' cried Mrs Moustakas as her husband came rushing from the living room.

'A gas installation?' he said. 'It came from upstairs!'

'Upstairs, yes. Get inside and shut the door,' said Gorsky and ran upstairs.

The door of his flat was blown into pieces and thick, black smoke filled the hallway. A large chunk of the wall was missing too and a cloud of smoke lingered on. Gorsky walked in. The explosive device had been placed next to the door and probably connected to the lock. It allowed a dozen seconds from the time you inserted the key. You insert the key, walk in, turn around and ... Boom. Off you go.

'Knyaz saved my life,' he thought as he inspected what was left of the living room. He found the case with the sword in a corner of the room and he picked it up. He went through the bedroom, the improvised gym, bathroom and kitchen, collected a handful of personal documents from a drawer next to his bed and put them in his pocket. With the case in one hand and the fist closed of the other he left the flat and ran downstairs.

'It looks like someone threw a grenade into my flat,' he said without paying any attention to Mrs Moustakas' screams and Mr Moustakas' questions.

'It must have been a mistake,' explained Gorsky. 'I have to go. It's urgent. Take care of Knyaz while I am away, please. Thank you.'

He tapped the dog on the head. The interphone rang and Stavros picked the receiver up.

'Yes, sure, come in,' he said and pressed the button to open the door. 'It's for you,' he said looking at Gorsky.

With a quizzical expression on his face, Gorsky turned around and made his way down the stairs. A shadow was coming up the stairs towards him. It was a skinny man whose movements looked disjointed.

'Senka?' said Gorsky in disbelief.

'Alex,' said Senka Golovkin standing in the middle of the smoke-filled stairway. His eyes were large and full of fear, his tie undone and over his right shoulder he carried a little red rucksack.

19

At the Army and Navy club

Jack Sailgood's ancestors had been members of the Army and Navy club for several generations. The club occupied a building in Pall Mall Street designed in mid nineteenth century as an imitation of the famous renaissance Corner Palace that overlooks Canal Grande, the main Venetian thoroughfare. The club did not allow women in, of course, and the only exception to the rule was made in 1855 for the visit of Queen Victoria and Prince Albert.

Sir Jack chose to meet with his associates, Tom Deutsch and Lord David Mintbatten, at the Club. Private and friendly, it was the ideal venue to discuss something as secretive and delicate as the Khatanga enterprise. A car was sent to pick Deutsch up from Pimlico and Sir Jack greeted the guest at the entrance.

'Very few people get the opportunity to visit this place, you know,' he said while walking down a corridor with portraits of important uniformed people.

'Sure,' said Deutsch. 'Sure.' Being an American he wasn't easily impressed by pictures, stern tradition and ceremonial behaviour.

Sailgood had booked the Crimea private room on the first floor. He led his visitor up via a narrow, private stairway and they managed to reach the room without meeting anyone. The chamber was well appointed, with wooden panels on the walls covered with more stern-looking, uniformed men. A sumptuous Afghan rug covered the floor and on top of it stood a large oak table. The fireplace was lit and two corner tables featured decanters and half a dozen glasses. Sailgood sat his guest in one of the leather armchairs facing the fireplace.

'A Scotch?' he offered. '

'Of course,' said Deutsch.

Sailgood poured the whisky and raised his glass.

'To your health,' he said.

'To yours too,' said Deutsch. 'When is Mintbatten coming?'

'Should be here in quarter of an hour,' said Sailgood and cleared his throat.

'Right.'

'How is the family doing, Tom?'

'The elder son is in his final year of law. The younger one is into IT and is also quite entrepreneurial. He's an interesting character. He designed with some friends an online game environment, the Drone Zone. They're developing the business model now as they want to become millionaires before their eighteenth birthday.

'Clever little buggers,' said Sailgood. '" The Drone Zone"... sounds cool. What does one do in this 'Drone Zone'?'

'Well, they apparently developed a virus that can penetrate the Pentagon operative network and take over the commands of US Army drones.'

'And what's the business plan?'

'Well it's a joke, a game obviously...'

'Yes, I am really, curious, if it's not a business secret?'

'Ha, ha, no, of course not. Not for you at any rate. Via a secure web site anyone in the world can hire a drone to take out people, institutions, and vehicles... You know? If you are dealing with some evil, nasty guys you hire the 'Drone Zone' guys to take the baddies out.'

'Something like the Ghostbusters?'

'Yeah, just like the Ghostbusters!'

'Are you sure this is legal, Tom?'

'Come on, Jack. It's just a game. Anyway, one could argue that this is only a model for the privatisation of state assets, right?'

'Right,' nodded Sailgood as the two raised the glasses and drank some more.

At that very moment, there was a knock on the door and Lord Mintbatten entered the room.

'Gentlemen,' he said.

'Lord Mintbatten,' said Sailgood, 'we finally meet'.

After a swift round of introductions, Mintbatten was presented with a drink and sat in an armchair.

'So,' said Deutsch. 'What is the latest on the death of this Kaganov?'

'Well, the body that was recovered was charred, burnt beyond recognition. The wife made a positive identification based on the wedding ring he wore but...'

'But what?'

'Something is not right and I don't know what. I don't like it when that happens.'

'And the woman is now in charge?'

'The widow? That woman is a dangerous beast!' affirmed Lord Mintbatten in the authoritative manner of a psychiatrist who had just examined a mass-murderer.

'The Kaganov widow?' said Sailgood.

'Yes,' nodded the Lord. 'The woman is a prime example of the Asiatic kind of barbarism normally associated with Mongol hordes. She makes me think that Napoleon and Hitler were right about the Russians and Slavs in general... all Tatars, all Genghis Kahns!'

'You obviously met her?' said Sailgood.

'Yes, indeed, I had that dubious pleasure,' said Mintbatten and took a sip of the whisky as though the liquor could protect him against the evil spell of Milla Ivanovna.

'What did she do to you?' said Deutsch whose idea of darkness was closely associated with southern Voodoo dolls, pins and Caribbean dances.

'What she said or did to me is nothing,' said Lord Mintbatten. 'Compared to what was done to her last night. There is justice after all.'

Both Deutsch and Sailgood held their breaths.

'What happened to her?' said Deutsch.

'Mr Medina, the Mexican, was there and he brought the jewel, the Russian Soul.'

'Yes?' said Sailgood.

'Well, it vanished.'

'The jewel?' said Deutsch.

'The egg?' said Sailgood.

'Yes, the mad Russian adviser, Goloffkin -- or similar -- vanished with the jewel.'

'The jewel's gone!' concluded Sailgood and downed his whisky in a single mighty gulp.

The three bade farewell before midnight. They shook hands on the pavement in front of the Club's entrance. Tom Deutsch said he was in a hurry as he had another appointment that evening. He entered a long-base black limousine and quickly vanished around the corner while Lord Mintbatten and Jack Sailgood boarded Mintbatten's Bentley.

Tom Deutsch sat comfortably in the back seat of the limo. He checked the fridge and took out a small bottle of water that he opened and took a sip from. Between the front seats and the rear section of the car, there was a panel with various flashing lights and knobs. He pressed a button underneath the LCD screen and watched it come to life. He navigated the on-screen controls, inserted several passwords and reached his destination. The face of an old man appeared. He sported a yellow Hawaiian shirt and could have been eighty or a hundred and fifty years old. Deutsch had the sensation that the man was aging in a parallel universe. Indeed, Mr Hank aged differently. He was different.

'Does Sailgood suspect anything?' said the old man and put a piece of Kiwi fruit into his mouth with a fork.

'No, nothing,' said Deutsch, 'And Garriburton is on track to win the concession rights.'

'That is good. If that is the case, that is very good,' said the old man and took his dark glasses off. He had pale blue eyes and the piercing look of a rapacious animal. He produced a faint smile in one corner of his dark, thin lips.

'However,' said Deutsch and cleared his throat.

'Yes?'

'There is a problem that we didn't anticipate.'

'You didn't?'

'The Jewel...,' said Deutsch, 'Seems to have disappeared.'

'The egg disappeared, you say?'

'Yes, I am afraid so.'

'And... Who might have disappeared this jewel, Tom?' said Mr Hank. His face came closer to the camera and filled the screen. Deutsch could see the deep wrinkles, the dots and the pores.

'A guy called Golovkin,' said Deutsch. 'He is... He was Kaganov's secretary and had access to the house.

'What was the Jewel doing in Kaganov's house?'

'Milla Ivanovna, the wife, invited Medina and asked him to bring over the Jewel and he did.'

'The Mexican brought the Russian Soul to Kaganov's widow and lost it?'

'Well, yes. Lord Mintbatten was there. He told us the story.'

'Who does this Golovkin work for?' said Mr Hank.

'He used to work for the Boss; now, there seems to be only one man he is constantly in contact with.'

'I'm listening.'

'A certain Gorsky. In Kaganov's employment, too.'

'Russian?'

'Yes, former military, now security officer. I asked the Central Office for details on him.'

'I see.' said Mr Hank.

The screen blinked and Tom Deutsch pressed the receive message button. 'Here it is,' he said.

'Who is the man?'

'Alexander Gorsky, retired Major of the Russian army, Paratroopers and SPETSNAZ, served in Chechnya and Caucasus, highly decorated. In 2008 suddenly appears in London and takes up employment as security officer of Mr Kaganov.'

'The FSB has the Jewel,' said Mr Hank and clinched his fists. 'Damn, I should have known it from the very beginning. Ah, the damned Russians!'

'The FSB? You think so?'

'You bunch of imbeciles!' said Mr Hank and swallowed another piece of kiwi fruit. He then took a blue pill. Deutsch kept silent. It didn't look good. Things had somehow taken the wrong turn. The stupid Jewel, the mad woman, the Mexican and oh, all those terrible Russians!

'I want that Jewel found. Is that clear? And no more blunders and infantile excuses. We are dealing with professionals, Deutsch. The FSB, the meanest of the mean, subversive mother-fuckers all-around!' said Mr Hank, hit the

189

keyboard with his right index finger and his face vanished from the screen.

'Of course, Mr Hank, of course,' said Deutsch nodding at the black screen. 'I need to find those guys. Now!'

Tom Deutsch wasn't very fond of talking to Mr Hank. That man had the uncanny ability to identify someone's shortcomings, put them under a magnifying glass and multiply by a thousand.

'Damn,' he mumbled and began hitting his on-screen telephone pad.

20

Dirty video tapes and jewels

Gorsky grabbed Senka Golovkin by the arm and dragged him down the stairs. Once in the street, they turned left and swiftly vanished in the narrow Cambridge street. One carried a long case and the other a small, red backpack.

As soon as they were several blocks away from the building engulfed in smoke and the sirens of oncoming fire engines, police and ambulances, Gorsky grabbed Golovkin by the lapels of the jacket, pushed him into a dark entrance and pinned him against the wall.

'What the hell do you think you are doing here?' said Gorsky into his friend's face.

'I had to!' Golovkin tried to justify himself.

'You had to?' said Gorsky, let the lapels go and stepped back. 'Had to what? Take a deep breath and tell me what happened.'

'Right,' started Golovkin, 'I was at the house with Milla Ivanovna. We were waiting for the partners on the Khatanga project, the Lord and the Mexican, when she started blackmailing me.'

'Did she now?'

'She knows about the old tapes.'

'The tapes?' said Gorsky who knew that Golovkin and Kaganov went way back but was never interested in the details. 'The blackmail tapes?'

'Yes, she has the tapes now and I don't trust her. I cannot trust that woman.'

'So, what did you do?' said Gorsky not without hesitation.

'I took the jewel,' said Golovkin.

'You... took the jewel. What jewel?'

'The Russian Soul!'

'You did what?'

'The Mexican brought the jewel for Milla Ivanovna to see it and while they were busy looking at her collection of diamonds I took the jewel and sneaked out of the house.'

'And where is the jewel now?'

'Here it is,' said Golovkin, took the backpack from his shoulder and opened it to show the green box. Gorsky glanced inside the backpack, grabbed Golovkin for the collar and pulled him off the ground: 'Let's go.'

'Where are we...?' Golovkin tried to inquire but was dragged out of the entrance into the street. Gorsky walked quickly dragging the moaning Golovkin behind him. As they reached the little park next to the Zionist Church they took the diagonal path to Mill Road when a group of hooded shadows appeared and blocked their way.

Gorsky went off the path and onto the grass with Golovkin behind him but the shadows moved too. There were five of them. Two carried big beer or cider cans, one had a baseball bat and the fourth who smoked a big, hastily rolled joint pointed a finger at Gorsky.

'I know you,' he said, 'You're the Russian fucker who jumped me!'

The man wore a sticking plaster across the nose, had a bruise on the cheek and a dark ring around the left eye. The one with the baseball bat raised his weapon and grabbed it with both hands while the other two took sips from their cans and laughed. It was just another evening on the streets, their idea of fun.

'I don't think we know each other,' said Golovkin who failed to notice the body language.

'Shut up, Senka,' said Gorsky, pushed his friend back and turned to the gang. 'Move it, we are in a hurry.'

'What did ya saaay?' said the baseball-bat hoody.

'Are you running away from the explosion?' said one of the can hoodies.

'Yeah,' said the hastily rolled joint hoody, 'What's the rush? You afraid of some boom, boom and fire?'

'Let's check your backpack,' said one of the gang throwing away his can.

Gorsky didn't like bullies. He took the sword out and raised it up in the air. As everyone froze looking at the unusual weapon, Gorsky stepped towards the gang leader and brought down with some force the flat side on the man's head. The knees just gave in and he fell still holding the oversized joint between his fingers. As the rest of the gang stood immobile, Gorsky stepped towards the baseball-bat man and made a stab with the sword. The hoody gasped for breath and concluded it was time for retreat.

'A fuckin' Samurai,' he cried and ran into the safety of the bushes at the other end of the park. The two can-hoodies concurred. They dropped their cans and ran towards the bushes themselves:

'The fuckers are armed!' cried one of the two before they vanished into the dark.

'I know you!' said the gang leader who in the meantime managed to get onto his feet. He held his head with one hand and pointed the finger of the other at Gorsky: 'I know you. You are the one who...'

'I don't like it when people think they know me,' said Gorsky raising the hand with the sword again. The man turned around and ran into the night.

'They are always wrong,' mumbled Gorsky.

Gorsky and Golovkin walked out of the park and down Mill Road where they entered a Middle-Eastern coffee shop with a half a dozen of shishas in the shop window. The interior was narrow and long with a counter and kitchen at the bottom. It featured wooden tables and small stools. Gorsky chose a table away from the entrance, sat on the stool with his back against the wall, his knees high above the table itself, and he dropped his reassembled bundle on the floor. Golovkin sat opposite and placed his backpack on the table. There were two other groups of people in the shop, both smoking shishas close to the entrance. Gorsky raised a hand giving his partner a signal to be silent. He listened to the merry chatter coming from the other guests of the parlour and once he ascertained they were safe he nodded to the waiter and asked for two Turkish coffees. He had been to this place before. It was close to his flat and yet secluded enough to offer sanctuary for at least a quarter of an hour in case there were more police or other 'entities' roaming the area.

'Who are those men?' asked Golovkin.

'Morons,' said Gorsky. 'Talk to me, Senka. What else did you or didn't you do and who else might be happy to see us dead?'

'Well, you see, Alex,' began Golovkin. 'I never mentioned to you the existence of a certain video tape...'

'I think you also failed to inform me of the levels of stupidity which you are capable of.'

'I understand, Alex. You must be upset with me and you are right to be so. However, you must listen to me. The

Boss, when we first met, managed to film me in some stupid situations with girls that I had no idea where underage.'

'You? With underage girls?'

'I didn't know. I swear I didn't know,' said Golovkin. 'I swear on my parents' grave I didn't know.'

'And the Boss had these tapes all these years?'

'He did and he called it his collateral, just in case. You know the drill.'

'I know the drill.'

'But I never had any intention of double-crossing him and I knew that he wouldn't use them. I trusted him. As much as he could be trusted. He was predictably unpredictable, if you know what I mean.'

'And now?'

'Now that the Boss is no more, the tapes are in the possession of that woman.'

'Milla Ivanovna?'

'Correct,' said Golovkin. 'That woman is not someone I can trust with my life, definitely not.'

'So, you decided to steal the jewel and exchange it for the tape?'

'Yes...'

Gorsky leaned against the wall. Golovkin opened his mouth as to say something but Gorsky stopped him by raising his middle finger. 'Shhhh,' he said. 'Do not talk to me.'

After a couple of minutes, Gorsky made a sudden gesture and asked to see the jewel. Golovkin obliged by extracting the box from the backpack and opening the lid. They looked at the jewel in silence.

'The Russian Soul,' said Gorsky, 'Here it is, in all its simplicity and beauty.'

'Sure,' said Golovkin. 'But the real soul is different and to understand it you need to understand the poetry, the music, the history...'

'I am not stupid!' interrupted Gorsky with a frown.

'This is just an expensive artefact, a jewel that happens to be called that. Thank you, Senka, where would I be without you? Probably wasting my time on a Volga riverbank, fishing, drinking vodka and feeling like the king of the world. This is a unique jewel that only a complete imbecile could attempt to steal from the claws of Milla Ivanovna and the king of drugs and mass murder himself!'

A gas cylinder had exploded in Golovkin's head. A mighty punch had landed in his plexus. He gasped for breath and slowly slid down the wall.

'What are we going to do now?' he muttered.

'Now? What are we going to do now?' said Gorsky. He grabbed Senka by the lapel. 'Listen to me carefully now. We have a problem here, a very big problem that we need to solve before the problem solves us.'

'Because of the jewel?'

'Because of the Russian Soul, yes!' said Gorsky and went on to tell Golovkin about Mark Hodayev's visit, the existence of the Report and the explosion in his flat. The only thing he didn't mention was the sword, Caravaggio's sword.

'And why do you carry that thing around?' said Golovkin pointing his finger at the wooden case under Gorsky's arm.

'That's all I have left now,' said Gorsky. 'An old sword.'

'Alex,' said Golovkin, 'That's the same people - Mark's killing and the explosion. That must be the same people.'

'Probably.'

'If Mark worked for the FSB and was after the jewel... The agency's interest diverges from those of the Boss and Milla Ivanovna.'

'How can they be different?'

'The FSB works for Myshkin, right?'

'Right,' Golovkin agreed.

'The Boss wanted the jewel to help get the Kremlin job, for instance. Milla Ivanovna and company now want it as a bargaining chip to soften Myshkin and get into Khatanga.'

'Better with the Soul,' nodded Golovkin.

'Much better. And now...' said Gorsky and looked at the long case that was sitting on top of the red backpack. 'We have it.'

'The Khatanga mine,' said Golovkin, 'The Boss wanted to cut a deal with Moscow, I know that much. He wrote letters and tried to establish contacts. He wanted to barter the jewel for a safe return to Russia where he would agree to release his ownership rights to a state-run company for the exploitation of resources. On the other hand, he might have had political ambitions'

'I see,' nodded Gorsky. 'The Kremlin and the Boss become partners and our dearest Aleksey Kaganov returns safely to Russia, hands over the Russian Soul and the keys to Khatanga in return for immunity from any prosecution and, of course, a nice slice of the diamond cake.'

'A sound, simple and robust plan with only one tiny crack in the armour?'

'What do you mean?'

'Someone else is in the game and that someone can't afford to be hung out to dry, Alex. Garriburton will squeeze themselves in if it were the last thing they do in this life. Their deal with the Boss was that he wins the elections with their help and repays by handing over Khatanga.'

'And the Lord, what was his name?'

'Mintbatten and his crew are the financial purifiers...'

'Purifiers?'

'Aha, money comes and goes through his hands.'

'Where does it come from?'

'The money comes from the Mexican, Medina, and is invested in the exploitation of the Khatanga site inclusive of heavy machinery and bribes to government officials.'

Golovkin picked up the green box from the backpack and lifted the lid. The Russian Soul lay bare before him on its velvet bed. He knew that each Fabergé Easter egg contained a surprise such as a scaled down golden model of a train, the Winter Palace in Sankt Petersburg or the Hermitage Museum. He found the little lever that he pressed releasing the lid. Golovkin tried to look inside and lifted the top. A cleanly cut, solid diamond the size of a large chicken egg stared at him. Golovkin gasped in admiration and turned the jewel towards Gorsky.

'This is marvellous!' he said.

'This is the Orlov,' said Gorsky.

'The legendary diamond, the Orlov? Catherine's diamond?'

'Yes, Senka, it's all in the Report,' said Gorsky. And then after a brief pause he continued: 'It all started in Rome with Vatayev's murder. There's a method to it. Nothing is accidental. Vatayev killed and his killer shot at the spot. This requires high levels of organisation, weapons, manpower and training. Motifs too. All professional stuff. The Neapolitan was hit by high velocity sniper fire and I wouldn't be surprised if it had been a Russian Vintorez gun. Stripped down to the smallest element, the gun is easy to transport and can be found anywhere. At the time, I wasn't important and the shooter walked away. What happened in the meantime? What made me so important?'

'Mark Hodayev,' said Golovkin.

'Mark Hodayev's visit,' continued Gorsky, 'And most importantly, I think, the Report he left with me. The Report connects the jewel with the Khatanga mine.'

'Zakhar taken out, the Boss... dies...'

'The body was never found though?'

'No, it wasn't.'

'I don't trust that man,' said Gorsky. 'Even if he's dead I don't trust him. He must have had a scheme of some kind?'

'So, you think that the same people killed all three of them?'

'Not sure, Senka. The simplest explanation is often not the right one.'

'You know that the two Garriburton people are agents?' said Golovkin.

'What side are they on?'

'One British and one American. They are in it for themselves, though. They run a diamond business, might use the MI6 and CIA labels and logistics but they are essentially a private operation.'

'Did the Boss know that?' asked Gorsky. He didn't like the sound of these words and the flavour of their implications. It was all getting too muddled, too complicated, multipolar, whatever... As a former soldier, he was used to receiving and giving clear instructions and orders, to being surrounded by trusted people in uniforms of the same colour. He hated traitors, liars, spinners and untrustworthy weasels... Even Mark Hodayev was a bit too much for his taste for he considered intelligence officers, spies and eavesdroppers to be no more than spineless cowards. That was the lesson he learnt in Chechnya.

'He did know,' confirmed Golovkin, 'of course the Boss knew.'

'And the FSB also knew that he knew?'

'Oh, they know lots of things, you would be surprised.'

'And what are we going to do with that egg now?'

'I'll send an e-mail!' exclaimed Golovkin with pride and assurance as though he had finally found the winning course of action.

'You will send...' said a much less enthusiastic Gorsky, 'a mail?'

'Yes, to Milla Ivanovna, and offer to exchange the jewel for the tape,' said Golovkin obviously proud of his scheme.

'You do realise, I hope,' said Gorsky softly with just a hint of irony, 'That tapes can be copied?'

'I'll ask for money too, Alex, and with that money I'll change my identity and vanish.'

'With the combined efforts of the Mexican drug cartel, the MI6, CIA and FSB, not even cloning yourself thousand times will get you out of the trouble,' explained Gorsky.

'I'll use a local machine,' said Golovkin and pointed his finger to a computer in the corner of the coffee shop. 'And open a new mail account.'

'Do that quickly and we get lost,' said Gorsky and put the case on the table. He then placed both his elbows on it and the head between his hands. The situation required thinking and there were situations, that much he knew for sure, when not even thinking hard helps.

21

'I can make one like that!'

Two shadows crossed Mill Road and entered a narrow street where they ran into one of the porches. The bigger shadow wore a long coat and carried a large wooden case underarm. The smaller shadow carried a backpack over the right shoulder.

Gorsky knocked at the door. By now, their phone records and the documents on their confiscated laptops would have been analysed and all contacts identified and placed under surveillance. They had nowhere to go except perhaps...

After the second knock on the door, steps were heard coming down the wooden staircase. Aptin opened the door, looked out into the dark at the two men standing in front of him.

'Hello,' he said and smiled.

'Hi,' cried Gorsky and Golovkin.

'Come in,' said Aptin and let the two guests step into the corridor from where all three entered the living room. Gorsky dropped the bundle on the floor and sat down while Golovkin placed the red backpack on the coffee table and sat in one of the two armchairs. 'Something happened to you?'

Before anyone tried to answer, an Andean tune echoed in the room and Aptin turned to detect the origin of the sound. Gorsky recognised it and took his mobile out of the pocket. 'It's Kathy,' he said. 'I have to take it.'

'Hi,' he said and for a moment just listened to what seemed to be a flood of words. 'No.' Golovkin and Aptin looked at him with interest.

'Listen to me, just listen,' he said. 'I cannot mention your name or any other references. I must to destroy this mobile. They might be tracking me... I'll call you from a disposable phone, right... Bye.'

He then opened the telephone, extracted the SIM card and tore it to bits, squashed the telephone with both hands and placed the lot on the coffee table in front of Aptin.

'Drop it in a rubbish bin somewhere far from this house, will you?' he said and immediately continued, 'my flat has just been blown into smithereens.'

Golovkin confirmed with a nod and moved the backpack a couple of inches to the left.

'A bomb?'

'Yes, a bomb,' continued Gorsky. 'We don't have anywhere else to go'.

'Who are those people?' asked Aptin.

'It's better if you didn't know,' said Golovkin. 'It's my fault.'

'The bomb is not your fault,' interjected Gorsky with a dry smile. 'The rest might well be.'

Aptin felt the need to sit down. Not much of what he had just heard made sense. An explosion in Gorsky's flat? People you can't talk about? He finally noticed the object on the table.

'What's that?' he said pointing a finger at the backpack. Gorsky looked at Golovkin who picked up the pack and took out the green box. He opened it and showed to Aptin the shiny, egg-shaped jewel. He then pressed the lever and lifted the top.

'This is the Orlov,' he said. 'The great diamond, the favourite of Catherine the Great.'

'May I,' said Aptin and Golovkin gave him permission with a nod. The Iranian took the diamond into his hand and began to scrutinise its weight, colour, cut... He turned it around several times with the flair of someone who knew what he was doing.

'It's fine,' he finally said and smiled. 'I can make one just like this in a couple of hours!'

Golovkin attempted to smile but he only managed to produce an even more worried facial expression.

'Say that again,' said Gorsky and leaned forward towards the host. 'You can do what?'

'Make a synthetic gem stone,' said Aptin.

'This is a synthetic gem stone?' cried Gorsky.

'Yes, it's a very well made synthetic gem stone, grown in a lab but it is a synthetic stone.'

'Are you sure?'

'Well, I can test in my lab and be absolutely sure.'

'Now!' said Gorsky and jumped on his feet. 'Can you test it now? It is very important that we know if this is the real Orlov or a fake.'

'Now? Let me see the time...' said Aptin and looked at his watch. 'Well, yes, I could test it now; my department is around the corner and it takes no more than ten minutes to get there. I have access to the building and the keys to the lab.'

'Let's go,' said Gorsky.

'Let's go,' said Golovkin jumping on his feet.

'No,' said Gorsky and pushed Senka back into the chair. 'You wait here!'

Gorsky walked to the door and. while Aptin was putting his coat on, he extracted a bunch of papers from the inside pocket of his coat and turned to Golovkin.

'In the meantime, you read this,' he said and dropped the papers on the table. 'Read this carefully as our lives depend on it. You understand?'

'I understand,' said Golovkin as he glanced at the title on the front page. It read: Strictly Confidential: Fabergé's Lost Jewel.

22

A paradigmatic shift

The MI6 headquarters dominates the south bank of the Thames. Thanks to its post-modern design, the building is an easily recognisable symbol of the British Secret Intelligence Service. Not that a secret service needs a recognisable symbol though.

Sir Jack entered the building through the entrance off Albert Street. He produced his ID, had his eyes scanned, passed through the x-ray hub and finally continued to the lifts. He arrived on the seventh floor, nodded to the young woman at the desk and continued towards a door to her right. She pressed a button and announced: 'Sir Jack Sailgood is here.'

The visitor pushed the door handle and stepped in.

The office was wide and it featured a glass wall that offered a view of the Thames and the nightline of north London. Behind the desk sat a man in his early sixties. He had a shiny, clean shaven head and he wore a white shirt with the sleeves rolled up above the elbows. He seemed ready to throw himself into a brawl.

'Welcome, Jack,' said Gideon Dickinson getting up from behind the table and the two men shook hands.

'Always a pleasure,' said the visitor and took a seat. 'I love this view and this city. I also hate Moscow, Gid. We can sum it up in one sentence: I just hate the place.'

'Can I offer you some vodka to alleviate your pain?' said Dickinson, stood up and walked to a little cupboard in the corner of the room.

'That's what I call a sense of humour,' said Sailgood, 'make it a whisky, please. Neat too.'

Dickinson chuckled and opened one of the bottles.

'Here it is,' he said and offered a generously full glass to the guest. 'What's big bear up to these days? Is the government falling any time soon?'

'Not exactly, Gid. Not exactly.'

'I thought you were working very hard on supporting the development of democracy?'

'Yes, we sure are, but the Ukrainian and now the Syrian situation got slightly out of hand. Nasty business.'

'Did we do anything wrong?'

'No,' said Sailgood and the two raised their glasses and took a first sip. 'It's the Americans I guess, the Germans... It's a mess.''

'What are you saying?'

'I am saying that with our usual diplomatic and intelligence contacts we're not getting anywhere. There seems to be a paradigmatic shift in... '

'Paradigmatic, you say,' mocked Dickinson.

'... In international relations,' continued Sailgood. 'But you can read all of that in my report.'

'Sure! Now give me the good news,' said Gideon Dickinson, 'you must have some good news, right!?'

The one thing Sir Jack Sailgood couldn't stand about his long-time associate was that he seemed to know things in advance. The man could not be taken off-guard, ever.

'I probably do by now. Anyway, you remember Elizabeth, the girl from your office?'

'Sure, Dudley-Vernon, we sent her to Teheran.'

'Yes, you did...' said Gideon. 'She has a sister, did you know?'

'Sister? I don't think I did, why?'

'Nothing, she works around here too, Jack. Isobel is the name and she is here with us. Works on this case actually!'

'You have the whole family working for you, do you?'

Gideon leaned over his desk and pressed a button on the interphone.

'Will you ask Isobel to come over please,' he said looking at the surprised face of Sir Jack Sailgood. 'She is attached to the unit that monitors the movements of the Russian immigration with special reference to the business migrants and...'

'Oligarchs, you mean?'

'If you prefer to call them that, yes,' confirmed Dickinson. 'This unit came up with some interesting findings. I want you to have a look at the intelligence for yourself and tell me what you make of it.'

Is this some sort of trap? The thought ran through Sailgood's mind. If Elizabeth's sister is here so might be the report which means that the whole of the bloody MI6 knows about the Russian Soul. Do they know about Garriburton too?'

Gideon Dickinson pressed a button and the door opened. A young woman stepped into the office. She wore a trouser suit and appeared taller that the last time Sailgood saw her.

'My God,' he thought, 'It wasn't that long ago.'

'Good evening or night, I suppose, Sir Jack,' said Isobel Dudley-Vernon standing in the middle of the room.

'Nice to meet you, Isobel. Liz spoke so often about you,' nodded Sir Jack while Dickinson pointed at the free chair for her to take a seat.

'Let's start with the report from our man who infiltrated the Cambridge gang. It has to do with our Russian connections in the underworld,' said Dickinson.

Isobel got up from her chair, placed the thin black folder that she brought with her on the table and opened it. Both Dickinson and Sailgood leaned forward to see its content.

'These are hidden camera shots from a park in Cambridge last night,' she said as they began going through the set of large black and white photographs. 'As you can see here, two men enter the park. The taller one carries a long case or a box under his arm and the shorter one carries a backpack. We have identified the second man as one Semyon Golovkin. He was in the employment of the Russian oligarch Aleksey Kaganov. He was his secretary and is now in the service of Kaganov's widow, Lyudmila Ivanovna.'

'And the other one?' said Sailgood.

'The other one is Alexander Ivanovich Gorsky, also an employee of Kaganov.'

'What are they carrying here?' asked Dickinson.

'Well, the tall man, Gorsky, as we can see on these photographs,' she said and displayed the prints on the table, 'Carries a weapon...'

'A sword?' said Sailgood. 'My God.'

'A sword dipped in poison?' Dickinson interjected in an attempt at being funny.

'Well, we don't know if it's anything of the kind, Mr Dickinson. What we do know from these shots is that the man walks around with what appears to be a sword fit for a museum. He dispatched the group of hooligans without trying to cut or seriously injure any of them.'

'What did he do?' said Dickinson.

'Kicked them!'

'He kicked them?' said Sailgood and looked at Dickinson.

'Karate kick, I guess, martial arts anyway,' said Isobel 'The man seems to be an expert of a sort.'

23

Iguanas, vultures and coyotes

A black limousine entered Park Lane and pulled up in front of the Dorchester. Two liveried attendants sprang into action to open the doors. As they approached the vehicle, a rear door suddenly opened and an enraged man jumped out of the vehicle. He screamed and turned back to slap or shove someone on the back seat.

The man wore a white suit and a red, unbuttoned shirt. He had a Mexican moustache and swore in Spanish. When this man finally approached the main entrance, a second man came out of the car carrying a briefcase. A large tear was coming down his cheek.

As the first man approached the entrance, the attendant bowed and said: 'Good evening, *señor* Medina.'

El Guapo stopped and looked at him as if trying to find an excuse for another shouting spree.

'You're kidding me?' he said.

'No, *señor* Medina,' replied the man. 'I would never dream of doing so.'

El Guapo then turned to the teary man who walked at a safe distance behind him and barked: 'Do you see, *abogado*? These people in England are all *cabeza loca*, brain-dead!'

Ituribe nodded and the attendant, who happened to be Chilean, opened his mouth to say something but then reconsidered his options.

'*Sí, señor,*' he mumbled with a bow.

'Having said that,' continued El Guapo while entering the hotel lobby, 'Compared to those Russian *cabrones* they look nice and fresh like a rose.'

'Russian women seem to be particularly mean,' said Ituribe in agreement.

Once in the lobby, Medina seemed to have remembered something important as he turned to his companion and started to shout attracting the attention of a couple of Arab sheiks, Hollywood producers and German bankers who found themselves in the vicinity.

'You stupid, drugged moron,' he said. 'You couldn't keep an eye on one silly little jewel for fifteen minutes!'

'*Señor* Guapo, I can assure you that...' tried the abogado.

'Don't you *señor* me,' roared the King of Drugs. 'While you were snuffing up your angel powder those despicable Russians, the witch and her lowly adjutant...'

'You think they are in cahoots?' asked Ituribe.

'Do I think so? You vile, stupid creature,' said El Guapo making a gesture as if to slap the abogado again but refrained when he realised that all eyes were on them. 'Where was my brain and what did I think when I employed you? Ah? Tell me, don't stare at me, talk to me. I pay you rather handsomely to answer my fucking questions, do I not?'

'Of course, El Guapo, of course. I am not sure though, that Milla Ivanovna planned the heist.'

'You are not sure,' said Medina and looked around as if a bat, a plank or some other weapon to strike his helpless advisor.

'The woman is a great lady,' stated Ituribe as if this were a matter of fact. 'She looked genuinely surprised and upset. And why would she want to do that in the first place? You had already promised to leave the jewel with her overnight.

She could have taken it later. It would have been much easier for her to come up with some sort of funny story.'

Medina considered taking out his gun and disposing of the abogado right then and there on the marble floor of the Dorchester's lobby. Being so busy, he failed to notice that the door of one of a lift opened and a lady in an elegant crimson dress walked out of it. She had long black hair and wore red lipstick. She walked as if she owned the place. Guadalupe demanded attention.

'Oh, *mi corazón,*' said El Guapo managing to produce a wide, disarming smile. María Guadalupe had seen too many of those.

'So, what do we have here, a great lady, ah?',' said María Guadalupe making a sudden upward gesture with her chin. She disregarded El Guapo completely and turned her gaze at the Ituribe. 'Tell me more about this lady *abogado?*'

'Well,' said Ituribe, 'the lady in question is a Russian business partner, you see... We were supposed to meet the husband who mysteriously disappeared... He is dead, actually, and since he is unavailable...'

'Since he is dead, right?' said Guadalupe.

'That is correct, yes. He seems to be quite dead and we met his widow Milla Ivanovna...'

'Russian?'

'She is indeed...'

'Let me explain, *mi amor,*' tried El Guapo but Guadalupe cut him short with a hand gesture. She then said: 'You keep your mouth shut and you, abogado, tell me. Is she pretty this widow of yours?'

'Oh, yes,' the advisor acknowledged, nodding, 'Very pretty. Green eyes, blonde, with an elegant figure and dignified posture.'

'Dignified posture, you say...' she said looking now at El Guapo who realised that his chances were rather slim. He knew Guadalupe well enough to understand that this was the wrong way to talk to her. 'If only this moronic Ituribe could get off his stupid white cloud for a second...' he mumbled and shrugged his shoulders. 'Too late now anyway.'

'The jewel has gone missing but it's not our fault,' asserted Ituribe with, given the circumstances, an enviable degree of confidence.

'What was the jewel doing there in the first place?' said Guadalupe with a frown.

'We took it to the meeting with business partners as a proof of our good will,' explained El Guapo.

'We did,' concurred Ituribe.

'So, you are telling me now that the whole egg is gone missing?'

'Yes, the man took it while we were...' said Medina but was cut short by Guadalupe: 'And with the stupid egg the man took the diamond, right?'

'Yes,' said Ituribe.

'No,' said Medina and met Guadalupe's quizzical stare. 'The diamond was replaced by a fake. I still have the original you see. Did you really think that I would walk around with that diamond and leave it to the first stranger I meet?'

'You might have saved the diamond but the egg is gone. Hasta la vista! And all of this because of this green eyed, elegant Russian *señora,* right?'

Medina shrugged his shoulders and declined to admit that Milla Ivanovna, *la señora*, did have such eyes and that, well yes, she had an elegant manner of walking, talking, gesturing... He glanced around the lobby and only then realised that they were standing in its very centre attracting too much attention.

'Shall we perhaps go to our apartment and...' he suggested tentatively, making a gesture as if to touch Guadalupe's arm.

213

'Get your filthy fingers away from me!' she hissed.

'Guadalupe, please,' let's go upstairs.

'You gave the jewel to that whore!'

'No, it was stolen!'

'But you wanted to give it to her in the first place!'

'No, I just wanted to show it to her.'

'Just to show it? Ha, ha, I can imagine. You are despicable!' she cried raising both her arms in the air. 'You traitor, you snake, you desert rat and low life vermin... After the ambush in Santa Clara, you come to me and ask me to patch your bullet holes. When those Maratrucha animals tried to sharpen their machetes on your stupid head and cut your arm off you ran bleeding and crying to me. You and your green-eyed Russian whore. Next time go visit Siberia, you dirty *hijo de puta, te chingaste,* low-life scumbag. I hid you in the basement of my mother's house from the *federales,* smuggled your dirty guns, brought you lunch in jail and served you and your bunch of useless *banditos.* And this is what I get in return from you. This? Another false step *señor* Guapito, another step in the wrong direction and not even Siberia will be vast and cold enough for you to hide from me. Do you hear me? I hope the Aztecan gods see this and descend upon you to tear your chest open and rip out that rotten, black, small heart of yours and eat it while I watch, you...'

At that very moment, the tirade was interrupted by the arrival of Mr Morrison, the hotel manager, who humbly apologised and asked, with a broad smile and a discreet bow, if they wanted perhaps, to move to one of the private rooms on the ground floor and have a glass of champagne. Compliments of the house, of course. Mr Rupert Morrison was a very discreet and sensitive man. Guadalupe who spoke enough English to understand his body language thought she heard the word 'quiet'. It was a word she didn't like. She gave the manager a penetrating stare and, as the man kept on smiling innocently, she slapped El Guapo's arm and turned back towards the lift

'We'll continue upstairs' she said with an air of righteous indignation. 'You are not getting away from me this lightly.'

Mr Morrison tried to explain that one of the adjacent apartments was now occupied by his sanctity the Archbishop Edelberto Valencia who had just flown in after a terrible ordeal involving bombs and terrorist threats as well as a thirty-hour-long-journey from La Paz in Bolivia on his way to the Vatican.

'Hell,' crossed Medina's mind. 'The Archbishop and his entourage speak Spanish and if this woman continues the fracas, the other half of the hotel will also be briefed about our business in detail...'

As the party got into the lift, Medina turned to Ituribe: 'I want the jewel back. No police, no inquiries, no more Russian bullshit, I want that jewel back by tomorrow evening or I will strangle you both with my bare hands. Is that clear?'

'Of course,' confirmed Ituribe.

'You two cage monkeys to return the jewel by tomorrow evening?' said Guadalupe. 'Ha, ha, I am really looking forward to having another good laugh over your dead, rotten bodies before they get pissed on by iguanas and eaten by vultures and coyotes!'

24

The big bang

Gorsky had spent a couple of hours on the sofa and he suddenly felt he had done enough introspection for a lifetime. He picked up the TV remote control and pressed the red button. He heard voices and then the picture appeared. There was an item about Prince William's visit to a local farm, the death of two British soldiers in Afghanistan and a scandal involving dishonest bankers. Then the time came for the local, Cambridgeshire news. There was a group of people standing in the street and the journalist, a young woman, was just about to interview one. Aspiring to the image of intellectual reporter, she wore a pair of black-rimmed glasses. She explained that an explosion was heard in central Cambridge and that the TV crew managed to arrive at the spot at the same time as the fire fighters whose station was just around the corner and well before the ambulance coming from the not so distant Addenbrooke's Hospital. But without further delay, she would now interview a woman who lives in the very building where the explosion took place. After the witness, the journalist said that she would interview the local police to see if they suspected a terrorist attack or gang related crime.

'Will you introduce yourself, please?' said the reporter to the woman in a colourful nightgown.

'My name is Paraskevi Moustakas,' said the woman, 'I live here with my husband Stavros and...'

'Thank you, yes, of course. Could you please tell us more about the explosion? It is my understanding that you were at home at the time of the blast, it that correct?'

'I was right there in the corridor and just about to get out to water the plants, you see? I had my water can ready and I was just about...'

'Right,' said the blonde reporter who held the microphone in one hand and, with the other, tried to hold an unruly lock of hair that was falling on her spectacles. 'Could you describe the explosion for us?'

'Well,' said Mrs Moustakas tidying up her hairdo with one hand and the nightgown with the other. 'It was a very powerful explosion. So powerful that I nearly fell over in the corridor.'

'And what can you tell us about the tenant of the apartment number seven where the explosion took place?' said the reporter while still struggling with the lock of hair.

'Mr Gorsky is a fine young man,' said Mrs Moustakas. 'I know him quite well as my son takes care of his dog, you see. He comes quite often to talk to me and my husband... A fine young Polish man, yes.'

'Does he live alone in the flat?'

'Oh, yes, he did,' said Mrs Moustakas who by now was fully aware of the possible nationwide exposure of her performance. 'He only had one visitor, a young lady... Brown hair, not too long, very slim body like that of a gymnast...'

'Do you know her name?' asked the reporter.

'Oh, no. I never spoke to her, you see.'

'And what did you talk to him about?'

'Oh, he often speaks bout international politics, you see? I come out to water the plants and he stops to have a chat and starts talking about corruption and the banking crisis, the war in the Ukraine, the financial crisis in Greece... You see?

I don't know much about politics. I am not that interested, we are simple people, we mind our own business,' said Mrs Moustakas about her conversations with Gorsky.

'Thank you, Mrs Mustikis,' said the blond reporter before turning to the camera. 'As we have just heard, the tenant of the flat number 7 here is a young Polish immigrant who appears to be a political activist but we still don't know where he worked or what he did for a living.'

The reporter then waved her hand and a bearded middle-aged man in a dark blue winter jacket joined her in front of the camera.

'Good evening, inspector McGallen. Are we potentially looking at a terrorist attack? This whole situation bears the hallmark of...'

McGallen raised a hand and interrupted her.

'No need for speculations. The fire fighters are securing the site and my men are taking statements from potential witnesses. I'd like to use this opportunity to invite anybody who saw anything unusual in this neighbourhood in the past days or even week to come forward.'

'I saw some people in the street the other night,' interjected Mrs Moustakas who was still standing next to McGallen. When the camera switched to her, the reporter thanked the woman in the nightgown and turned to McGallen.

'Inspector,' she said, 'what are the chances that something more sinister than a gas boiler explosion happened here?'

'I would like us to keep our minds open as all the options are still on the table. However, I would certainly like to speak to the tenant of this flat, Mr Gorsky.'

As the wind blew and the reporter tried to fix her locks, McGallen looked straight into the camera and said: 'There are indications that this explosion tonight might be related to a murder committed earlier today in London and the activities of an international crime syndicate that we have been monitoring for some time now. The victim of the said murder was a Mr Mark Hodayev, a Russian art dealer. Mr Gorsky, if you are watching this broadcast, do contact me personally at the Cambridge Constabulary phone number and ask to talk to me directly. My name is McGallen, Robbie McGallen.'

'Well thank you...' began the reporter when Gorsky switched the TV set off and leaned back in his seat.

On the coffee table lay the case with the sword. Next to it was the box with the Fabergé jewel. The apartment was dark and only a tame ray of light penetrated the cracks between the curtains and the wall. In the distance, he could hear the steady, reassuring flow of traffic.

'He wants to talk to me...' rang in his ears. 'Why would a police inspector want to talk to me? To the owner of a flat that was blown up,' thought Gorsky. 'It could have been the gas installation. It's too early to be sure it wasn't. Could be a gang related crime, a random act of violence or... Did inspector McGallen perhaps, know something that he couldn't disclose to the public? Is he trying to connect the dots of a different trail? A trail that brought him to my doorstep. Inspector McGallen... The law.'

Gorsky was calm. 'It's easy when you have a purpose and a clear vision,' he thought. 'Once you find yourself in a fight you fight to the end. Mujahedeen warriors ran towards him yelling. He couldn't hear the *Allahu Akbars* anymore, he couldn't hear or feel anything. He pressed the trigger. And again, and again... Then, the clouds cleared, the night sky appeared with millions of cold, distant stars – one for each man who ever lived, his grandfather had told him. Before this night is over, he said to himself back then in Argul, there will be many more.'

He heard steps on the corridor. They were coming closer. Light, the steps of a woman. Quick. They stopped outside, in front of the door and a key entered the lock. The door opened and the light from the corridor illuminated part of the room.

'Hello,' said Niusha and switched the central lighting on. Gorsky didn't move from his spot. He had a plan. Not something you could articulate in words or on paper, no. He had a plan that made sense to him and that he could follow.

'An intuitive plan,' he would call it. 'Alex, what are you doing here in the dark, all on your own? Where are Aptin and your cousin?'

'Senka, yes... He and Aptin had to go, they will be back soon.,' said Gorsky.

'Where did they go?'

'They went to the lab for Aptin to check something he left there.'

'Really?' she said with an expression of utter surprise. 'It has never happened to him to forget anything in the lab. That's his sanctuary. He only forgets to bring his head home from that lab.'

'He didn't forget anything,' said Gorsky who didn't care for the subtle difference between telling lies and not telling the truth. 'They went there to test an item... The jewel.'

'What jewel?' she said and sat next to Gorsky on the couch. 'You think it's a fake?'

'I don't know; Aptin just suggested it would be good to be sure.'

'Of course, to be sure. Of course,' said Niusha and jumped from the couch and took her short jacket off. 'Steve is doing the night shift at Canary Wharf, I imagine. Can I get you tea or coffee?'

'No, thanks. Have you seen again those fools who attacked you the other night?'

'No, I haven't but I know them anyway,' said Niusha from the kitchen where she was pouring water in a jug. 'They often come to the shelter, you see?'

'The shelter where you work?'

'Yes. One of them, the one who said he remembered you...'

'He will remember me now, that's for sure.'

'He used to be my local dealer, you know, in the old days. He is lucky to be alive. Aptin wanted to kill him, then you...'

At that point the phone rang the *El Condor pasa* theme. 'Sorry,' said Gorsky and picked the gadget out of his pocket. It was Kathy and he nodded while she spoke. He then nodded some more and put the phone back in his pocket.

'Was that your girlfriend?'

'Yes, that was Kathy.'

'You love her?'

'I think I do, why?'

'I don't know, just curious, I guess.'

'You're always that curious?'

'Oh, yes. You bet!' said Niusha and began laughing.

'OK,' said Gorsky, 'interesting...'

'I think I do,' said Niusha with mocking a serious facial expression, 'I think I love her.'

Gorsky shrugged his shoulders. There was no discernible way out of that predicament.

'You don't have children?' she said.

'No,' he replied.

"How did you meet?' she continued, 'let me guess, you saved her from the claws of a one-eyed Moroccan assassin and...'

'Why Moroccan?'

"Don't know, sounds exotic. Was he not?"

'?'

'... Moroccan... the killer?'

'I have no idea what are you talking about and where is this conversation going!'

'Just chatting, small talk, getting to know each other... relax!'

'OK,' said Gorsky, 'I'll tell you how we met and that's pretty much everything you need to know. Is that alright? If you must know she was the one who saved my skin.'

'Alright, go on...'

'Kathy was in my martial arts class. That's how we knew each other, so when she overheard a phone conversation featuring my name and the word hospitalise in the same sentence she thought of alerting me. She helped me. OK? Happy now?'

'Sure,' exclaimed Niusha, 'that's the version you normally tell your aunty, I bet, ha?'

Gorsky didn't say anything. Would it help using more words?

The television was switched off but the images he saw last remained ingrained in Gorsky's mind. 'Call Scotland Yard, inspector McGallen, Robbie McGallen.' The game was on. No boundaries though, no time limit, no rules or uniforms. Zakhar killed, the Boss dead, Mark Hodayev murdered, the flat destroyed... 'I am in it and they want me out. They want me dead. They didn't mind me walking away in Rome but they do mind my presence now. Are we talking about the same people or are there several outfits contesting the same turf? What was the trigger? Why am I so important now? Because of Mark Hodayev's visit. The report. That's why he is out and I am next in line. Not to mention Senka's antics with the jewel... That must have been the peak of their despair. Different players. There are different players in this but they all have something in common – the Russian Soul.'

'What are you going to do?' Niusha interrupted his flow of thoughts. She held a cup of tea and she sat next to him. 'To wait for Aptin's analysis, I imagine, and then?'

The case with the sword and a blanket were on the table and the time was running out. They want the jewel. They will get the jewel at any cost. There was a scheme, though. There was one little scheme that might, just might do the job.

'Can I ask you a favour?' said Gorsky.

'Of course,' said Niusha. 'Shoot.'

'I'd rather not present myself in the street and I need something. Would you go and buy it for me?'

'Yes, what?'

'I need two pre-paid, disposable phones.'

'I see,' said Niusha. 'You are going high-tech!'

'Yes,' said Gorsky, 'you got it. That's the nature of modern warfare!'

25

The new driver

Milla Ivanovna took the lift at the top floor of the One Canada Square building on Canary Wharf. She pressed the level -3 button and enjoyed the feeling of a controlled fall. When she exited the elevator she nodded to the car park attendant and walked straight towards her limousine. The man came running after her, threw himself forward and made it just in time to open the door for her. Milla Ivanovna entered the car and flopped into the back seat.

'Let's go,' she said and crossed her legs to admire her new acquisition - a pair of 6-inch heel, knee high Miu Miu boots. She was pleased with herself.

The car moved slowly, got out of the underground facility and entered the traffic flow. After a couple of minutes instead of taking the M11 route north, the car turned left into the A406 orbital. Still busy admiring her footwear, Milla Ivanovna didn't notice the change at first. When she did, she clinched her fist and pressed the interphone button.

'Goran,' she yelled, 'Where the hell are we going? You, Serbian dimwit, I said I wanted to go home!'

The driver pressed a button and lowered the glass separating the front seats from the rear and a familiar voice replied. It wasn't Goran.

'Hello, Milla. Surprised to see me?'

'Alex? What are you doing here? What do you think you are doing here?'

'I have the Russian Soul, Milla,' said Gorsky holding the wheel tight with both hands. 'The jewel!'

'Ha, of course. That little toad Senka Golovkin ran straight to his dearest cousin. Oh, wait, wait, wait a moment! How silly of me not to understand that this little charade is your doing,' said Milla Ivanovna in a rapid-fire fashion.

'FSB or private business? All I really needed now was a lunatic war hero who suddenly remembered he was a Russian patriot and decided to steal my jewel and send it back to mother Russia, the Kremlin, uncle Myshkin and the Communist Party, I guess! How much? How much do you want for the jewel? Name the price. Just say the price, give me the egg and take the money. And I don't want to see either of you two anymore again in my life. Ever!'

'And as soon as I give you the jewel you will post Senka's tape on YouTube and alert the police, I imagine,' said Gorsky looking at Milla Ivanovna in the mirror.

'What?' cried Milla Ivanovna. 'Alex, you and I have so much in common we could...'

'We don't have anything in common, Milla. Never had, never will and the longer it stays that way the better. I understand that the Boss had in his possession a certain videotape and that he blackmailed Senka with it. You know anything about it?'

'No, Alex, first time I hear of such a thing.'

'Milla, I know you have the tape or that at least, you know where to find it.'

'Alex, I...'

'I don't have the time for you, Milla,' said Gorsky and dodged a delivery vehicle that crossed on his side of the road. 'I want that tape.'

'OK, what else do you want? How much money? I don't have much cash at home...'

'Cut it. All I want is the tape. I don't want any money.'

'What?'

'I don't think it's something you would understand,' said Gorsky pulling the car at the roadside. He stopped the car and took the key out of the ignition. 'One thing, Milla. In case a copy of that tape appears anywhere, any time. Believe me that I'll come looking for you and I'll find you. You know I will.'

'Of course, Alex,' said Milla Ivanovna. 'When will you bring me the jewel?'

'I will bring the jewel to the meeting on Friday.'

'The meeting at...'

'Yes, to the meeting. '

'But I need it before so I can...'

'Those are the rules, Milla. You'll have to trust me, I guess. Bring the tape and I'll give you the Russian Soul. Make sure I am on the list of invited guests as Boss' chief of security.'

'But the Boss, Alexey...'

'Sure. Tell the Boss when you speak to him...'

'But he's dead!'

'Of course, the Boss is dead. You just pass the message, will you?' he said and turned to face Milla Ivanovna who sat speechless on the back seat.

'Whatever agreement we had, the Boss and me, whatever contract, it's not valid any more. The murder of Mark Hodayev was a mistake, a big mistake. Blood has been spilt and there is no way back now. Someone will have to foot the bill for it.'

'Who is Mark Hodayev?'

'Just remember the name. That's all I need you to do... And, yes, keep the mobile switched on,' said Gorsky, opened the door and got out of the car. He shut the door, pressed the activating card double-locking all the doors on the vehicle and walked away. As he was turning around the first corner, he saw a group of local hoodlums approaching the car. Milla Ivanovna was trying to open the door and was then banging on the windows with both fists. Gorsky dropped the car's start card in the first manhole he came across. He needed to get away quickly. He needed to be somewhere else.

'Time, time!' thought Gorsky, while reconstructing the trip and visualising the tube stations. He had a plan. Precision, timing and resolve, that's all it takes to complete a mission. There will be variables, things no one can possibly predict, that's true. But the plan was simple. All he had to do is to move swiftly, very swiftly.

Tired of hurting her fists on the bullet proof windows, Milla Ivanovna watched in horror the local gang members bringing in the gear to start dismantling the car. Crowbars, spanners, hammers, monkey wrenches... They were gearing up. She picked up her handbag and started fishing for her mobile phone. A minute or two later she dialled the security officer at One Canada Square. 'You be here in a minute or you are dead!' she screamed at the phone and then started giving her coordinates. Except that she had absolutely no idea where she was. The car was shut down and the GPS switched off. Her phone did have one too but she had never used it...

A monkey wrench hit the front window and bounced back. A screwdriver tried to find its way between the front and the back door. Spanners were working hard on the tyres and someone was jumping on the roof of the car. Milla Ivanovna picked up her phone again and dialled the only number in the memory without a name against it. The number ended with fifty-two - 5 and 2. When the call was answered she said: 'I have managed to trace the jewel... No I don't have it yet, it will be brought to the meeting on Friday... Gorsky, Alex Gorsky, yes, he has it... He did say things, yes, he did, but... I trust him, yes.' The chap jumping on the car roof had company. There was another one jumping on the bonnet and Milla Ivanovna lost the connection. She crouched in one corner of the back seat, put her hands over her ears and shut her eyes. Milla Ivanovna was facing a couple of very long minutes now. Very long minutes indeed.

26

AK - 107

Early in the morning, two scruffy looking men walked into the hotel lobby. They were in a hurry. The smaller of the two carried a little red rucksack over his shoulder and kept turning his head around as if he expected a deadly attack. The bigger man wore a dark grey coat and carried a black carry bag. A porter approached them and they mentioned the name of a hotel patron. They were shown to a green sofa in the corner and told to wait. The gentleman in question would be contacted immediately. He was in his suite. The two dropped their luggage on the marble floor and took a seat. The Dorchester was already buzzing. People were coming and going, chatting in half a dozen different languages. A couple of minutes later, the doors of the lift opened and José Saldero Medina walked into the hotel lobby, like a bull entering the arena and scanning for toreros, banderilleros and picadores to slay. His trusted lieutenant Ignacio Pachenga followed suit.

Gorsky saw the Mexicans and elbowed Senka Golovkin straight in the ribs. 'Here we go,' he said and the two stood up to make themselves known. El Guapo spotted Gorsky and marched straight towards him with a menacing expression on his face.

'Are you that son of a bitch who has something that is mine?' he cried from metres away and approached fast gesticulating widely as Pachenga followed. As he reached

Gorsky he suddenly stopped as he realised that the Ruso on whom he zoomed his hostility was taller and considerably larger. El Guapo stopped at a safe distance, waited an instant to make sure that his trusted lieutenant was behind him and rephrased his question: 'Are you the Russian who wants to give me back my property?'

'Yes...' Senka mumbled and was interrupted by Gorsky who pushed him back on the sofa.

'My name is Gorsky and I have a business proposition,' he said to the Mexican.

'Say no more,' cried Medina mockingly. 'You don't seem to understand, amigo. El Guapo does business when and how he pleases. Understand?' He said and Pachenga nodded in approval.

Gorsky raised one hand as a sign of good faith and with the other pointed at Senka Golovkin. 'It's all my cousin's fault and I apologise for it,' he said.' He's not very bright, you see, and I often have problems in controlling his unusual temper.'

For a couple of brief moments, El Guapo scrutinised the Russian duo. Pachenga raised his eyebrows.

'However,' continued Gorsky, 'I have in my possession something that is possibly worth more than a simple piece of jewellery or a diamond to you. You are a man of action, Mr Medina, a native son of the Mexican planes.'

'Right,' nodded El Guapo. 'You think that there is such a thing, worth more than diamonds and gold?'

'Bravery and pride?' said Gorsky.

'Bravery and pride, ha, ha... I like that. You are not stupid. What a pity that you will be dead so soon,' said the Mexican. Pachenga nodded in approval. He was a man of action.

'I will give you the best weapon in the world. The weapon that killed two hundred in one night,' said Gorsky.

'What kind of weapon is that?'

'It's a Kalashnikov, a special edition machinegun designed and produced for the Russian special forces, SPETSNAZ. This specific piece bears the signature of its maker, the engineer Mikhail Kalashnikov and was used in the Chechen war.'

'It bears Kalashnikov's signature?' asked El Guapo.

'On the barrel.'

'How many did you kill with this toy, you said?'

'More than two hundred,' said Gorsky, 'in one night.'

'In one night??'

'In one night,' confirmed Gorsky. 'This is an absolutely unique piece. Just taking it out of the country gets you a lengthy prison sentence for high treason.'

'And why do you want to give me this... Gun?' asked El Guapo who was obviously impressed by the war record of the weapon. 'Your friend had already stolen the jewel from me. So, you have.... Or rather, had them both.' He added with a sinister and menacing stress on the word had.

'I only have the shell of the Russian Soul, señor Medina. Its heart is missing. The diamond in the egg is not the Orlov. It's an excellent piece of synthetic gemstone probably produced in a Mexico City lab, but not the Orlov. So, I am pretty sure that you have the real stone and that's why I came to offer you a deal.'

Medina cast a glance at Gorsky. A rattlesnake sizing his pray.

'How would you know that?' he said.

'We have labs in this country too, señor Medina. Let's keep it at that.'

El Guapo sized Gorsky up starting with the boots up to the top of the hair. He then turned to Pachenga and the two exchanged glances. Senka Golovkin summoned the courage to get up from the sofa and stand on his feet.

'Where is that miraculous piece?' said El Guapo.

'In a van around the corner,' said Gorsky. 'Let's go.'

The four walked through the busy hotel lobby without exchanging a word. They were in a hurry. Once in front of the hotel, they turned left into Deanery Street and walked for a couple of hundred metres until they reached a small white van. The sign on the side of the van was red: RentDirect, Van Hire. Gorsky produced a key, opened the back door and invited the guests to jump in. Medina and Pachenga exchanged glances. At the back of the vehicle there was a single wooden case with writing in Cyrillic script. Medina sized-up the Russians and decided to enter the van. Pachenga followed suit. Once all four were in the back of the van, Senka shut the door and Gorsky lifted the lid of the case. The Mexicans leaned over its content. Medina asked for permission and picked the machinegun up in his arms. Both he and Pachenga scrutinised the weapon. They turned it around, found the safety, released the clip and checked the bullets. They opened the butt and put in position. Medina took aim at a dot on the wall of the van. Looked down the barrel. Pressed the trigger, switched from single to rapid fire. 'Why is this the best machinegun in the world?' he finally said.

'What is the worst it can happen in a fight?' Gorsky asked him. 'When your life depends on the weapon.'

'The worst thing... the gun doesn't fire, gets stuck.' said El Guapo. Pachenga nodded like a real connoisseur.

'Give me the gun. Look at your watch and time me,' said Gorsky to Medina and kneeled. 'You keep the weapon in your left hand. Like this. Then you disassemble it and lay all the parts one next to the other. You reassemble the gun and you pull the trigger. Ok?'

'Ok,' said the King of drugs.

'Now,' said Gorsky. He then disassembled and

reassembled the gun. He pooled the trigger and the AK - 107 said: 'Click'.

Medina stopped the watch and looked in disbelief. Pachenga looked at the watch and then at his boss. Senka shrugged his shoulders. He has never been fond of violence and war games.

'So?' said Gorsky.

'Twenty,' uttered Medina.

'You're in combat, under incoming enemy fire. You need luck, you need skills and you need a weapon to keep you alive. Guns jam. They misfire when you need them the most. I fired bursts of three to four rounds on fully automatic for fifteen consecutive hours in sub-zero temperatures and used ten thousand rounds. The barrel turned red and stayed red for most of the night. This weapon jammed once, only once. I disassembled it in the dark, fixed and continued to shoot. I killed hundreds of rebels. They were armed too. Brand new flashy American weapons. They misfired, froze, jammed, got stuck and broke. I kept on shooting and that's why I am now here talking to you. You fix this gun in under thirty seconds, señor Guapo. You live. That's the only difference that counts.'

'Where did you fight, you said?'

'I fought in Chechnya in the Russian army, airborne regiment. This was in the Caucasus, the now famous battle of the Argul gorge.'

'Famous?'

'Yes, that's what I said, famous.'

'Why would I believe you? The story is good but how do I know it's true? How do I know that you were there?'

Senka Golovkin who, up to that point, had been sitting completely silent and motionless, picked up his rucksack and took out of it a tablet computer and switched it on. He opened the browser, scrolled through the bookmarks and found the right one. He put the tablet down on the van floor and played a YouTube video. The title was Vysota 776 and the video showed the aftermath of a terrible battle that took place in the Caucasus between a Russian platoon and two thousand Chechen and Arab fighters. A couple of minutes into it, the journalist interviewed the two Russian survivors - two nineteen-year old privates. One of the two was seated on a fallen tree trunk, smoked a cigarette and had an obviously heavily used machine gun at his feet.

'That's you!' cried Medina and looked at Gorsky.

'That's me,' said Gorsky.

Medina then looked at the video again and asked Golovkin to play it again. He checked the faces again, rewound the video and scrutinised the weapon and compared it with the one they had in the van. 'It's a young version of you.' He concluded looking at Gorsky.

'That's me, yes.'

'And the Kalashnikov seems to be the one.'

'It is the one.'

'How many people were there with you before the battle?'

'Ninety.'

'And how many survived?'

'The two of us.'

'How many enemies were killed?'

'Six hundred.'

'Six hundred!' repeated Medina, obviously impressed. 'How many did you kill?'

'Two hundred, I think,' said Gorsky modestly.

Medina and Pachenga exchanged glances. Gorsky picked up the machine gun and offered it to the Mexican who took and began looking at the many scars on the weapon's body.

'It fired all night and killed two hundred, you say?'

'It did.'

'So, you must be a big hero in your country, ah?' said Medina.

'I was, for a short while,' said Gorsky. 'As you can see, this weapon is unique. It brings luck. I was lucky that night, Mr Medina, very lucky and that's why I am here with you, now. It is unique and very, very precious. That's why we are here. I propose and exchange. A small friendly exchange, I will give you this fine weapon and the synthetic diamond and you will give me the Orlov. The original, mind you.'

For a split second, El Guapo considered his options and then turned to Pachenga: 'Go upstairs and bring the diamond from the safe.'

His right-hand man seemed to be startled.

'El Guapo,' he said. 'What if Guadalupe finds out... We...'

'Don't you worry about Guadalupita. She is still sleeping and when it comes to the diamond, she can't tell the difference anyway.'

Pachenga left the scene running.

'You will give me the synthetic copy, of course,' said Medina to the Russians and they both nodded simultaneously. Gorsky took out of his pocket a velvet tissue wrapped around an object the size of a bigger goose egg. He opened the wrapping and showed its content. It was a perfect example of a synthetic diamond of a world-class production. A piece of art that required a scientific lab or a diamond professional to establish it was not a genuine gemstone. Gorsky offered the stone to Medina who picked it up and just slid into the pocket of his jacket.

'What does Guadalupe know about diamonds anyway!' Medina uttered and continued playing with the Kalashnikov.

When Pachenga came back, he handed the little box with the diamond to Medina who passed it to Gorsky. El

Guapo liked the gun. He liked the aura of invincibility too. Diamonds were for girls.

Gorsky pulled a key out of his pocket and threw it to Pachenga.

'This is the key to the vehicle. Unload the crate with the weapon and drive the vehicle back to the rental agency. The details are in the glove compartment. OK?'

Pachenga nodded and Medina mumbled something that sounded like he agreed. Gorsky and Senka got out of the van, went down Deanery Street, left into Park Lane and took the underpass to Hyde Park. They took a short cut across the lawns and reached the tube station. They changed lines at King's Cross and continued north on the City line. They got out at Redbridge where they found the blue Volkswagen Golf in the car park. A couple of minutes later they were driving towards Cambridge.

'The scribbling on the barrel,' said Senka interrupting the long silence, 'It doesn't say Mikhail Kalashnikov!?'

'No, it doesn't,' replied Gorsky. 'It's Cyrillic, he'll never know.'

'What does it say?'

'Mark Hodayev.'

'Why is that?'

'When Mark vanished, I took his weapon. It was better balanced than mine.'

'I see,' said Senka who for a moment turned pensive only to come back with a new question. 'How did you smuggle the weapon out of that and into this country?'

'I didn't.'

'?'

'You did, Senka.'

'What do you mean, I did?'

'Well,' said Gorsky. 'Do you remember the one time when you asked for some furniture and your other belongings to be transported from Voronezh to London?'

'You put that case with weapons among my belongings?'

'Well, yes,' said Gorsky. 'I hope you don't mind.'

'No, of course not,' said Senka with a wry smile. 'Why would I mind? What could have possibly gone wrong? Me arrested for arm trafficking? Well, minor details in the grand scheme of the things?'

'Thank you, Senka,' said Gorsky. 'I knew I could trust you.'

'Yeah, right,' mumbled Senka.

In less than an hour they arrived in Cambridge. They got out of the car and walked around the corner. As they were approaching Niusha and Aptin's house, Gorsky noticed a couple of unusual shadows that appeared to be sneaking through the dark. When they were near their destination, a large shadow jumped out of a doorway with a shrill cry.

'Ha, here you are!' the shadow appeared to be shouting. He had a hood over his head and a baseball bat in his hands. As he jumped out of the cover and onto the path of Gorsky and Golovkin, an additional four or five shadows popped out and surrounded the pair. They wore hoods over their heads and waved chains, crowbars and wrenches.

'Where is your sword now, samurai, ah?' said the baseball bat hoodie and produced a sinister sound that he probably felt was laughter, 'Ha, ha, ha...'

One of the others cried, 'Yeah,' and another one added, 'Sucker!'

Senka Golovkin squeezed his rucksack tight against his body and got closer to Gorsky.

'Alex,' he said. 'There are a couple behind us too!'

Gorsky was in a hurry. They had the diamond, they would get the tape, the meeting was on and there was still a tiny, outside chance that...

'Step aside,' he said to Golovkin.

'Ha,' cried the baseball bat hoody waving his tool through the air. 'You must be joking, Mr Knight of the fucking Russian samurai order. It's time for you to taste some of your own medicine. What did you think? You can just come here to beat up and bully whoever you please? Tough luck, mate. Tough luck,' he said and swung the bat.

With his right hand, Gorsky reached under his coat and pulled out the Sig-Sauer. Before he knew it the baseball-bat man faced serious proposition, the ominous, dark mouth of a '38 calibre gun. He froze and remained with the bat raised in mid-air.

'Don't you move,' said Gorsky and turned towards the other members of the little welcome committee who had all made their first step towards the two and found themselves now stranded in the 'no man's land'.

'One move, one word and you're dead,' Gorsky said. No one moved and no one said a word. They could have been transported directly to Madame Tussaud's and exhibited under the title - The Clueless Gang.

'I count to three,' said Gorsky and pulled the safety on the gun off with, what it sounded the hoodies, a thunderous click. 'Now turn around and run.'

And, of course, run they did. Not in the same direction, they just ran back into the dark and as far as possible from the Russians.

'Fuck'n criminals,' cried one.

'Murderous bastards,' complained the other one. They swore and moaned but never looked back.

'And don't come back,' yelled Senka. He then turned to Gorsky.

'We gave them a good scare,' he said.

'Yeah, we sure did,' said Gorsky putting the gun back into the holster. 'We need to get ready, Senka.'

'You mean, *that* ready?' said Senka and pointed his finger at the holster.

'Yes,' said Gorsky, '*that* ready!'

Senka Golovkin shrugged his shoulders.

'It was always meant to end this way,' he mumbled, 'always.'

27

McGallen's visit

Gorsky and Golovkin reached their shelter in Collier Street. Senka took the key out of his pocket and rushed to the door. He turned around once more just to make sure they weren't followed. Once they entered the corridor, Aptin came out of the living room and stood in the doorway. He was pale and his big dark eyes were even bigger than usual. He tried to say something but no sound came out of his lips. Gorsky put a hand into his inside pocket. The Sig Sauer was there. He stepped towards Aptin, moved him aside to cast a glance at the room. There was a man sitting in the armchair. He wore a short coat and smoked a cigarette. Gorsky removed his hand from the gun and entered the room. The man shook the cigarette and collected its ash in the palm of the other hand.

'Good evening, Mr Gorsky,' said the man. 'You know who I am?'

'I know,' said Gorsky. 'Good evening, Inspector McGallen.'

'Please do sit down,' said the visitor and, with a wide gesture, showed the available seats. Senka and Aptin moved silently into the room and sat on the couch. Gorsky stood next to the door looking at the visitor. He wasn't quite sure what to make of his presence. Too many questions and too few answers, he concluded and decided to hear the policeman out.

'I realise that I come here uninvited,' said McGallen, a man in his mid-fifties with broad shoulders, a flat, boxer's nose, a mightily square jaw and short white hair. 'We have a couple of murders on our hands though, and, as you will appreciate, there is a sense of urgency about it.'

'We have nothing to do with those murders,' cried Senka Golovkin and jumped a couple of inches from his seat.

'Of course not,' said McGallen. 'That's why I am here on my own. Let's say this is a social visit, shall we? Mr Golovkin, I believe?'

'Yes, this is Senka Golovkin and my name is Gorsky as you, I am sure, already know,' said Gorsky.

'I was disappointed to see that your righteous Fravashi friends were not at home. They must be away plotting something...' said McGallen with an ironic smirk. 'But worry not, Mr Gorsky, I am not interested in your friends.'

'Not my friends really,' said Gorsky. 'Acquaintances perhaps.'

'Sure, sure. They are an interesting bunch, though. They feel they have been rejected by the society. Unjustly, of course. Except the one who decided to kick society in the arse. A completely new situation in my line of work, you see?' said McGallen.

'What do you mean?' asked Gorsky.

"Well, most of them were left on the margins, you see. Alcohol abuse, drugs, unemployment, nervous breakdowns, failed marriages...'

'Ok, I get your point,' said Gorsky. 'Niusha and her lot are victims of your society.'

'Niusha?' said McGallen and turned to Aptin. 'You didn't tell him?'

Aptin shook his head, 'No. Never had the chance and it's not important anyway.'

'It's not. It's not that important, you might be right,' said the policeman. 'But there you go.'

"What is it?' said Gorsky.

'You think Niusha is a victim, persecuted by society? You see Mr Gorsky, that's where you got it wrong. It's my job to know, you see. Niusha Khanbaghi was the best student of her generation and completed a BA and PhD in Chemistry at Cambridge in under six years. It seems to be a world record. She won a gold medal at the Chemistry Olympiad. And that was apparently not good enough. She wasn't happy with such achievements, you see? The only reason she completed her studies in record time was to be able to 'dump the system,' her words mind you, from the Facebook page. So, she 'dumped the system,' the career prospects, the academia, the whole Oxbridge prestige thing, the high tables, the gowns and the port and the champagne. She volunteers in the shelter these days, the hospice for homeless people. Isn't that right, Aptin?'

'It is right,' said Aptin and shrugged his shoulders looking at the floor.

'So, we now have Aptin here to carry the scientific torch of the Khanbaghis,' said McGallen. 'Interesting family, isn't it?'

'I didn't know,' said Gorsky. 'Didn't look that way when I met Niusha.'

'No, of course not. The young lady is inconspicuous, shall we say. Yes, inconspicuous is a good word,' concluded McGallen who was obviously amused by the story and was showing signs of admiration too. But he was first and foremost a policeman.

'As I said, four murders in Rome and one in London,' he continued, 'An apartment in a peaceful residential block of a university town blown up. You see, the police don't like such behaviour.'

Gorsky moved from his position next to the doorway and sat in the other armchair facing McGallen. This encounter was becoming interesting. 'The murders in Rome and in London in the same sentence,' he said. 'That's quite a leap, inspector McGallen.'

The policeman meticulously extinguished the cigarette on the lid of a silver cigarette case and coughed a couple of times. He then returned the case to his pocket and coughed once more.

'Sure,' he said. 'Apart from data gathering, analysis and decision-making skills we also possess the power of imagination, Mr Gorsky. As you can see by my presence here, we did gather the relevant data, analysed it, and here we are. Even more so, I used my, if I may say so, imagination and decided that the best course of action was to come here on my own and have a little chat with this Mr Gorsky who happened to find himself at several murder scenes and who had his flat explode. Lots of coincidences, you see. I may also add here an interesting observation. The said gentleman has also been in the employment of the Kaganov family. No need to remind you, of course, that Mr Kaganov himself apparently perished in a car crash.'

'I understand, McGallen,' said Gorsky. 'but, why not send the police force in and arrest everyone? That's more like standard police procedure. Why bother with visits?'

'Mr Gorsky,' he said. 'Could we have this conversation in private, please? I appreciate that these are your closest acquaintances but I think it would be better if we could...'

Senka Golovkin immediately assumed an upright position and looked at Gorsky as if asking: 'May I?' Aptin Khanbaghi looked around without blinking.

'Sure,' said Gorsky before turning to his friends. 'Wait for me in the kitchen.'

'Mr Gorsky,' said McGallen and moved forward, placing his elbows on his knees and assuming a confidential posture. 'I am not a very popular person among my superiors, you see. There's a body in the Tate Modern next to the Kandinsky or one of those Russian paintings anyway. A dead man's body, mind you. In Italy, a Russian businessman with political asylum in this country had been shot dead. His wife too. Same time and place, a man got killed by high calibre rifle fire and another one executed in a car. Call me superstitious but these are bad signs, very bad signs. So bad that my superiors insist on apprehending the culprits while I can't help noticing that four of the five dead people are Russians. Interesting coincidence. Or, is it, Mr Gorsky?'

Gorsky sat in the armchair and listened carefully. He knew how to lower his heart rate to below forty beats a minute and keep it that way. He knew how to increase the oxygen intake. The one thing he knew he couldn't afford to be was to be nervous. People make mistakes all the time, people fail in their judgement, they do all sorts of wrong things at the wrong time when they are nervous. Gorsky was aware of that. He liked to think of himself as being beyond such frailties.

'I came far, too far, to be stopped here,' ran though his mind. He knew how to keep calm and focused. 'Think,' he whispered to himself. 'Think, Alex.'

He nodded and McGallen continued.

'I don't think it is a coincidence, you see. No such things as coincidences. If there were such things, there would be no organised crime, gangs, Russian and Italian mafia, oligarchs and the rest of the fraternity. There would be only random crimes and great police work. No, Mr Gorsky, there is a pattern to these and to many other crimes. You know there is such a pattern and I know that you know. So?'

'So, what?' said Gorsky.

'Talk to me,' said McGallen, leaned back in his chair and took the pack of cigarettes and a lighter out of his pocket. He put the cigarette between his lips and lit it. He inhaled a mighty drag and puffed the smoke in the air.

'No smoking in this house,' said Gorsky.

'I know,' said McGallen and produced a wry smile.

'Good,' said Gorsky. 'Let's talk!'

28

A different kind of war

Gorsky got out of bed before dawn. The streets were quiet, the whole town still sleepy. Senka and Gorsky were left on their own. Golovkin slept downstairs in the living room and Gorsky in the guest room. All the regular occupants were in London attending the pre-demo meet and coordinating the event. Listening to their conversations and observing the preparations for the anti-globalist protests, Gorsky thought they looked like getting ready for Chechnya rather than for the London tube and perhaps the water cannons. They had water bottles, mobile phones, tablet computers, sleeping bags, thermal underwear and trekking boots. They had communication systems, procedures, passwords, user names, code names. They owned credit cards and passports and they bought regular rail and tube tickets. They wore shirts with the iconic Che Guevara image and red, green and yellow stars, Russian army fur hats with the sickle and hammer. They would shout *'no pasaran'* while greeting each other at the door.

'Desirable opponents, desirable. They imagine they pose a threat to people like the Boss and his partners in the City, I guess,' mumbled Gorsky while looking at his own reflection in the glass. 'They will be treated as a threat, that's for sure. But do they really represent an imminent danger to the system? No, they don't.'

Gorsky took the Sig Sauer out of his coat and went to the kitchen. He put the gun on the table and next to it a small box of ammunition, a container with oil, a piece of cloth that he ripped off a kitchen towel and a pencil. He opened the window ajar and sat at the table. The fresh morning air made him feel at home. He disassembled the weapon carefully, placing the parts one next to the other, from left to right. He examined every piece and used the cloth on it to take off any dust particle or gunpowder residue. He wiped every single surface with care, wrapped the piece of cloth around the pencil and pushed it up and down the barrel. He then inspected the tube against the kitchen light and reassembled the weapon, reloaded the ammunition and put the safety catch on. He moved the gun to his right and looked through the window. There was still an hour before dawn. He took a deep breath. He could hear the noise of a helicopter in the distance. Then came the sound of mortar shells exploding and rapid machine gun fire. The air he breathed was cold but not as cold as the one on the Argul. No, never that cold. The days of the Beslan siege ran in front of his eyes. No more war. No war, he thought. The gun was ready though, right there on the table. A different kind of war was coming.

The army taught him to listen to the night and unlock its clues. Gorsky knew the sound of the wind and the gurgle of the stream. He learnt to tell animals by their call and movements, people by their deeds under extreme pressure. He knew the pulsating feeling of blood that runs through your veins and the moment in time that, like a sword, cuts life into what was and what is. Unlike in the Caucasus, he had a choice. It did seem like he had a choice. The endgame was nearing and Gorsky wanted to make sure that he had a good grasp of the relevant details. Any, even the tiniest detail, might prove to be of crucial importance.

'The Italian was planted to take Vatayev out,' he thought as he went through the possible scenario. 'Irina was collateral damage. The Italian killed Sergey first. He earned his trust and it was then easy to pull the gun behind his back and shoot him. My absence made this possible. Why was I not there? The Boss asked me to pay a visit to the antiquarian and collect an item. The Boss. Why would the Boss want Vatayev out? The missing link number one. The Italian is shot dead by the sniper. Fine work, very professional. Double safety, kill the killer. The sniper had to leave his position and wasn't interested in me. I got out of there and contacted Senka who informed the Boss. The Boss was unfazed. No hurry to collect the items from the antiquarian. It seemed urgent when he asked me to pick them up. Hours later it wasn't anymore? The old man said that the Boss was interested in the letters first, he picked up the sword along the way or... He did so just to hide his interest in the letters? The old man said that the Boss sat in his shop and read a good part of the papers. That would explain why he wasn't in a hurry to have them. He knew the content for he had read them. He just wanted to make sure that no one else had access to them. Then the Boss in Scotland. What was he doing in Scotland? Coming back from a business meeting with North Sea oil corporations his car skidded off the road and all three passengers died. The other two were local, petrol people, not our regular security men. In both Rome and Scotland security was compromised intentionally. I was sent away and the regular security was kept away from the Scotland trip. Interesting. Did someone take both the Boss and Vatayev out? Why and who would that be? Now we get to Mark Hodayev. Mark must have known much more than he gave away. He needed my assistance to get hold of the Russian Soul. He had to ask me for help? Did they not have a plan A? Or, maybe they did. They must have had a plan A that went badly. Something didn't work out for the FSB. The Boss wanted to return to Russia as a presidential candidate, he needed the jewel. Vatayev? What did he want? Did Mark Hodayev contact Vatayev? Is that it? Treason? Was he promised something in return for the Russian Soul? Did such a deal cost him his life? Did such a deal cost them their lives? Mark Hodayev dies at the hand of a man I remember seeing somewhere. I know that face and it will come back to me. Milla Ivanovna is cutting the deal - access to the Siberian resources, Kremlin politics and international finance. Enough reasons for many more people to get killed. Including me. I spoke to Hodayev and had the letters. I had a copy of the Report too. I became a target. Now that I have the jewel I am even more of a target. The Russian Soul. The spell of the Russian Soul. Four people died in Rome, the Boss and his escort in Scotland and Mark Hodayev. Eight people dead. If we count the Boss of course... Milla Ivanovna identified the charred body. If he is in hiding, who is after him? The same people who killed Vatayev? If both were targets, why not take the Boss out first? That would be a more logical sequence. Unless there is a pattern. There must be a pattern and a hand that pulls the strings, a puppeteer. They will come to the meeting, that's for sure, as no one can afford to miss out on a piece of this cake.'

While Gorsky was trying to imagine every conceivable scenario, and work out the possible outcomes, Senka Golovkin was having a turbulent sleep. He turned and frowned, sweated and breathed heavily. He fell into a bottomless pit, drowned in a red waterfall and hid from a kimono-clad Japanese secret agent. He then ran through the desert trying to escape a bunch of blood thirsty, camel-riding Bedouins and got stuck in a pit of quicksand where he was being strangled by an anaconda. He wanted to scream but his mouth would not produce a sound.

Thankfully, a clock somewhere in the building rang and woke him up. He was alive and grateful for it. He gasped for air and rushed to the bathroom where he splashed two handfuls of cold water onto his face and looked at the mirror. Right.

He recognised the face - Senka Golovkin. He walked out of the bathroom.

As he entered the kitchen, Gorsky got up from the chair and closed the window. The streetlights went off and the first passer-by hurried down the street. Someone turned the key in the ignition and the sound of an old diesel engine rumbled.

'We'll leave at nine,' said Gorsky. 'Put all your documents and the jewel in the rucksack and get ready. It is likely that we will not be coming back here so don't leave anything behind.'

'Right,' said Senka while pouring water into the kettle. He needed a black coffee and not even the prospect of the imminent Armageddon would make him reconsider his priorities.

A couple of minutes after nine the pair left the house on Collier Street. Golovkin carried the rucksack with the jewel and Gorsky the case with the sword. In one pocket, he had the Fabergé letters and in the other a Sig-Sauer with twelve reassuring rounds. They decided to take the train and leave the blue Volkswagen Golf parked in the street.

They walked to Mackenzie Road and turned left into Mill Road. It was early morning and the street was buzzing with delivery trucks bringing supplies to Middle-Eastern bazaars, Turkish coffee shops, Gyros takeaways, Indian, Tandoori and Chinese restaurants, Pizza places and convenience shops. The traffic was heavy.

Gorsky was focused on the day ahead. In front of his wide-open eyes there was a procession of murderous and treacherous characters wrapped up in layers of intrigue. He had a sword, he taught, and swords cut through smoke screens. In one pocket of his coat he had the Fabergé letters. He had the jewel too.

Before the rail overpass they turned right into Devonshire Road at the bottom of which they walked under the pedestrian bridge, through the parking lot and arrived at the railway station. The early morning rush of London commuters was over. They purchased the rail and tube tickets and boarded the train. Gorsky put the case on the luggage rail and took his seat facing in the direction of the train. Golovkin sat down opposite and held the rucksack firmly in his embrace. The two sat in silence, each with his own thoughts and fears. There was a sense of inevitability about their trip to London and the unfolding events. Like sitting in a bobsled that is racing towards the bottom of the mountain. The track is frozen and narrow, the bends sharp and deadly.

'It's about self-control,' thought Gorsky. 'You always stand a chance in life, at least one. The thing is, you have to be quick and take it.'

As the train entered London Kings Cross, the passengers picked up their belongings and hurried up the platform. Gorsky and Golovkin boarded the Northern line that took them south of the Thames. Half an hour later they arrived at Canary Wharf station. They took the escalator, reached ground level and spilt onto the street joining a wave of protesters that was moving towards the Canada Square Park.

Gorsky made sure he had a firm grip on his case and Golovkin, under his friend's watchful eye, embraced the precious rucksack tightly. They moved slowly with the tide of people towards the park. Their destination was the Canada

Square One building. The meeting was taking place on the top floor of the skyscraper. While Gorsky walked with a straight face trying to focus on the task at hand, Golovkin was eager to read the slogans on the protesters' placards and banners. A bearded man with a woollen hat was asking 'What would Jesus say?' While another behind him wore a decommissioned German army uniform and carried the slogan 'Eat the Rich.' Next to him was a woman in flowery gumboots who declared that 'Robin Hood was right!'

Senka found it all very amusing. It felt like the good old times he had read about. May '68, flower power, the Hippies... As Karl Marx put it, Capitalism contained its own contradictions. The way the system decided to deal with such contradictions was to make protests permissible and thus contain their critical and subversive edge.

'Let them Eat Big Macs!' cried a rainbow coloured banner carried by a very skinny young man. 'Spare the Horses, Ride the Bankers!' shouted a slogan on the shirt of a middle-aged man with long, white hair. In one hand, he carried a bottle of water and in the other a whip.

'If Not Now, When?' screamed the banner carried by two Jamaican men in Rasta hats who danced and sang along a reggae tune coming out of a Smartphone. They were followed by a man who beat a small drum that he carried attached with a piece of string around the waist.

The stream of people flowed towards the Canada Square Park between two banks of police in full riot gear. 'Pigs,' yelled a man next to Senka. 'They come to peaceful protests geared up and armed as if we a bunch of bloodthirsty marauders or an occupying force. The real criminals are sitting in the very buildings they protect - swine!'

One protester waved the flag of Brazil and another one of that of Jamaica. Alongside a red Ferrari flag, there was the Welsh dragon as well as a red flag featuring a green star. T-shirts bore images of Che Guevara, the Dalai Lama, David Beckham and Jimi Hendrix. People spoke different languages, clapped their hands and shouted slogans.

'Noah's Ark and the Tower of Babel put together,' mumbled Senka Golovkin towards Gorsky who was a step ahead working his way through the crowd. 'This is what anarchy and the end of the world look and sound like.'

Gorsky didn't say a word. He understood Senka's preference for a world without ferment that runs like a well-oiled machine, for a system that operates without disruptions and for people who keep their opinions to themselves. Gorsky, on the other hand, wasn't afraid of change or the consequences of his own actions. He understood the nature of struggle.

Eventually, they reached their destination and stepped out of the human river. Gorsky grabbed Senka by the jacket and nearly lifted him to the safety of a concrete plant pot. From this vantage position, Gorsky began to scrutinise the crowd. From here he could see the police cordon, the metal fence and anti-vehicle concrete barriers in front of the building he was going to. He spotted the antiterrorist unit, standing next to a couple of armoured vehicles. While the noise level increased by the minute, Gorsky remembered that the Fravashi team was allocated a place right in front of the covered stage towards the northern side of the park. That area was clearly full and he was sure that Niusha's friends arrived in good time to claim their strategic spot.

The two jumped down from the pot and continued the march towards the entrance. Did Milla Ivanovna instruct the security officers and the police? thought Gorsky. Well, there was only one way to find out.

'No entrance, no jewel, Milla Ivanovna,' mumbled Gorsky and continued to clear his way through layer upon layer of ecstatic demonstrators. When they reached the first line of policemen, Gorsky showed his British passport and gave the officer a piece of paper with an address, telephone number and the name Milla Ivanovna on it. As he and Senka stood waiting to be admitted to the building, Gorsky spotted a tall, blond man exiting the building in the company of a policeman. The man wore a dark green velvet jacket and jeans. He tapped the policeman on the shoulder and vanished in the opposite direction.

'Senka,' cried Gorsky grabbing Golovkin's arm. 'You have to reach the Fravashis.'

'Fravash... What?'

'Niusha and her crew, it's important.'

'And how do you think I can find them in this mayhem?' he said making a wide gesture towards the adjacent sea of people.

'We know exactly where they are. You will find them in front of the stage,' said Gorsky and pointed in the direction of the stage. 'Right there.'

'But...'

'Senka, I know what you want to say but this is important. Listen to me. Leave the rucksack with me. I will deliver the jewel. You go over there and pass a message to Niusha, Aptin or Steve. No one else, do you understand me? You must find one of those three.'

'And tell them what?'

'Tell them that we saw Nick Hershaw coming out of this building in the company of an agent. They are up to something and I don't like it.'

'I thought Nick was one of them? What are you talking about?'

'They suspected him of being an infiltrated agent for quite some time. Don't worry. They will know what to do. You just go there and pass the message. Give me the jewel,' said Gorsky.

Senka hesitated. He then took the rucksack off his shoulder and passed it to Gorsky.

'Don't do anything too stupid,' he told Gorsky.

'Senka, no matter what happens, you hide and wait for me to get in touch. It might take a day or two, a week or two, but I'll find you. Keep in touch with Niusha and you'll be fine.'

'And the jewel?' asked Golovkin with an anxious expression on his face.

'Go, Senka,' said Gorsky and turned towards the entrance of the skyscraper where two security officers were looking at him and exchanging words.

'Fiftieth floor, RM & CEN security officer to attend a meeting. My name will be on the list,' he explained to the officers, trusting that Milla Ivanovna stuck to their bargain. The name Gorsky was indeed on the list and one of the officers ticked it. Gorsky produced his passport and the permit to carry arms. He was on duty, he said, as per the strict instructions from Milla Ivanovna. He opened the case and produced the artefact belonging to the Kaganov widow. He displayed the Russian Soul and said that it was his duty to deliver the jewel. While he was at the security check point, he saw a man waiting in the lobby. Mid-height, stocky and bearded, he was scrolling through his mobile phone. As soon as he cleared security, Gorsky rushed towards the elevators and stood next to the man. The lift arrived and the two entered the cabin. The man put his phone in the pocket and said: 'Which floor?'

'Fiftieth, Inspector McGallen,' said Gorsky. 'Fiftieth.'

McGallen pressed the buttons for the forty-ninth and fiftieth floors. 'We'll be downstairs,'

'Sure,' said Gorsky. 'Just don't forget whose side you're on.'

29

One Canada Square

The lift came to a stop. It was the top floor of One Canada Square building. Gorsky stepped out and on to the marble floor of a lobby. To the right there was a welcome desk with elaborate flower arrangements and immediately next to it the emergency exit that led to the internal emergency stairs. To the left of the lift was the cloakroom and straight ahead a milky glass door with Art Nouveau ornaments. Two young ladies greeted the new arrival with a smile, asked for his coat and if he wanted to deposit the belongings.

'No, I'll keep my coat on,' he replied but decided to leave the case. He would keep the rucksack, though.

They asked for his name and when he obliged they ticked a box on the list. 'Please come in,' they said and one opened the entrance. The sound of a piano came through.

'Chopin perhaps or Shubert or... one of those,' thought Gorsky.

'To the right,' said the girl and pointed at the next glass door. Above it, a golden plate read - the Atrium. Gorsky found himself in a vast room with marble flooring, a high ceiling and glass walls that left the visitor in a state of levitation and awe above the city. He felt like he was sitting on Aladdin's magic carpet. The music came from a concert piano at the opposite end of the Atrium. There was something ethereal about this office that sat in the clouds, overlooking the Thames and half of the London amenities.

The city lay within reach and yet it was stuck behind a thick protective glass.

To the right of the entrance, there was a long red wall that featured some contemporary art work as well as a large, flat TV screen showing logs burning in a fireplace. In front of the wall, further from the entrance, there was a large aquarium with tropical vegetation and a couple of piranha fish. In the middle of the room stood a massive totem-like phallus mounted on a wooden pedestal.

As he entered and observed this spectacle, Gorsky heard a tall, elegant gentleman explaining to the party that this sculpture was borrowed from the Phallological Museum in Reykjavik. It belonged to his good friend and business associate, Dr Sigurdsson.

'It's a young blue whale phallus, you see. A grown-up male's member can reach the length of up to five metres!' the elegant, learned gentleman informed his listeners.

Beyond the group there was a long, glass table and chair, several armchairs and a large couch. The room probably featured hidden cameras and microphones as the RM & CEN considered it good business practice to record the proceedings of all the meetings and keep an accurate record.

Several floors below, the Global Monetary Fund spread over a couple of levels and was hosting an important conference: Global Resources and Global Responsibilities. The Conference was that morning opened by Stieg Rasmussen, the president of the Euro-American Investment Bank, who drew the attention of the delegates to the responsibility that financial institutions have in the forthcoming division of natural resources with special reference to the Arctic, Antarctic, Amazon and Siberia. After Rasmussen spoke the Chairman of the Global Enterprise Investment, the retired USA general, John P. Schwarzwald. He elaborated on the strategic rationale for an uncompromising war against terrorism, Russia and China and the criminal supporters in our midst. He concluded by stressing the importance of a regulated internet.

In front of the building, the little Canada Square Park and the adjacent streets were filled with protesters. The BBC announced a ten thousand-strong crowd while some bloggers operated with the figure supplied by the protest organising committee: fifty thousand and growing. The sea of people shouted slogans, waved flags and posters, danced and yelled. They protested the militarisation, financialisation, fragmentation and occupation of their free minds and living space, against the global rule of an irresponsible minority.

Gorsky took notice of the city below and the clouds above, the aquarium and the concert piano, the large TV screen, the collection of artworks, the sacred totem, the piranhas and the people gathered in that space. He stood and watched, waiting to be noticed. Under his arm there was a small, red rucksack. In the rucksack, there was a box.

Further down the room, at the long table, Ituribe sat next to a young woman, his head buried in paperwork. Beside them there were two other lawyers, one from Garriburton Inc. and one from RM & CEN.

Two waitresses in smart outfits stood in the corner holding trays with drinks and light snacks.

'Nice to see you, Liz,' said Tom Deutsch while placing a hand gently on the waist of a young woman talking to Jack Sailgood.

'Isobel, the name is Isobel,' she said removing his hand with an expression of distaste on her lips, then turned her back and walked away. At first, Deutsch held his nerve.

'What the fuck was that?' he then said as he watched Isobel leave. The ever-so-helpful Jack Sailgood was happy to oblige.

'It's the sister, Tom,' he whispered into the American ear. 'The sister.'

'Sister? I didn't know she had one? They look the same!'

'Of course, Tom. They are twins.'

'You kept this as a secret?'

'Classified information, yes.'

'And what happened to Liz?'

'Tehran happened to Liz. She just helped secure a nuclear deal with Iran. Haven't you noticed?'

'I noticed the deal, not her role in it.'

At the other end of the room, behind the totem and closer to the piranhas, Lord Mintbatten was discussing the advantages of owning one's own stable of racehorses with El Guapo Medina who appeared to be a great admirer of the English countryside.

'It is so unlike my native Sonora,' the Mexican moaned. 'If only we had some rain back home!'

Milla Ivanovna stood next to the concert piano. She wore a black jacket, trousers and a pearl necklace that she kept touching with her left hand.

Deutsch was interested in obtaining from Medina the names of the United States Senators on the Sinaloa cartel pay list. Since Sinaloa was the competition to Medina's own interests in the Senate, Deutsch figured that this would be a win-win situation. It would strengthen both men's positions in their respective lines of business. The Mexican listened to the proposition carefully and then exploded in laughter.

'Ha, ha,' he said. 'For a small fee I can throw in a couple of names of your own, personal foes. Ha, ha, that would be very elegant. Ha, ha, what do you think, ha?'

'Sure, excellent idea, why not continue this conversation later, in a more private location?'

As the newcomer walked into the room and stood at the entrance, the murmur slowly died out and the heads started turning. Even the touch of the pianist seemed to turn softer as the music paled into the background.

Ituribe stopped writing his notes.

At that point, Milla Ivanovna noticed Gorsky's presence and stopped talking to Lord Mintbatten in mid-sentence. The rest of the party followed suit. The chatter died out and everyone turned towards the newcomer with the rucksack.

'My dearest Alex,' squealed Milla Ivanovna and made one step towards Gorsky with her arms wide open. 'We are all so happy to see you.'

'Who is that?' asked Tom Deutsch who was standing next to Medina and Ituribe.

'The Russian guy with the jewel,' explained Medina.

'Gorsky,' said Sailgood. 'The Kaganov security man.'

'Ah, here comes our man!' exclaimed Lord Mintbatten.

'Where is my jewel?' cried Milla Ivanovna who had, by now, reached Gorsky and extended her arms towards the rucksack. Gorsky sidestepped her and approached the long table where he dropped the bag and put a hand on it.

'The Russian Soul is here,' he said, took the green box out and placed it on the table. 'First, you, Milla Ivanovna,' he said. 'You owe me something.'

In silence, they all gathered around the table. This was the moment they had waited for, the unveiling of the Russian Soul, the most precious jewel that would open wide the gates of Russia and of Khatanga, the largest diamond mine in the world. Milla Ivanovna clapped and asked a waitress to bring in the 'parcel'. In the meantime, she stood next to Gorsky looking at the green box. When she tried to reach out for it, Gorsky grabbed her wrist and pushed the hand back. Tom Deutsch forgot about the Isobel episode and managed to win a position on the other flank of the Russian. The moment they had all waited for so long had come. The Russian Soul was the key to the future and that key was there, sitting on the table on the fiftieth floor of a London skyscraper. Next to the table stood Medina, eager to see if his jewel changed shape, colour, size or substance. He was a great chemistry buff, Medina, specialist in synthetic drugs and heroin production.

On the other side stood Sailgood. Ever so calm and collected, he was aware of at least two endgame scenarios for this little drama. Experience taught him that one could never foresee all the variables and that contingency plans were a sign of sound organisation and wisdom. He didn't trust anybody and that was his strongest card. His hands were sweaty and he wiped them off his trousers making sure no one noticed. Isobel stood next to him.

'When I get hold of that treacherous son of a bitch...' she remembered her sister's e-mail from Tehran. Yes, there was a sort of dispute but...'

'Is this really the greatest jewel... ever?' said Mintbatten and walked around the table where he found a place next to Ituribe. The abogado was writing his detailed notes as if they were the exact instructions for getting off Noah's Ark after the deluge.

'The jewel is in there?' said Tom Deutsch.

Milla Ivanovna darted an unfriendly and possibly lethal look in his direction.   'Better be,' she said.

'I already saw it the other day,' said Mintbatten to Sailgood.

'Did you know?'

'What is it like?' asked Isobel.

'Well, if you ask me it's an egg. Made of gold and diamonds, though. Yes,' explained the Lord.

'I found it in Frida Kahlo's blue house, in the monkey's cage,' Medina reminded everyone. 'I did.'

Gorsky listened, observed, said nothing and glanced at his wristwatch. In fifteen-minutes all the pieces would be deployed on the chessboard. He had a gun. The jewel was on the table, the sword in the cloakroom.

The faces of some of the participants were new to Gorsky but he remembered Boss's comments and was able to guess that Jack Sailgood was the stocky one with white hair. Next to him the girl, an MI6 trainee... Then Lord Mintbatten who was so obviously lordly while Tom Deutsch was easy to pick up. He was the American guy who thought he was in charge.

'How many guns around this table?' Gorsky started counting. All men except Ituribe and Mintbatten. Abogado Ituribe wouldn't know what to do with one. The Lord? What's wrong with him, anyway? The women are not armed but there is security next door, two, perhaps three men. Security cameras are not visible but they are on. Microphones...

'Open that box,' ordered Deutsch.

'Oh, here she comes,' cried Milla Ivanovna as the waitress approached the table. She then grabbed the plastic bag out of the girl's hands. "Here you are,' she said passing the bag to Gorsky.

'The jewel is yours,' said Gorsky, grabbed the bag and moved away from the table.

Milla Ivanovna laid her hands on the green box. Everybody gathered as close as possible. 'I want to see this,' said Isobel and pushed Jack Sailgood slightly.

'Open that thing!' he exclaimed while Mintbatten oversaw the proceedings with a sneer. Symbols, jewellery, names. All nonsense, he was more accustomed to counting millions and trusting fat, diversified portfolios.

Ituribe stopped writing his notes and raised an eyebrow.

Milla Ivanovna opened the box and buried her hands in it. She held the jewel with both hands and lifted it.

'I can feel the power!' she cried.

'That's it?' said Mintbatten. 'All this mayhem about this little egg?'

'Ha, ha,' chuckled Medina.

'The Russian Soul,' said Sailgood.

'Now we're talking,' contributed Deutsch.

'Is that all gold?' asked Isobel.

'The diamond,' said Milla Ivanovna, pressed the little lever and lifted the upper half of the jewel.

'Let's see the diamond!' agreed Medina.

'Ladies and gentlemen, I present you the greatest jewel of all time, the Russian Soul and at its heart the legendary Orlov!' announced Milla Ivanovna and raised the jewel above her head as if she were a priest in a mystical Aztec ceremony where you rip the heart out of the prisoner's chest to offer it as a gift to the god of thunder.

The Fabergé masterpiece now shone bright in the heart of London.

Isobel sighed. Sailgood, Deutsch and Medina sighed too. Mintbatten and Ituribe stood silent, in awe and relief. It was a magic moment and, sadly enough, such moments are never destined to last.

'My jewel,' said Medina pumping his chest 'I like it. I might change my mind and keep it, you know?'

'It's my present. You, vile creature,' objected Milla Ivanovna moving the jewel away from El Guapo. 'And I'm not giving it back. It's my present.'

'I left it with you as a gesture of good will and what did you do with it? You let that diabolical Russian steal it!'

'I did not let anyone do anything of the sort. That was pure treason and I got it back, didn't I?'

'That's all fine,' intervened Tom Deutsch. 'But you are forgetting that I was the one to contact my man in El Paso and give him the task to source the jewel!'

'Over my dead body, Tom.' said Jack Sailgood and produced a gun. He then took the jewel out of Milla Ivanovna's hands. They all went quiet while Sailgood walked around the table and placed the jewel at its very end.

'What the hell you think are you doing, Jack?' cried Deutsch.

'Did you really think that you and your mates would get away with this mess?'

Everybody stood motionless, taken aback by Sir Jack's move. Gorsky didn't expect such a development. He didn't expect a split to show in the two agents' relationship. He assessed the situation and made a step towards Sailgood who was still talking to Tom Deutsch.

'Did you really think I was that dumb, Tom?' said Sailgood, 'disappointing, very disappointing, I must say!'

'Hold on, I think you misunderstood the whole thing,' said Deutsch.

'You didn't expect me to be able to work out the connection between General Enterprise International, Garriburton and the Kremlin? Thanks so much for having faith in your ally's abilities,' said Jack Sailgood.

At that point, Mintbatten picked up the remote control and asked for everyone's attention. 'If I may, please. We have Mr Hank online,' he said. 'He would like to salute you all personally and express his gratitude for all the good work we are doing.'

Mintbatten switched on the TV screen and the image of an old man seated at the desk in an office appeared. His head was cleanly shaven and shiny, his face thin and sickly. He wore a black shirt and spoke with a southern American drawl that seemed to have gone through many incarnations. It was the accent of people who got uprooted at some point in life never to return to their lands of origin.

Gorsky made another step and was now in the proximity of the jewel. He leaned on the table while monitoring as the party gathered in front of the screen.

'I wish I were in London and engaged more fully in your important work. Unfortunately, I had a transplant scheduled for this morning but I decided to postpone it so I can personally express my gratitude...'

While Mr Hank kept the audience busy with his vision of the future and their respective roles in it, Gorsky noticed a shadow behind the milky glass door. There was an exchange of words with the two attendants. Gorsky observed the shadow approaching the door and pulling it open. A middle-aged man with greyish hair and a week-old beard walked into the room. He strolled across it as though he owned the place.

'What a charming reunion,' said the man. 'I hope no one missed me too much.'

'Aleksey, finally!' cried Milla Ivanovna and rushed with her arms wide open to embrace the newcomer.

The rest of the party turned around and followed the scene with vivid interest. None of them had ever met the Boss. Was the man who just walked in the room the mighty Russian Oligarch who owned the reaches of Khatanga and was earmarked to become the next President of the Russian Federation? Gorsky knew the answer and he was ready for it.

'Mr Aleksey Kaganov, I presume?' said Jack Sailgood still holding the gun.

'Really?' added El Guapo.

'I see,' contributed Lord Mintbatten.

Tom Deutsch and Isobel said nothing and made a couple of steps with the others towards the newcomer. Ituribe found the whole spectacle entertaining and a faint smile appeared in a corner of his lips. 'And I thought the

Gringos were crazy,' crossed his mind. 'Just look at these confused Axolotls.' He then took his silver snuffbox out of the pocket.

'Yes, Alexey Kaganov is back from the dead and is very happy to see you all here in this room courtesy of Lord Mintbatten,' he said. 'And let me guess, you must be Jack Sailgood, Sir Jack, and you are Tom Deutsch of Garriburton Global. Who else do we have... Mr Medina, of course and...'

'Isobel, Isobel .... I work with Sir Jack.'

'Pleasure,' said the Boss.

'That is Mr Ituribe,' said Milla Ivanovna and pointed at the man in striped suit with an unusual expression on his face. He was seated at the table and quickly put the snuffbox back into his pocket. 'Mr Medina's trusted aide.'

'And, to complete this beautiful family portrait here is our very own Alex Gorsky who, as I am informed, retrieved the Russian Soul for us and saved it from an uncertain and possibly tragic fate,' said the Boss.

'And who is the man incinerated in the car? The one wearing your wedding ring?' said Gorsky.

'Ha, ha, you have always been too soft, Alex. A true Slavic soul, always thinking about the abstract and neglecting the practical aspects of life.'

'Why did you have Zakhar killed?' said Gorsky.

Kaganov looked at Gorsky and, obviously displeased by the question, turned to the rest of the party.

'I never had the pleasure to meet some of you personally and I humbly apologise for this grave omission. Entirely my fault. As some of you already know and others have guessed, I am Alexey Dmitrovich Kaganov and despite some recent controversies about my whereabouts, I can assure you that I am here and that I am ready to bring our plans to fruition. Before we proceed though, I must clarify a subtle point for I don't want any speculations to get in the way of our business relationship. Some time ago, I received the information that a prominent and somewhat hostile organisation was planning to replace me as CEO of my company, as well as the Gubernator of Khatanga.'

Jack Sailgood and Tom Deutsch listened attentively. There were many versions of the events of the past week floating around. What was the official Kaganov version? Milla Ivanovna stood a couple of steps away from the Boss, scanning the faces around for possible reactions. That was her general role in the life she chose to live next to Kaganov. She monitored everyone except Alex Gorsky. After all, he was one of them, a foot soldier in the Kaganov team. What could he possibly know about global affairs, corporate interests and international business? She smiled. She beamed. She had the power. She had the jewel and with the jewel came more power, limitless power... Power.

'So, Vatayev was earmarked to replace you?' said Gorsky and everybody turned their heads to him.

'Vatayev was a traitor,' said Kaganov. 'I did not order his murder but I was not disappointed to hear about it.'

'You were so not disappointed that you decided to vanish from the scene. Who were you afraid of? Is that why you ordered the murder of Mark Hodayev too?'

'Hodayev? Who is Hodayev?' said the Boss. 'Ah, the FSB agent who solicited your collaboration to get hold of the Russian Soul. He was good, you know. He figured nearly everything out and had to be stopped, for the greater good of course. We don't want Russian agents roaming freely in London, do we? Well, Alex, I can only say that I am very glad and proud that you decided to do the right thing and return the jewel to its righteous owner, the future President of Russia – myself, of course. What an elegant and symbolic gesture. Give to the Tsar what belongs to the Tsar, didn't your grandfathers use to say so, Alex, didn't they? In this case, not much has changed. Instead of the Tsar we have a President! Ha, ha... You have no idea how funny you people are with your little ideas and fears.'

'I know the man who killed Hodayev. He is on your pay list, Boss,' said Gorsky.

'You read too many, what do they call them... Thrillers, yes, crime fiction,' said the Boss and a few people laughed. 'We are business people, that's all. Aren't we, Mr Sailgood, Mr Deutsch, Mr Medina, Lord Mintbatten? Gentlemen, we have some important business here waiting for us, don't we?'

'And you also tried to kill me by blowing my apartment up,' Gorsky was relentless.

'This is what I call fun,' said Medina with a grin. 'People accusing each other, insults flying... I thought only we in Mexico had that sort of fun. Thought it was part of our... folklore. Shame no one is armed, though. That element is missing, not quite the same...'

Isobel followed with great interest the exchange. There was also the small matter of the body found in the sports bag in the bathroom of a Pimlico flat. Her Majesty's intelligence services were unhappy about this episode and no amount of hush-hush would do.

Jack Sailgood and Tom Deutsch exchanged a couple of nervous glances. They both looked worried.

'Shall we take our seats and start the proceedings then?' said Kaganov and made a wide gesture towards the table that Ituribe had transformed into his office and drug store at the same time. Milla Ivanovna approached Gorsky with the obvious intention of kicking him out. The jewel sat on the table. Kaganov was in charge and questions were superfluous. The stakes were sky-high.

'Just a second, Mr Kaganov,' said Lord Mintbatten. 'We have Mr Hank online. He will be pleased to see that you are alive and well.'

The party moved away from the table and gathered in front of the large screen. The man in the picture had a long and wrinkled face. He had followed the discussion patiently through the live feed and possibly found it entertaining. Mr Hank was a man of principles, the most important of which was to gather and store all information.

'Mr Hank,' said Kaganov shouting across the room. 'Nice to have you here with us. As you see, thanks to you, everything is ready for the next phase of our operation.'

'Who's this guy?' Medina whispered in Milla Ivanovna's ear.

'The mastermind,' she said.

'I see,' said El Guapo not without admiration.

'Mr Kaganov,' said Mr Hank calmly. 'I must confess that for a moment I was worried.'

'Ha, ha, no need to worry, Mr Hank,' said Tom Deutsch and all heads turned to him. 'The jewel is finally and firmly in our possession and we can proceed with the next phase of our operation.'

'Is that so, Tom?' muttered Sailgood barely audibly to his colleague and business partner. 'I thought this was the final phase of our little Russian operation. But of course, you have another deal going on here, right?'

'What the hell are you talking about?' hissed Deutsch.

'I'm talking about the deal that supersedes the diamond deal. I'm talking about the deal that you and your pals from the dark side of the moon have cooked up to privatise the natural resources of Siberia inclusive of water and air. That's what I'm talking about.'

'Are we talking subtle ethical points here or...?'

'I don't give a flying fuck about your ethical points. I'm telling you that the deal is off!'

'Is it you or is the whole family like that?'

Sailgood grabbed Deutsch for the arm. 'You're a swine, you know?'

'Well, buddy...' began Deutsch but was interrupted.

'Sure, whatever,' cried Medina. 'I appreciate this heart-breaking and tear-jerking spectacle but the jewel is mine and will stay so until I see money coming out of the washing machine nice and clean, comprende? Lots of money. I want to build a couple of skyscrapers like this one in Sonora.

By then, the party forgot about Mr Hank and moved back towards the table and the jewel. Ituribe was surprised to see this crowd advancing. Gorsky stood his ground next to the jewel. The Boss approached it and picked it up. There was a glassy shine in his eyes when he raised the green box above his head.

'I am the heir of the Romanov throne!' he cried. 'And I have an appointment with destiny!'

Of all the people present in the room, Isobel was the one who never uttered a word. She did want to say something to Sir Jack, but he turned to Tom Deutsch and she overheard the exchange they had about the Siberian resources.

'Liz was right,' crossed her mind. 'For Christ's sake, she was right. Jack and Tom are running a racket on their own behind the façades of state-sponsored intelligence services. That's what all your talk about privatisation is about. It's about the ultimate expropriation of natural resources. That's their business model and...'

'That's right, Boss,' said Gorsky, interrupting the long-awaited moment. He held the Sig-Sauer in one hand and with the other he pointed at the jewel. 'Now put that back on the table, please.'

'How did he get in with a gun?' cried Lord Mintbatten.

'He is our security officer,' explained Milla Ivanovna who suddenly felt short of breath.

Kaganov put the box back on the table. A gun was aimed at his guts and he was a reasonable man.

'Move away,' said Gorsky and made a gesture for everyone to retreat from the table. Ituribe too.

'Miss...' he said nodding at the young woman.

'Isobel ...'

'What's the time, Isobel?'

'It's,' and she looked at her wristwatch, 'Half past twelve.'

'Good, your friend, Mr McGallen of Scotland Yard will be here any time now. I am sure you will have lots of explaining to do.'

'You cannot do that!' cried Jack Sailgood and stamped his foot on the floor. 'I'll contact my office and...'

'Put the phone down,' said Gorsky aiming the gun at Sir Jack who returned the phone to his pocket.,

'Wait a minute young man,' said the dark man from the screen. 'What do you think this is? A Boy Scout's party? Put that jewel back on the table and you better apologise to these fine people.'

Gorsky raised the aim of the gun straight towards the screen and Mr Hank.

'Don't be silly, boy,' the man said. 'We are in charge and there's nothing you can do about it.'

'I don't know you,' said Gorsky aiming at Mr Hank. 'But from the little I saw and heard from you, I decided not to like you.'

Gorsky fired the gun straight into the screen and ended Mr Hank's virtual presence. Moments later, as no new shots were fired, everyone raised their heads from behind the pieces of furniture while checking their faces and hands for possible cuts or wounds. The door suddenly opened and detective McGallen walked in the room in the company of four policeman.

'I believe you are involved in a string of murders as well as illicit financial activities,' said McGallen. 'You are all under arrest.'

'What do you mean, under arrest,' said Jack Sailgood. 'I am...'

'I know, I know. I know everything about you and your diamond deals in Mozambique too.'

'I am an American citizen!' declared Tom Deutsch.

'That doesn't exempt you from UK law,' McGallen was quick to reassure him.

'On my own premises?' Lord Mintbatten was perplexed. 'I want to call my lawyer.'

'Of all the bastards around the world that I could do business with I managed to find this bunch of useless amateurs...' complained Medina bitterly. Ituribe nodded.

'Alexey,' said Milla Ivanovna. 'What's going on?'

'Mr Superintendent, you are making a huge mistake,' said Kaganov approaching the policeman. 'Please check with your superiors, contact the Foreign Office before...'

While this scene was taking place somewhere between the phallic totem and the piranha aquarium, Gorsky used the opportunity to put his gun back into the holster, collect the green box with the jewel and walk straight towards the milky door. When he passed next to McGallen they exchanged glances, something that didn't escape the attention of the Boss.

'You, dirty little traitor...' he yelled at Gorsky, 'I saved you from your stinky Siberian hole and this is how you repay me, by betraying the whole country and... Me! Even me!'

He howled and fell in the embrace of Milla Ivanovna who felt a strong urge to kick him out of the window.

Gorsky walked out of the room, and collected his silver box from the cloakroom. He walked past the elevator and opened the door to the stairway.

'The lift,' cried the two girls, 'it's here!'

'No, thanks, I'll take the stairs,' he said, exited the lobby and took the stairs up. In a couple of long strides, he reached the flat roof of the building and the helipad platform. There was one man standing next to the chopper and another one seated in the pilot's seat. The man next to the aircraft was mid-height, overweight and bald. As Gorsky opened the door and stepped onto the platform, the man turned around holding a gun.

'Good day, Vargas,' said Gorsky.

'I didn't expect to see you here,' said Vargas and lowered the gun. 'Where is the Boss? I thought he would come on his own.'

Gorsky put the silver case and the jewel down on the green tarmac.

'He sent me instead,' said Gorsky. 'He sent me to deliver his expressions of deepest gratitude for murdering Vatayev, Sergey and Mark Hodayev. With a bit of luck, he said, you should be able get rid of me too.'

'What are you talking about?' said Vargas.

'And of course, I forgot to mention people killed in the car accident in Scotland.'

'I obey orders, Alex,' cried Vargas. 'Same as you.'

'Oh, no, Vargas, no. Not same as me.'

At that very moment, Vargas raised his hand and fired a shot aiming at Gorsky who managed to throw himself to the ground and land at Vargas' feet. Before his adversary realised, Gorsky hit him with the forehead straight on the nose, then placed his right leg behind his left and pulled the man down. As Vargas lay with a bloody face on the ground, Gorsky picked his firearm up and got on his feet. The pilot in the chopper sat immobile, like frozen and Gorsky assessed him as of no risk. As he picked up his case and box and threw them on the back seat of the chopper, Gorsky noticed a strange expression on the Indian's face. He turned around, moved sideways and pulled the Sig-Sauer out just in time as he heard a bullet impacting the haulage. Vargas was up on one knee and aiming again. He didn't have enough time though, as Gorsky's bullet hit him straight into the left side of the chest. He fell on his back and stayed prostrate.

With a couple of quick steps, Gorsky approached the body. Vargas had a gun in his hand and blood on his chest. His eyes were glassy. He was gone for good.

'Never keep family photographs on display in public places,' said Gorsky. For that was where he saw Mark Hodayev's killer, in one of the photographs that Vargas kept on the wall of his Bella Patria office. Gorsky decided to leave the gun in the dead man's hand. It would look tidier in the eyes of McGallen and his associates.

He jumped onto the front seat of the chopper and said: 'City airport.'

The pilot nodded and in a matter of seconds they were airborne. He was more than happy to listen carefully to the man with the gun. As the chopper flew from the rooftop of the skyscraper, a blast shook the air and the chopper shuddered. Gorsky looked down and all he could see was a cloud of smoke coming from the Canada Square park and people running in all directions. As the pilot directed the chopper away from the skyscraper and towards City airport, the wind blew the smoke away and Gorsky could tell the location of the explosion. It was just in front of the stage. There seemed to be charred bodies on the ground and people running in panic.

30

Agathon Fabergé

The city was covered in snow and the waters of the harbour undulated under the weight of heavy, winter clouds. The green dome of the Uspenski Cathedral dominated the small Helsinki harbour peninsula. Gorsky stood on the Cathedral steps and looked at a sailing yacht passing between two nearby islands. To the left, he saw the city roofs and somewhere in the distance the polar horizon that dwindled and merged with the frozen forest.

Behind the Cathedral lay the Russian cemetery in the middle of which stood a small church with an onion-shaped dome. The church was light blue, in gentle contrast with the tall, leafless birches and the slim, dark pine trees. Gorsky walked from the chapel down a narrow path in the snow. He carried his green box and the long case and used them to keep his balance as though he were walking on a plank. It was Saturday morning and he only saw two elderly people busying themselves around a grave. They brought flowers, took the old ones from the vase and cleaned the tombstones with small brooms and wipes.

It took Gorsky more than half an hour to find the stocky, black marble tombstone with an egg-shaped ornament on top. He kneeled and made the sign of the cross. With his bare hands, he brushed the snowflakes from the golden lettering. It read Fabergé on top and below were listed the names of Agathon, Maria, Oleg and Liisa. There it was,

Agathon Fabergé, the last of the creators of the greatest jewel the world has ever known, the Russian Soul.

He extracted a knife out of the inner pocket of his coat and dug a little hole in the frozen ground. He then worked to make the hole larger and deeper. It took him some time to penetrate the soil and reach the lid of the tomb itself. Once he did, he inserted the edge of the knife between the lid and the wall. He made sure the knife could slide left and right and then applied pressure; too much, for the blade snapped in half.

'Safari gear store,' mumbled Gorsky exasperated. 'This steel wasn't made for polar temperatures, that's for sure.'

Unsure how to proceed with his plan he sat in the snow. After a couple of seconds, he spotted his long, silver case that sat on a snowdrift. He picked the case up and took the sword out of it.

'Sorry, Caravaggio,' he said and continued to work on the lid using the long blade of the renaissance sword. After a while he managed to gain access to the interior of the tomb. He could tell the coffins and little more in the complete darkness of the grave. The opening was wide enough, he concluded, and picked up the box with the jewel. He opened it and checked the diamond. It was all there. The Russian Soul was the same egg-shaped jewel that Nicolay II Romanov gave as a present to his wife Alexandra. Gorsky placed the top back, locked it and then closed the box. The gap in the tomb was wide enough and through it he lowered the box into the grave. He took his Sig-Sauer out of the holder and placed it next to the box. He then moved the marble lid back on and placed the soil on top of it. In his cupped hands, he brought some snow from the surrounding area and made the disruption look minimal. No one would have guessed that this tomb had been tampered with. Happy with his work, he cleaned the sword and put it back into the case.

He walked back, up the path in the snow towards the church and then to the cathedral. He entered the cathedral and bought two candles. He went to the little sand pit where a couple of candles were already burning. He lit his first candle, pushed it into the sand and made the sign of the cross.

'Agathon, you can rest in peace now,' he said. 'Your art will bring no more misery and death.'

He then lit a second candle and placed it in the pit, making sure it wouldn't fall. He made the sign of the cross.

'For Mark, the Mark of old.'

He stood on the granite stairs looking at the white surface of the Helsinki harbour and the frozen mist carried by the wind. The light was scarce and the clouds so low that they seemed intent on turning the cityscape into a pressure cooker. Behind the harbour and ice-locked ships, Gorsky saw the grey façades of the Port of Helsinki buildings and in the distance the dark roofs and chimneys of the private houses. Beyond the city, and even further there were the immense Finnish forests and the polar circle.

31

Two swords, one purpose

Gorsky got out of the bus and walked through the automatic gate of the Helsinki airport terminal where he found himself in a brewing sea of people and a cacophony of sound.

He had lost his phone during the Vargas episode and he had no contact with Senka and the Fravashis. After a couple of minutes, he found a phone booth and dialled the only mobile number he knew by heart, Kathy's. There was no reply. He then managed to find the Internet access room. There was a blast in that park, right in front of the stage where the group had gathered. Steve the drummer was right. He smelt the rat but couldn't stop it. Gorsky sat in front of one of the computers, logged on and went to the BBC website where he found a report on the London terrorist attack. That's what they called it - the London Terrorist Attack. Muslim elements radicalised in the UK, international links and sleeping cells... The attack triggered many other attacks on mosques, Muslim people and property around the country.

In the video, a woman escorting the daughter to an evening class said: 'We breathe fear.' She spoke with a London accent, wore a hijab and gesticulated frantically.

Gorsky stopped reading and leaned back in the chair. Nick was not a Muslim fundamentalist. Nick was an inside operative, he was one of us. The terrorist attack was designed to cast the blame on the jihadis, the extremists, the

Muslims, the whole lot. This was the usual pretext needed for more war. Gorsky had seen this line of thinking before, the crude maths of adding and subtracting human lives - the minute pieces on the great, global chessboard. Senka Golovkin would cherish such a chess challenge. Just feed him some data and leave enough breathing space. You could solve lots of pressing problems by deploying that simple method. If no physical activity or danger were involved, Senka was your man.

Gorsky tried to Skype but there was no reply. He then opened a new Gmail account and sent e-mails to both Senka and Kathy asking Senka about the explosion and telling Kathy to reply to the mail and pick up the bloody phone. She is switched on and she knows what to do. She saw the news and connected the blast, the arrests made at the World Trade Forum and his disappearance. The Boss's face was all over the front pages. Kathy was a clever girl, no need for detailed explanations.

'By the time the agencies work out where the mails were sent from I'll be gone,' he thought. 'Sending my name to the Finns won't help either. The Boss wasn't a stupid man, the multiple name and passport policy is a sound operating principle, very sound.'

The next news item seemed to be from a kind of political gathering. There was on old man giving a fiery speech and the crowd was waving thousands of green, white and red flags as well as some symbols. The man was pumping his chest and waving his fists. The subtitles ran fast at the bottom of the screen... 'The leader of the Italian Padania, Fazio Bombardelli, spoke against immigration from northern Africa and the south of Italy and asserted the historical duty of the leadership of his party to free Northern Italy from the shackles of the tragic Unitarian ideology. He went on to mention the example of the great Padanian artist,

Michelangelo Merisi Caravaggio, who is a shining symbol of the spirit, and works that should be reclaimed from the vile, centralist Roman claws.

'Give me Caravaggio's sword,' the madman shouted, 'And I'll cut our way through the perennial poisonous weed to a prosperous and dignified future.' The crowd cheered and waved huge flags. The politician waved back and smiled his artificial, Hollywood smile.

'After all, Italy might not be the right destination for me,' thought Gorsky, squeezed the handle of his case even harder and walked away from the computer station.

While he was considering his options and possible destinations, he passed by a Cowboy themed bar featuring a five-piece live band. The girl on stage was dressed as a cowgirl with proper boots and hat. She was singing a country music standard that Gorsky found familiar but couldn't pick up the words.

'It sounds like a different language, but not Finnish. This is not Finnish?!'

He then spotted the large poster advertising the session. These were the Helsinki Cowboys. Then, there were the names of places, dates and hours and the explanation that their repertoire was made of traditional American folk songs sung in Latin.

'In Latin,' mumbled Gorsky and walked away. 'In Latin?'

A couple of minutes later he bought a ticket to Rio de Janeiro and went to the counter to check in and drop off his case. He took his place in the queue behind an oriental looking gentleman who wore a tailor-made coat and wide brimmed hat. The man carried a silver case. He approached the counter and placed the case, his only piece of luggage, on the conveyor belt.

'It's a precious item,' Gorsky heard the man say. 'It's a Japanese sword.'

The man checked in and turned to leave. He saw Gorsky and never blinked, just walked away.

'Strange,' thought Gorsky. 'This is the man from the antiquarian shop in Rome. He recognised me, I'm sure...'

32

That's when…

An hour later, Gorsky sat in the middle of the Airbus aircraft en route to Rio via Madrid. As always, he had asked for an aisle seat. He needed more legroom and he liked to monitor the cabin. It was an old and useful habit. A flight attendant asked him to place his luggage in the compartment. He didn't have any luggage. The attendant then asked if he wanted to take off his coat.

'The cabin is warm,' she said. 'And you won't need it in Rio.'

'No thanks,' he replied. 'I'll rather wait till Rio to take my coat off.'

Gorsky didn't know anybody in Rio. He didn't know much about Rio full stop. He had never been to South America and that was probably the only reason for choosing it as a destination.

He finished the conversation with the attendant as the last passengers were boarding the plane and finding their seats. Gorsky spotted the Chinaman coming up the corridor. He had taken his coat and hat off and was carrying them in a hand. He stopped before reaching Gorsky and checked the row and seat numbers. He placed his coat and hat in the luggage compartment and, as he was taking his aisle seat on the other side of the aisle from Gorsky, a woman with a small child passing down the aisle dropped a milk bottle. Half way to the ground, the Chinaman grabbed it. Quick reflex, a lightening move and Gorsky saw it. The man smiled, handed the bottle back and took his seat.

'He knows I'm here, three rows behind him,' thought Gorsky and found the idea entertaining.

The plane took off and after a while the crew served the dinner and then coffee. It was then, one and a half hour into the flight, that Gorsky noticed some strange commotion. Nothing happened but it was one of those situations where silence is the best indicator that something was happening. The Chinaman was browsing a flight magazine without reading it. That much was clear. Somewhere behind, a child cried. Some passengers turned the lights above their heads on and began reading. Others had tablet computers and laptops. Kids had smart phones... All sorts of gadgets appeared on display.

Suddenly, two men in dark blue overalls appeared in front of the pilot's cabin door. They wore keffiyehs on their heads and had guns. Two more in identical outfits appeared in front of the rear cabin crew area.

A passenger screamed and the four men began shouting instructions. A male attendant who stood in front of the pilot's cabin waved his hand and was struck forcefully on the head by one of the terrorists. An axe appeared in the hands of the other terrorist and he started hitting the pilot cabin's door.

A wave of shouts and screams suddenly inundated the passenger cabin. No-one moved, though. People sat in their seats. Some crying, the brave shouting, the not so brave screaming.

'Glock 17s, standard issue,' observed Gorsky, 'seventeen rounds each. If they start firing they will turn this plane into Swiss cheese. We would plummet in a matter of a minutes.'

One of the armed men picked up the microphone. He yelled for everyone's attention and then said: 'We are the commando unit of the Holy Caliphate Army! We took control of this aircraft. Remain seated and calm and you'll be safe. The captain and the crew will comply with our requests and so will you!'

Gorsky recognised the accent – British. Midlands, probably.

'We are redirecting this flight to the Holy city of Idlib,' the man continued, 'We'll land in three hours.'

The plane was being hijacked by people claiming to be soldiers of the Great Caliphate and Gorsky was aware of the procedure. Once in the hands of the local warlords, the lives of the passengers would become a commodity. They will be exchanged for someone or something or they will be killed. The crew was locked away. The captain probably had a gun pointed at his head or a bomb placed under his seat. Half of the passengers on board were screaming and the other half were trying to calm the first half down by shouting. One of the terrorists came down the aisle with a sack collecting the electronic devices. He stood next to Gorsky and shouted something in Arabic.

'No problem, no problem,' said Gorsky and dropped his broken mobile phone into the sack.

He then saw the Chinaman taking his smart phone out of his pocket and dropping it into the sack. The collector pushed the man and shouted. The Chinaman remained composed, nodded politely and responded by saying that he didn't have any other devices. As the collector continued moving down the aisle, the man turned towards Gorsky. Their eyes met and they nodded to each other. The collector continued to gather phones and gadgets. Two armed men stood in front of the cockpit. Two other men stood at the other end of the plane that continued to fly over Germany en route to Damascus. The Chinaman leaned back into his seat and closed his eyes. Gorsky put his hands into the pockets of the big grey coat. He extended his arms and closed his eyes. There were hundred and fifty people on board of the plane - five terrorists that he could see and probably another two among the passengers - three more hours before they landed in Syria. He pushed his hands even deeper into the pockets and tried to stretch his legs but there was not enough legroom.

'Bummer,' he mumbled, annoyed, as if this was the most serious of his problems. The middle-aged lady in the seat next to him started shivering and the man on her left was trying to comfort her. They were going on their honeymoon somewhere exotic.

'Finns,' thought Gorsky and smirked. 'This is his third and her second marriage, probably. Children grown up and left home. They are looking forward to a sunny destination so they won't mind the Middle-East that much.'

Gorsky recognised this state of mind and body. The heartbeat, the adrenalin, the calm, collected mind at work. He felt alive. He felt the wind of the Caucasus on his cheeks. He heard the battle cries and recognised the smell.

Thirty-three thousand feet above Germany, in a plane bound for Syria, Gorsky knew the answers. Living a quiet, normal life was a dream, an optical illusion and this is what was left of it now – another war zone. Sometimes you must pick a fight. Sometimes.

He then turned to the woman on his left and said: 'I'll be back, you know?'

She looked at him.

She was afraid and she just looked at him.

The collector completed his job and joined the other armed men in front of the cockpit. They began to argue and gesticulate. Gorsky turned his attention from them and glanced out of the little side window. In the dark, he saw the intermittent red light on the wing of the aircraft.

He turned to the woman again: 'I was right to keep my coat on, wasn't I?'

She kept on staring at him while her jaw trembled slightly and her big blue eyes filled with tears and horror.

'The Syrian desert must be very cold at night,' he added in an amiably serene fashion.

That's when she began screaming.

Printed in Great Britain
by Amazon